HAWK'S CRY

Satan's Devils MC - Next Generation Book #2

COPYRIGHT

Published 2020 by Trish Haill Associates

Copyright Manda Mellett

ISBN: 978-1-912288-63-2

Cover Design by Wicked Smart Designs

Edited and formatted by Maggie Kern at Ms.K Edits

Proof reading by Melanie Farrow at Professional Writing Services and Maria Lazarou

www.mandamellett.com

Disclaimer

This is a work of fiction. Names, characters, businesses, places, events and incidents are either the products of the author's imagination or used in a fictitious manner. Any resemblance to actual persons, living or dead, or actual events is purely coincidental.

Warning

This book is dark in places and contains content of a sexual, abusive and violent nature. It may not be suitable for persons under the age of 18.

CAST OF CHARACTERS

Officers
Wizard – President
Hawk – Vice President
Hound – Sergeant at Arms
Throttle – Enforcer
Heart – Secretary
Dollar – Treasurer
Joker – Road Captain
Mouse – Computer Expert

Patched Members
Drummer (ex-Prez)
Wraith (ex-VP)
Peg (ex-Sergeant at Arms)
Blade (ex-enforcer)
Bullet
Cast
Drifter
Jekyll
Lady
Marvel

Roadkill
Rock
Shooter
Truck

Prospects
Butcher
Nathan
Rascal

Old Lady's and Children
Olivia (Hawk's)
Sam (Drummer's): Eli (Hawk) and Zane
Sophie (Wraith's): Olivia, Zoey, Eliza and Hilda
Tash (Blade's): Sabrina and Mason
Darcy (Peg's): Noah (Throttle) and Lisa
Marcia (Heart): Amy, Jacob, Isabel and Alexis
Maya (adopted daughter of Joker and Lady)
Mariana (Mouse): Yiska, Maria and Tanya
Becca (Rock's): Rose and Aidan
Ella (Slick's): Faith
Allie (Truck's): Hope
Carmen (Bullet's)
Sandy (Viper's)

Members who've moved on
Hyde – left the club
Dart – transferred
Beef – transferred
Road - transferred

Deceased Members
Adam
Buster
Tongue

Hank
Viper
Slick
Kidder
Shortass

SATAN'S DEVILS MC

CHAPTER ONE

*E*li…

"I wondered where the fuck you were hiding. Took me ages to find you. What the hell are you doing up here all alone?"

I glare at Throttle, enforcer for the mother chapter of the Satan's Devils MC, as he comes closer. When my narrowed eyes and my teeth all but bared don't send him the message, I resort to words. "And that I was here alone didn't give you a fuckin' clue that I might want some solitude?" Here is in the forest up above our Tucson compound. I'm sitting on the trunk of a fallen tree contemplating my life, trying to get things straight in my head. Or that's what I was doing until I was so rudely interrupted.

Throttle doesn't take the hint. Instead of disappearing like most decent people would, he comes closer and sits his ass down alongside me. Stripping off a piece of bark and, giving his hands something to do, he starts to shred it.

"What the fuck is up with you, Hawk? You've been off lately." He taps his head as if to show me what he means.

Throttle, the son of the ex-sergeant-at-arms, Peg, who stepped down from his role a few months back, is only a couple of years younger than me. As club kids, we'd grown up together here on the compound. All our lives we've been as close as brothers, in and out of each other's houses all the time. I'm not surprised I haven't been able to hide my state of mind from him.

"I just…" I start, then stop. How can I explain? Why, when outwardly I have everything, do I feel so wrong? Why is it that some days, I find it hard to breathe, as though there's a heavy weight on my chest? Why am I not happy and content, but rather full of unease?

Throttle throws away the remains of the now destroyed bark and looks sideways at me. "Spit it out, Brother."

How can I put the impossible into words? I open my mouth, close it, then opening it again, finally spit out, "I'm not sure I'm where I should be." It's the best, *only*, explanation I can come up with. It sounds weak, even to me.

The enforcer turns his head to look at me. "What the fuck do you mean?" He barks a short laugh. "Here, in the forest? If you're lost, I know the way back." He winks. It's a joke. We spent our childhood playing amongst these trees.

I shake my head, take another deep breath, and admit, "In the club."

If anyone's eyes could open wider, I've never seen it. "You can't be fuckin' serious?" He stares at me again, trying to analyse the expression on my face. "You *are* serious?"

I nod. "Deadly."

Throttle stands, rakes his hands through his hair, and then tugs at the beard that's thick just like his father's. His voice is just as deep and controlled when he states, "You're the VP of the Satan's Devils, Hawk. You're the son of the ex-prez. You've just gotten married to the daughter of the previous VP and you're expecting your first kid. Now you're questioning being in the fuckin' club?" He shakes his head. "You were fuckin' born to this."

My hands clench into fists. "And that's just the fuckin'

problem. Can't you understand?" Rage that he doesn't immediately see things the same way as I do floods through me. Standing, I get up in his face. "Drummer's my dad. Drummer, the ex-prez. I was fuckin' groomed to be an officer in this club from the day he and Mom gave me life. It was expected that I'd follow in his footsteps. I never had a fuckin' choice, Noah." Unconsciously, I realise I've reverted to using his legal name, the name I'd called him before he'd patched in. Appealing to him as my friend, not the club's enforcer, I say, "Zane was never under the same pressure—"

"Your brother, Zane, took after your mom. He was different from you since the day he was born. He followed the rules blindly while you always questioned and challenged them. Just like a man ready to lead this club should."

It's true. I've always been the serious one while Zane's got a much lighter outlook on life. I know it amused everyone how much I resembled my father, in looks and in the way I got things done. But I question how much that was his influence. Oh, he loves Zane, don't get me wrong. But I was the son he'd never expected, but once arrived, he'd found he'd always wanted. The one who'd carry his legacy on.

I envy Zane, my younger brother. He's not part of the club, never having expressed any desire to become a member. He still lives here on the compound but isn't involved in all the shit that goes on.

I hadn't meant to share my thoughts with anyone, not today. While they weren't things I'd be able to keep to myself for much longer, I didn't think I was ready to share them. If Throttle hadn't come to find me, I'd never have opened up. But he's caught me at a weak moment, perhaps it's serendipity that he has.

So I look him directly in the eyes, take a deep fortifying breath, and give it to him straight. "I'm going to leave the club. I'm going to become a civilian."

I'd been wrong. It is possible for his eyes to widen further.

"What the fuck did you just say?" He growls and cups his ear as if he hadn't heard me right. He shakes his head like a dog shaking rain off its back. "Must be fucking hearing things. Thought I heard you say you wanted to walk away from this life."

I put it more definitively, "You'd heard right. I want to go. Get a proper job, move off compound."

His body is vibrating with anger as he rounds on me. "This life isn't something you walk away from, Hawk."

I shrug. I'm aware of that and the consequences of my decision. But something's wrong, and I can't see any other way to fix it. "I just can't do this anymore."

"You can't fuckin' do this anymore?" he roars. His head moves to one side, then the other, then back. I see his muscles tick in his jaw. "You're the fuckin' VP, the vice president, Hawk. You and Wizard lead us. You, of all people, can't just turn your back on the club."

"That's the fuckin' problem!" I scream at him, losing any control that I had. "I wasn't asked if this is what I wanted. I had no choice."

"Choice?" He looks astonished. "What the fuck are you talking about? You could have said no if you didn't want to prospect when the chance came up. You could have said no before you took the patch. You weren't let off lightly because of who you are. Both you and I went through a harder time as prospects, because of who our fathers were. You had to be pretty fuckin' sure that's what you wanted, else you'd have walked then."

He's right. No one had taken it easy on us. We should have been shoo-ins, already trusted, having known no life other than the club. But we'd been tested to the ultimate to make sure we weren't hanging onto the coattails of our dads. So the members could see our loyalty was real, not assumed, and that we expected no special treatment from the club. That we'd risen through the ranks so fast had been part of the dedication and commitment we'd proven to have.

"I'm too young to do this. I shouldn't have made VP."

"You're twenty-five, almost twenty-six," he replies, deceptively quietly. "Wraith was what, twenty-seven when he made VP? He ever say it was too much to handle? Fuck no. He ever want to walk away? Not that I've ever heard. From the day he became Drummer's right-hand man, Wraith's given his all to the club. You saying you can't give the same support to Wizard?"

"I'm saying exactly that." I've nothing to offer anymore. I feel like the club's sucked the life right out of me. I'm wrung dry.

Throttle kicks at the tree trunk as though he's kicking me. His steel-capped boot makes it rock. "How does Olivia feel about all this?"

I sigh as he mentions the woman I exchanged vows with just three months back. "I haven't spoken to her about it," I tell him, while acknowledging to myself, she's part of the problem. "I was groomed and prepared to become an officer from the day I was born, Throttle. From my first breath, this was what Drummer wanted for me. I was put into that fuckin' crib with Liv, the VP's daughter. She was my first friend. We learned to walk and speak together. We played together, shared toys. Of course we were fuckin' close. So I did what was expected, and now we're married. Now the cycle's happening all over again with a fuckin' kid coming along."

Throttle stares at me as though he can't understand any of the words coming out of my mouth. "You love her," he says after a moment, almost accusingly.

He's not wrong. I do. I love her as much as my ability to breathe. She's everything to me. But she wasn't a choice that I made. That's the point. Just another thing I was forced into.

What it comes down to is that I haven't been allowed to

make a choice over anything. Everything's always been mapped out for me. To keep everyone happy, I've done exactly what was expected. I've had to pretend to be someone I'm not, and I just can't do that anymore.

Throttle leans with his hands on his thighs. He looks like he's struggling for something to say. It's a few minutes before he speaks again. When he does, it's with something akin to disgust and disappointment in his eyes. "Do me a fuckin' favour, Hawk. Go speak to your wife." Then he straightens, gives me one last glare, and walks off with his shoulders hunched over. I catch his mumbled *someone needs to talk some sense into him* before he disappears.

I haven't any intention of ignoring his instruction. It's something I've already put off far too long. A conversation I'd known was coming, but also one I dread, and with fucking good reason.

I stay in the forest for about ten minutes after Throttle leaves, trying to get my thoughts in order. Whether the enforcer will keep what I said to himself or tell others, I've no idea. But I can't take the risk that he won't, and Liv, who was my first and who remains my best friend, deserves better than to hear that shit secondhand.

My wife is folding laundry when I step into our house that's built at the top of the compound. It sits in the midst of all those that have been constructed for anyone who wants to live here. Ours is a stone's throw away from the one belonging to my dad, and next to that, there's the home of her own parents. Another expectation I'd fulfilled, being swept along with the tide when it was taken as a given we'd live nowhere else. *No choice. No one asked for my opinion.*

"Hi." She looks up expectantly and raises her chin, offering her cheek to me.

Automatically, I step to her side and place a kiss to it.

Her hand moves down and touches her stomach. At six

months pregnant, she's sporting a definite baby bump. "She's active today. Do you want to feel her?"

I should reach out and caress where my baby's lying inside her. I should take delight in these moments. I should laugh when she alludes to the fact that as she's one of four sisters, girls run in her family. I should remind her that boys run in mine and insist she's carrying my son as that's all my sperm will give her.

But I don't. I can't. I feel frozen inside. Where once there was light, now it's all dark.

She looks at me carefully, then shakes her head. "You ready to talk yet?" Her teeth worry her lip.

That's exactly what I was intending, but something about the way she's holding herself, how her arms go protectively around her body, shows me my talk was anticipated.

I'm hurting her. I never meant to. She'd gotten swept along in the same way I had.

Giving a deep sigh, she prompts me. "Eli, this has been too long coming. You've got something to tell me, so spit it out." But she half turns away as though not wanting to hear it.

"Liv…" I start, then stop, finding it harder to tell her than it was to bare my soul to Throttle. Then, like a dam breaking, it all starts coming out. About how I've never been asked my opinion on anything. How I am who I am because of who I was born to. How I don't know what I want anymore. How I don't know *me* anymore, let alone my desires.

When I run out of things to say, at last I look at her and see a tear leaking out of her eye. From the day I was first conscious of her lying in the crib alongside me, I've hated to see her cry. It's no different now. The only change is when I step closer to wipe it away, she takes a step back.

"You don't get to comfort me," she hisses, "when you've just told me I'm not what you want."

"I didn't say that," I remind her quickly, certain I hadn't

expressed anything of the sort. Though perhaps that had been the implication.

But she ignores me. "Is it because of the baby? I thought we both were ready. It was you who didn't want to wear the condom. We both took our chances. Then Dad got out his shotgun and you proposed—"

"It's not the baby," I refute quickly, while acknowledging deep down inside, perhaps it is. Yes, I was the asshole who'd taken the chance. She'd reminded me when I'd forgotten but, to feel myself inside her unprotected for once? That, I'd thought at the time, was well worth it. Wraith hadn't needed to get his shotgun out; Dad would have killed me if I'd not stepped up and made an honest woman of her. Though why he'd wanted to see me married when he'd never officially tied the knot himself, I've no idea.

Though Drummer's enduring love for my mom is clear to everyone, she has never needed a ring on her finger. Wraith and Sophie, Liv's dad and mom, had made everything official, and their relationship had stood the test of time. Maybe, married or not, I'd be feeling no different.

My thoughts veer this way and that, and all the while *my wife* is trying to keep herself from crying. I'm an asshole, standing here, unable to take any of what I've just said back. I'd be a liar if I turned around and said I hadn't meant any of it.

"What do you want to do?" she asks, her voice breaking.

What do I want? I can't recall anyone before ever asking me that, or at least, not in relation to important decisions in my life. I give her the same answer as I'd given to Throttle earlier. "I want to step down as VP. More than that, I want to leave the club. I want to live off compound and get a proper job."

"Do you…" her voice catches. She tries again, "Do you want a divorce?"

"Fuck no," I tell her, my brows rising. "I want you by my side. I want us to bring Junior up like a normal kid. Have citizen friends he can play with. I want to keep him well away from the club. Let him have a future only he dreams of. No, darlin', a divorce is the last thing I want. I want you by my side in a bright new future."

Giving voice to what I desire makes me feel lighter than I have in ages. Liv goes to speak, but I stop her.

"Liv, sweetheart. We'll talk more later. I'm already late for church." Which, I realise, I'll now need to hurry to.

CHAPTER TWO

*E*li...

The minute I step into our hallowed meeting, I realise Throttle hasn't wasted a moment before he's opened his mouth. Some men, at least, are looking at me differently.

Wizard watches me approach and take my seat to his left, and the enforcer won't meet my eyes as he sits beside me. Opposite, Hound, the sergeant-at-arms regards me with a stern, calculating expression on his face.

A quick glance down the table makes me pleased weapons are not allowed into church else someone would probably shoot me. As for my dad? Well, Drummer's looking a mixture of disappointed and angry.

Most are looking puzzled, so Throttle's not enlightened everyone yet, but there's a definite atmosphere and every-one's catching hold of it even if they don't know the cause.

I hold my breath as Wizard picks up the gavel, bangs it, and after a quick shake of his head in my direction, officially starts the meeting. "Dollar. Over to you," he says tiredly.

Either he's letting me off the hook, or he's making me sweat. If my disclosure to the enforcer is going to be addressed, I'd rather he just get on and get it over with. I don't welcome the reprieve. I'd rather get my decision out in the open, but I won't disrespect my prez right now. If that's what he wants, we'll follow the agenda as normal.

I bow my head and only half pay attention as the treasurer runs through our finances, and various members give their updates, having already lost interest in the day to day running of a club I no longer want to be part of.

Shooter raises his hand. "Think it's common knowledge by now that Zane's come on board at SD Construction. We've made him a full partner."

"Great fuckin' news." Peg thumps the table and gives Dad a thumbs-up.

Dad, who barely seems to have taken his eyes off me the whole meeting, manages a chin lift back. Well, I suppose my brother hasn't steered clear of the club completely, though he is working in a citizen role. Dad's still managed to keep him close and under his eye.

Bullet leans forward. "Now Zane's taken more responsibility, I'm stepping back a bit. Want to take a few more rides with my old lady before we're too old to enjoy life."

"Anything we should know, Brother?" Wizard asks quickly. "Everything okay with you and Carmen?"

Bullet shrugs. "I've given close to forty years to the club. Built the business up with Viper..." he pauses, and gives a moment for everyone to remember my grandfather, who died a few years back. I join in when fists briefly rise to cover hearts, while wondering whether he'd be turning in his grave at some of the thoughts in my head. Bullet continues, "I joined this club thinking all I was going to do was ride my bike." Now everyone chuckles, that being what most people think we spend our time doing. "Instead, I spent those years working with my sleeves rolled up. Think it's time to take it easier, brothers. Not giving up, just reducing my hours."

"I can live with that." Wizard nods. "You've done a lot for the club, Bullet. You deserve something back."

"Carmen's giving up her business as well." Bullet grins. "She's giving up her shop but you can tell your old ladies she'll still be doing hair."

"Thank fuck for that," Peg murmurs. "Darcy wouldn't have liked having to go somewhere else." Other people agree with him, while I suppose Liv will have to find a new hairdresser in Tucson. I have no idea what our relationship with the club will be once I leave the compound. It's something I haven't thought about. But then, I haven't given much thought to the future, only how to escape the present.

"With all the women here, she may as well be working a full-time business." Throttle looks at the many brothers who have daughters, then pointedly at Wizard who'd gotten married on the same day I had. Yeah, the VP and prez had had a joint wedding much to everyone's enjoyment. Another thing I'd gone along with to please my club.

Once Dollar has finished with our finances, Wizard moves on.

"Got news that Archangel's reared his head. There's been word of him being seen near Nogales."

There's silence for a moment as brothers stare at the prez.

"He crossing the border?" Hound asks. "That would be fuckin' good news."

"It would," Peg agrees. "One less worry for us."

"Tucson's only sixty miles from there, Prez." Throttle is frowning.

"Too close for comfort," Wizard agrees. "Of course, Hound's right. The US is too hot for him, so he might be crossing the border and starting a new life. Or, he could be starting a new drug trade."

"Or, he's got a reason to be in Arizona," Dad states.

And that reason could be bad news for the club.

It's indeed possible he's dealing close by. The Herreras, the crime family that my father had had to deal with back when I was a kid, had ended up stepping on the cartel's toes a bit too firmly a few years back. A big falling out ensued by way of a blood bath, or more accurately, a massacre. Since then, while the cartel had tried to take over the city, they'd not completely filled the void. Archangel might well have seen a business opportunity. The Satan's Devils have never touched drugs themselves, but turn a blind eye to others dealing as long as it doesn't affect the club.

The problem we have is that the Satan's Devils were responsible for Archangel going to prison. Since his escape, the club has had cause for worry. If he knew about our part in sending him down, he's the type who'd want retribution. Learning he's back on our turf is concerning.

"Whatever he's doing, I don't like it."

Wizard grimaces. "I hear you, Drum. Need everyone to keep their eyes open."

Archangel will be their problem, not mine. I don't intend to be a Devil very much longer.

"I'd like the VP's thoughts on Archangel," Joker states.

The words wash over me.

"VP," Wizard snaps. "Joker wants your thoughts."

He probably doesn't, as I don't have any. "I'll support the prez," I offer lamely. My comment is rewarded by looks of surprise. Normally I'd contribute a lot more, challenging the prez on his assessment if I think he's taking a turn down the wrong road, but today I can't find it within me to care. I'm too tied up in the thought this may be the last time I'm sitting around this table, which would mean I'd turned my world upside down. The touch of regret and sadness takes me by surprise. *It's what I want, isn't it?*

Wizard asks for any other business. Turns out there's none. As everyone gets up to leave, Wizard shoots out his hand, his fingers curling around my arm.

"You're not going anywhere," he says sharply. Then before anyone leaves the room, he barks out, "Got some business to discuss. Stay close, brothers. I may need you all back in."

With a few curious looks, followed by chin lifts, most trundle out. But looking around, I see several others are staying seated as well. Throttle, Hound, Drummer and Wraith to be precise and Wizard himself, who waits only until Lady, the last one out, closes the door.

"What the fuck's going on with you?" Prez snarls, and Drummer and Wraith reposition themselves closer to the top end of the table.

"I spoke to Throttle in confidence." Well, I thought I had. I suppose I hadn't expressly told him to keep my thoughts quiet. In any event, I glare at the man.

"Throttle did exactly what he should. His role is to watch out for the safety of the club and enforce the rules as you very well know. And any member who is thinking about betraying us very definitely comes under his remit."

I feel like a kid with my dad and my wife's father in this meeting, both looking at me with the same disapproving looks they would use when I fucked up as a child. The familiarity of it makes me snarl, "Thinking of leaving isn't a fuckin' betrayal. And why the fuck are Drummer and Wraith here? I'm the VP. It should be officers of the club who reprimand me. Not fuckin' family."

"Every man seated around this table is your fuckin' brother, as well you know, Hawk." Wizard wipes a hand over his face, making me notice he looks tired and drawn. "I was of the mind to bring this up to the whole club in church, but I have a lot of respect for you and thought you'd appreciate talking shit through with a smaller group." He leans forward. "And yes, I wanted Drummer and Wraith here. Until a few months back they were sitting in the seats you and I now occupy, and have experience we haven't got. I'd like to get their input on something I've not seen handled before."

Hound clears his throat. "I, for one, have no fuckin' idea what's going on. Throttle informed us just before church that you were thinking of leaving the club." His worried eyes meet mine. "Has he got that wrong, Brother? Because I fuckin' hope he has. You want to step back as VP? Now that's something I'd vote to accommodate. But you walking away?" He shakes his head in answer to his own question.

My shoulders rise and fall. "It's the club I want to move away from." I speak slowly, carefully, not wanting to be misunderstood. "I don't want to be VP. Hell, I don't want to be a member anymore. I don't want to live on the compound—"

"You gonna leave Olivia?" Wraith snarls, and it's only Hound's quick thinking that pulls him back before he can reach over the table to grab me.

"No," I say fast. "Fuck no, Wraith. I'm not leaving my wife. She'll be coming with me."

"What's she got to say about this?" Dad asks, almost lazily. "She happy with it?"

Again, I shrug. "I only told her today."

"Told her?" Wizard's eyebrows rise. "Doesn't she get a say?"

I stare at him, explaining as though I'm talking to a child. "If I'm not in the club, we can't stay here long term. That's obvious. But there's no rush for us to move. I'll need to find somewhere to live, get a job. We can wait until the baby's born—"

"Ain't having anyone on the compound who's not club or family," Drummer snarls, then looks Wizard's way. He gives a little apologetic shake. "Sorry, Prez."

Wizard waves off his apology. "It's why you're here, Drum. I don't know what the fuck goes in a situation like this. Never had a man walk away from the club before, in any of our chapters. Not without good fuckin' reason, or unless they went out bad."

What are they talking about? Surely they're not going to kick us out? "Zane's not club, and he lives here." I can't stop myself from pointing out. "And Jacob's always welcome."

Drummer's fingers tap on the table. "Want my views, Prez?"

Wizard waves his hand. "Happy for you to tell your boy how it is, Drummer."

"Zane is club, he's family," Dad starts. "It wasn't news to any of us that he's a full partner in SD Construction now. He earned that on his own merits, and he's bringing money in. Money that goes into the members' pockets. You on the other hand are turning your back on the club." He pauses and tugs at his beard, and after drawing in air, lets it out on a sigh. "You swore, Hawk. You swore when you were patched in, you were in this for life. You swore you'd have the backs of your brothers, that you'd give your life for any one of theirs. You walking away means giving all that up. It would be bad enough were you a normal member, but you're the fuckin' VP." His hand slams down on the table. "You're leaving us in the lurch at the very time the club needs valuable men." His voice has been rising, and now it's almost a shout.

"If my heart's not in it, I can't be the man you want me to be," I cry out. "I shouldn't have made VP. I'm too young, too inexperienced—"

"Fuck, boy!" Wraith snarls. "I was little older than you when I gained the VP patch. Drummer about the same age when his old man died, and he stepped up to the top seat. How the fuck can you say you're not old enough?"

"We love you, Brother, always have." Wizard's voice has gentled. "You've earned that love by being family. You've earned respect from every man who sits around this table by proving your worth. You didn't get your position by nepotism. You earned your place by my side by being the man people look up to and trust. How the fuck can you doubt that you're anything but the man that I need?"

"Why don't you take a break, Brother?" Hound suggests reasonably. "Take Olivia, go on vacation. You might just need some time to get your head on straight."

"Good idea," Throttle agrees, giving what sounds like a sigh of relief. "Give yourself a chance to think about what you want, Hawk."

They're being reasonable, well, the enforcer, prez and sergeant-at-arms that is. Drummer's eyes are shining with disappointment, and Wraith's with anger and rage. Me? I just want to close this chapter in my life, fuck, open a brand new book and move on.

Not wanting to appear like a petulant child, I turn to Wizard and force myself to say calmly, "My mind is made up. I can't stay a club member. If I have to leave the compound, then so be it. But take this as my official resignation as your VP, and as a member of the Satan's Devils."

There's silence. A pin dropping would have sounded loud. It seems to stretch out until Wizard eventually breaks it.

"One chance, Hawk. One chance to take that back. Take a time out like Hound suggested. Talk to Olivia, sort yourself out."

"No," I tell them firmly. Their arguments have only served to convince me I'm right. "My mind is made up, and I won't be changing it."

With his eyes on me, Prez addresses to his predecessor, "What are the rules about this, Drummer?"

My dad's face has one of the coldest expressions I've ever seen him wearing, and grey steely eyes land on me. He might be my parent, but right now he's Drummer, ex-president of the mother chapter of the Satan's Devils as he replies icily, "All the members vote. The choices are that he leaves with a beatdown, or he loses his life."

A beatdown I'd accepted could have been on the cards, though I'd hoped I'd get a pass seeing as how I've been brought up as part of the club. Surely they'd have seen how railroaded into this I'd been, and that I'd never had the chance to be me? But that I could lose my life, leave my wife a widow and my kid without a dad, had never occurred to me.

"Get the members back in," Wizard rasps out, not giving me the opportunity to change my mind now I know what the consequences are.

I wouldn't, even if he had. The club, the compound, isn't where I want to be. If I end up meeting Satan in person, well, so be it.

Minutes later the room has refilled, men grumbling they've got drinks ordered and ready to be drunk or had old ladies or sweet butts they've had to leave warmed up and waiting.

Unsympathetic, Wizard bangs the gavel loudly to get their attention. When eyes go to him, he shakes his head. "Brothers…" he pauses, then pushes emotion back down. "The VP has just let me know that he wants to step down."

A stunned silence, then Shooter asks, "What the fuck?" His words then echoed around.

Wizard bangs the gavel again. "You need to hear the rest. Hawk wants out of the club completely."

Drifter looks completely stunned, Truck too. Peg's face has gone blank. Lady looks disappointed, Joker disbelieving. Heart and Mouse, two others I've known all my life, seem upset.

Blade snarls and stabs his knife down hard into the table where it lodges and quivers.

"I'm sure you don't need me to tell you the severity of this situation. We've got…" Wizard clears his throat. "We've got the VP who wants to walk away from the club. We've got to decide whether we'll allow him to. A nay means we don't."

"Can't force him to stay," Rock says.

Wizard looks around. "A nay means Hawk meets Satan." Without giving them a chance to respond other than for gasps, he continues, "A yay has to be for a beatdown."

Blade struggles to use his waning strength to pull the dagger back out of the wood, but when he does, he points it straight at me. "You prospected for the right to wear that patch. You prospected to prove your loyalty. We've shown that right back. You're disrespecting everything we stand for to want out of this life. Even thinking of that means you shouldn't be wearing that patch, *Eli*."

"Good point." Wizard nods at my cut. "Take it off." He has a silent conversation with Throttle over my head.

I knew this was coming. Standing, I slip out of my cut, and hand it to Throttle before it's forced off of me.

"You want me to leave?" I offer, trying to sound nonchalant, as though I don't give a damn, surprised how much I already miss the weight of the leather on my shoulders.

"Not just yet." Wizard nods to the enforcer.

As I retake my seat, it's to see Throttle slicing off the patches, the ones I worked so hard to attain. Each stitch he methodically cuts through wounds me, though I don't know why. He's symbolically cutting me off from all that I'd previously wanted from my life. I'm a man without a home, with no anchor. I've nothing left.

It's what I want.

Once the naked leather is on the table for all to see, Wizard instructs, "Leave us, Eli. Lady? Get a prospect to wait with him, please."

Rock looks up and shakes his head, then points at me. "Get two."

Drifter snorts.

CHAPTER THREE

*O*livia…

I knew something had been going on in Eli's head, I just hadn't known how grave it was and the far-reaching effect it was going to have on our lives.

Eli had always been there. There's only a couple of months between us in age and we've been inseparable since then. Eli had been my companion, my first friend, my protector from the moment we could walk. He'd been the one to pick me up each time I'd fallen. I suppose it's corny, but I never looked at anyone else. I'd always known he would be mine, that I'd marry him when we were old enough. My childish thoughts might have matured into those more fitting to an adult, but had never changed.

While similar to his father in so many ways, there was one major difference between Drummer and Eli. Drummer's reputation for banging everything in sight had earned him his handle. He'd continued that way until he'd met Sam, Eli's mother. After Eli had prospected and earned his patch, I had feared he might believe he had to live up to the family reputation. But he hadn't. He stayed faithful to me. We'd lost our virginity to each other.

We live in a club where sex is all around us. I can't even begin to count the number of times I've walked in and seen men taking one or two girls, or two men taking one girl together. I'd grown up where fucking wasn't just something done behind closed doors, it was a natural bodily function, nothing to be ashamed of. Everyone did it. Except when it came to the club kids, or, in particular, daughters of the club members.

Dad had been, and still was, the ultimate in overprotective fathers, knowing, as he put it himself, just what pigs men could be, and how little encouragement they'd need to take advantage. He'd have killed anyone, including Eli, who'd touched me or my sisters inappropriately. I'd been seventeen when I was first able to sneak off with Eli for sex. After that, we got together as often as we could, but had to hide from everyone that our relationship had moved to the next step. We were successful, or so it seemed, waiting another four years later until I gave up the pretence, and admitted it to my father. Two years on and I was pregnant which was when my dad figuratively and literally got the shotgun out.

Neither Eli nor I had minded. We were each other's and always had been. Making it official was just one more step toward the rest of our lives, or so I had thought. We teamed up with Wizard and Amy, went to the altar and said our vows, a double wedding the likes of which the Satan's Devils had never seen.

At first, Eli seemed over the moon about the pregnancy, as happy as I was myself. But as the months have passed, I've sensed him pulling away.

I'd thought it was me.

The good thing about living on the compound is that I always have family around me. Mom, Dad, and Zoey, Eliza and Hilda, my three sisters for a start. Then there are Drummer and Sam who are like second parents to me. Zane, my brother-in-law, Maya, Rose, Hope and all the other kids

I'd grown up with. I can't forget Amy, who's three years older than me. There's always someone to turn to, to talk to.

The bad thing about being here is that it's like living in a goldfish bowl. Everyone knows your business, sometimes it seems even before you do.

Sometimes I wonder whether if Eli and I had lived different lives, would we have ended up together? Our marriage was seen as a fairy tale ending, a natural culmination of a love that we'd shared all our lives.

I know the other old ladies, and my siblings by proximity, all think it's cute that while we've been brought up in an environment where sex was offered and taken freely, Eli and I have remained faithful.

I do feel pressure to maintain other people's fantasy of a perfect life. So when the cracks started to appear in our marriage, I kept that to myself, maintaining the pretence that I couldn't be happier. Even though as the weeks have passed since our wedding, it's become increasingly hard.

No one was surprised that Eli and I became pregnant. It was only a matter of time. My mom had joked she'd expected it to have happened earlier, but I'd waited until I was twenty-five. Then came the wedding, and soon after, my relationship with Eli started to fall apart. Who could I blame but myself? Was I not enough for him any longer? Did he not want to be saddled with a wife and child?

This afternoon's conversation had been a revelation. It had been a relief to be told Eli being closed off had nothing to do with me, but was down to the last thing I expected. His unhappiness stemmed from disillusionment with his club.

I'd been gobsmacked—the word used by my mom is the only way to describe it.

That he'd disappeared before we could have a decent discussion and left me hanging, but every Wednesday the members congregate for church. I knew he had to leave and attend it.

But as he'd walked out of the door to go to the meeting, I was left not knowing what to think. My first reaction was sadness, that he'd gotten to this point and I hadn't seen it coming. The second was fear. This club is all we've known all our lives.

My only experience of life off the compound was when I'd attended school and that was only a few hours a day, five days a week during the school terms. And even there, club children tended to stick together, mingling with citizens not discouraged, but why spend breaks with people who didn't understand your way of life?

Now the very thought of living among citizens and not having the support of family around me is so scary it takes my breath away.

In three months we'll become three. How could I cope with a baby without my mom living so close? Or without Sam, and the rest of the women here?

Our baby will be the first of the next generation born on the compound, but will be joined by Wizard and Amy's only three months further down the line. I'd thought our children would grow up together, just like Eli and I had. The thought that we won't be living in close proximity is soul destroying.

The third emotion I feel is anger. A blast of rage that he hasn't considered me overcomes me. *How dare he make such decisions on his own, ones which will have such a far reach for our little family?*

It seems he's given no thought that soon we'll have a baby to feed, while having nowhere to live, and perhaps no means to put food on our table.

Perhaps he'd lied. Perhaps, despite what he'd said, his unhappiness was down to me. Perhaps when he leaves, he'll go alone leaving me behind. Because I've become baggage he no longer wants.

Have we been growing so far apart without me knowing how serious it was?

"Olivia?" my mom calls from my kitchen.

"In here." I realise I'm still holding one of his clean shirts and place it down on the rest of the laundry I've taken out of the drier.

"Olivia? Are you? Oh, Ollie." Mom's arms come around me. "He's a bloody wanker."

My eyes go wide as I sob into her chest then pull away and take a deep breath. "You know already?"

"Yeah, we do. Want one of your disgusting decafs?" Eli's mom's voice comes from the kitchen.

This is part of why I love living on the compound. We might live in separate houses, but our doors are never locked, and people treat each one as their own home. Sure, it can be a bit embarrassing at times—it wouldn't only be the once Mom's walked in when Eli's been thrusting home. Or me interrupting her with Wraith. I'd had to bleach my eyeballs on that occasion. But when one of us is hurting, everyone rallies around.

"Yeah, thanks, Sam," I call back. With Mom's arm around me, I walk to the kitchen, unsurprised to see Sam's got three cups prepared. Proper coffee for her, decaf for me, and a tea for my still-after-all-these-years very British mom who hasn't forgotten her origins.

Mom picks up her cup, then puts it back down realising it's too hot to sip. She waves to the kitchen table. "Spill. What's going on with Hawk?"

"What do you know?" I take the offensive, not feeling ready to have this discussion, not overly eager to dissect what a failure as a wife I am.

Sam shrugs. "Not a lot." She eyes me carefully. "Drummer and Wraith spoke to us for a couple of minutes before disappearing into church. They said they thought Eli might have spoken to you about something that might upset you. They wanted you to have support, if he has." She waves her hands. "Looks like they were right."

I hadn't wanted to speak to anyone until I'd processed Eli's revelations myself. Now they've confronted me, it all spills out. "You mean that brief conversation where he told me he wanted to leave the club and live off compound? Yeah."

"Jesus!" Mom cries. "It's true. I was hoping Wraith was wrong."

Sam looks more resigned, as though she'd been more convinced by Drummer. "I'm so sorry, Ollie."

"It's worse than that," I admit. "Mom, Sam, I don't know what to say to him. I don't want to leave…"

Sam gives me a sharp look. "He may be my son, but you've always meant as much to me as a daughter of my own, Olivia."

"I'd have said I looked on Eli as my son," my mom remarks. "Though now I might just have to disown him."

"He's an asshole. Your place is here, where you've always lived. His too." Sam purses her lips. "What the hell has gotten into him?" She sits, pulling me down beside her and takes one of my hands in hers. "How have things been between the two of you?"

I press my lips together. There are things you can't say to your mom and mother-in-law. I can't tell them he's not touched me for weeks, or that I've been walking on eggshells around him. "Fine," I lie. "He's been a bit preoccupied, but I thought that had something to do with club business." Both women roll their eyes and nod sympathetically. "But to find out it's his feelings about the club?" I continue, "This has hit like a bombshell. I hadn't a clue what he was thinking."

A tear runs down my cheek. I wipe it away, uncertain whether the man I'm crying for deserves it. The man I've known all these years, well, I'd have said he does, but tonight I was faced with someone new. Someone I didn't feel I knew at all. Had there been signs that I'd been ignoring, that my fairy tale life was already broken?

"Oh, sweetheart." Mom sits to my other side. "I don't know what to say."

"I can't believe it," Sam says. "He's not acting like the son I brought up."

"Is it the baby?"

"Maybe it is," I answer Mom softly. "Perhaps Eli's been pulling away ever since I found out I was pregnant." Previously, we'd both been insatiable, but while my appetite for sex has increased, Eli's has diminished. I had told myself it was because he was scared of harming the baby, but maybe it was something else? Maybe he didn't want me as his wife anymore. Maybe my pregnancy belly is a turn-off. It clearly isn't a turn-on.

Mom looks annoyed, but Sam looks confused. "Eli always spoke about eventually having a family with you," she tells me. "I can't believe my son would walk away now. And from what you said, he wants to leave the club, not you. Will you go with him? You know you'd be welcome to stay here if you want."

The direct question—me having to confront a decision I won't want to make—has me flinging myself at my mom, tears flooding again now, and me unable to stop them. "I don't want to leave," I wail. "I want to stay here, close to you two, close to everyone else. The compound is all I've ever known for the whole of my life. How will I survive without it?"

"Then stay," Mom says firmly. "That Eli wants to leave has nothing to do with you. You're club, Olivia, with or without him."

I do have that choice. I won't be ostracised just because my husband has left me. But all my life, my fortunes have been intertwined with his. If he still wants me, how could I abandon him?

"If he does leave, I'll have to go with him," I sob. "I promised to love him, to support him, through good times and bad. Unless he doesn't want me with him, I don't see how I can do anything else."

Sam's eyes soften. "Leaving the club is serious, Ollie. He won't be welcome back." The sadness in her eyes shows she knows she'll be losing a son if he throws in his patch. Or, at least, have a very different relationship with him. I feel sorry for her as well. "If you go with him, remember, you can always come back if you need to. You'll always have a place with us here."

I raise my head enough to send her a grateful look. When Drummer was prez, she was the first old lady. Now Amy's married Wizard, Amy's taken that place now, but Sam still speaks with authority.

But to not go with my husband, or to rely on the safety net they've just offered me, means I'm not putting effort into making my marriage work. It might be a shock, but I have to deal with it. I married Eli for better or worse, for the bad times as well as the good. My place is with him, without question. I'm just scared as I can't envision what a life off compound would even look like.

"You'll always be welcome here," Mom starts. "Even if you move away, you can visit all the time."

But if Eli's intent on building a new life, isn't that what I should also be doing? When the baby's born, I should join a mom's group or something. Find new friends who don't live and breathe the scent of leather and motorcycles. But where would I start? Even at school I'd found it hard to form friendships with people who didn't understand our lifestyle. Citizens tended to be nervous around those picked up on motorcycles.

Though if we leave, it won't be my lifestyle any longer.

I pull away from the comforting arms of my mother and blot my tears once again. Maybe if he sees I'm so worried about leaving, he'll change his mind and stay. Or at least, put off any decision until after the baby's born. Perhaps, instead of giving in and letting him have everything his way, there's a chance I can stop this happening.

"I need to talk to him," I say decisively. "This has come out of the blue. Maybe I can change his mind. He could step down as VP, but stay in the club." I start to stand, but Mom pulls me back down.

"Olivia." Sam comes over and kneels in front of me. My attention is caught by the serious look in her eyes, and the wetness that threatens to fall from them. "Listen to me, will you?" When I raise and dip my head, she continues, her eyes hardening slightly as befits the ex-first old lady, "Remember what this club is about. It's about respect and loyalty. When Eli accepted that patch, he vowed allegiance to the Satan's Devils. If he turns his patch in, it will be seen as a sign of disloyalty. The brothers won't be able to trust him anymore."

I nod once again. "That's why I've got to make him see sense. See how serious this is. Because once he's gone, there's no coming back, is there?"

"No." Sam sniffs, and Mom hands her the box of tissues now.

"So, I'll go talk to him. He should be out of church now."

Again, Sam stops me. "Olivia, it could be too late."

"What do you mean?" My brow creases. Surely it's never too late for talking?

"The decision may already be made. Drum… Drum warned me. Eli is going to be asked about his intentions in church." Her lips press together. "The brothers will think even the thought of leaving shows a lack of respect. He's got to be called out on it. *If* he tells them he wants to go, then…" She sobs, and sends a pleading look my mom's way.

Mom swallows back a sob of her own. "I'm so sorry, Olivia." Her eyes glisten with tears. "I came to this club twenty-six years ago. I was a fish out of bloody water at the start. Of course, I've been shielded from club business. I might not like that part of it, but it's how the club works. It works because it's a closely bound family. We might live outside the citizen rules, but that doesn't mean we don't abide by our own. Following the club regulations keeps the club knitted together. If Eli wants to walk away, he'll be shitting over an important part of our lives. He'll have to take what's coming."

What's coming? I look from one to the other, seeing, understanding their distress for the first time. I'd been so wrapped up in my own, I didn't realise the pain they, themselves, were feeling. Sam, because Eli is her son, and on Mom's part, she's regarded him as her fifth child. A feeling of dread settles inside me, as I recognise I'm seeing another side of Sophie and Sam. The determination of these old ladies who've accepted this way of life, and who would condone, while not like, any retribution that's coming to one who's threatened it. *Whoever* that might be.

"What do you mean?" I ask, holding my breath for the answer I don't want to hear.

Sam struggles, but puts it into words. "There's no retirement plan for Satan's Devils. A man who steps down won't be welcome on the compound." Her face hardens as if readying herself to accept it.

I protest, "Jacob lives here, he's not a Devil. Neither's Zane. It's home to Mason and Aidan."

Sam looks at me sadly. "You're right. The difference is they've never made promises that they've now decided they won't keep. They've never sat around the table and learned the inner secrets of being a Satan's Devil. Blade's son and Rock's are serving as Marines. When they've done their time, they might become prospects. Zane does work for the club."

"Eli had to have known," Mom interrupts. "Men don't walk away from the club unscathed. It's you I'm worried about. He bloody knew what to expect."

Sam stares at her, and something passes between them.

"What to expect?" I seem incapable of using many words. My heart feels like it's going to stop beating.

"You're club, Olivia, always have been. You know how men settle their disagreements."

Now the organ pumping blood through my body does cease working as my fist goes to my mouth.

I do indeed know. With their fists. "He's going to get a beatdown."

Sam's openly crying now. It's my mom who puts it into words. "If Eli has told them at church, then there's no going back on this, Olivia."

I stare at my mom and mother-in-law in horror, suddenly understanding why they're here. Not just to discuss Eli's revelation, but to support me through whatever will be the outcome for my husband.

Men don't just walk away from the club.

CHAPTER FOUR

*D*rummer...

Like Eli, I'd been born into the club.

The Satan's Devils MC had originally been formed by Bastard back in the nineteen seventies when he and a group of his friends had returned from the Vietnam War. Society had no place for such men, so they'd made their own. Bastard was president from the start. He met my mom, made her his old lady, and they'd had a baby. Me.

In those days the club was into everything and anything they could make money from. When men patched in, they knew their lives could be cut short any moment from a bullet, or other various options that all ended up six-feet-under. The club had been into drugs, guns and prostitution. It wasn't the life I would have chosen for myself, but I'd prospected, gotten my patch. Then I'd tried to change it from within, knowing the men I was living alongside deserved more, and I was determined to try to give it to them. Despite garnering support from some quarters, it had been impossible to steer the club in a different direction. Back then, the prez and many others liked the easy money.

In the end, change came but not as a result of my efforts.

The police had cooked up charges that led several of us spending a few nights in jail. When we'd gotten out, the clubhouse had been raided, laid waste, and burned to the ground. Bastard, my father, was dead. His old lady, my mother, had taken a bullet to the heart meant for him.

We lost eleven men that day. Three went to jail. They didn't get to live out their sentences. For the eight others, their time as Satan's Devils had ended more quickly—they'd lost their lives defending the club.

I could have walked away, but I didn't. The handful of men who were left, Peg, Tongue, Beef, Digger, Dollar and Viper—and Rock who was just finishing up his year in jail— were lost without being part of an MC. So I kept us going. I found this compound we bought for a song as nobody else wanted it, changed the direction of the club and accepted the role of prez.

For the past forty years, I've given my all to this club. Sure, I stepped down as prez last year, but only as age was catching up with me, and it was Wizard's time to lead the club. I'm still a full member, though, and that I will remain until such a time as I can no longer ride.

Wizard, quite rightly, had wanted his own team of officers around him. While he hadn't come out and said it, we could see the way the wind was blowing. So, also deciding they'd served their time, Wraith, my reliable VP who I could rely on one hundred percent, Peg, my sergeant-at-arms and Blade, my enforcer, chose to take a back seat along with me. None of us resented giving up the responsibility. It was time for us to relax and enjoy what remained of our lives. Oh, and have a bit of fun while doing so. It had earned us the name of F.O.Gs—Fuckin' Old Guys who run rings around the prez.

None of us would leave the club voluntarily. We'd signed on for life.

I never expected Eli would be anything different.

Had I forced him to join? Had I directed his life, so he had no other option?

Is it my fault he's now going to suffer the fate that the club decides?

"I still don't fuckin' believe it." Rock's shaking his head, and then lowering it into his hands. When he looks up, he's staring at Throttle. "You've always been closest to him. Didn't you have a fuckin' clue? Couldn't you have talked some sense into him before it came to this?"

The enforcer's face goes red. "Don't you think I fuckin' would have if I'd had a clue what was in his head?" He bangs his hand down on the table. "Hawk and I were fuckin' tight." He crosses his fingers as if to demonstrate how close. "He's not been himself; anyone could see that. But the man's got a lot on his plate. He's always been serious, now he's got a kid coming. Just thought it was that." His anger slips away, and he grimaces. "I saw he had something on his mind, but I'd left it too late. When I dragged it out of him, his decision was made. Took the wind out of my sails when I'd thought he was having doubts about the fuckin' baby or something. Never dreamed it was this."

"What about you, Drum? You're his dad?" Peg asks.

I pull myself back from my memories, and like Throttle, get annoyed at the implied criticism. "Don't you think I'd have fuckin' talked him out of it if I'd known?" They must see how much it hurts that my son hadn't come to me. "I don't know what the fuck's going on in his head." I stare at Wizard. "That's my son, and I don't know him anymore."

Prez looks down the table at me sadly. "You may need to recuse yourself from this discussion, Drummer."

Perhaps I should. It's the fate of my first born they're going to be talking about.

"Drummer's always put this club first." Dollar glances at me, then his eyes go to Wizard. "I trust him to vote for the club."

That pulls me up. *That's what he expects me to do? Put the club first in front of my son?*

Problem is, he's right. I can't not do that, and maybe that's what I've always done. Maybe it's why we've come to this point. The club has got to contend with a member who carries our innermost secrets in his head, who's proposing to walk off with them fuck knows where. What would I do if it were someone else instead? *Can I divorce my relationship with my son with what's right for my club?* The answer, I'm afraid, is yes.

"I trust Drummer," Heart also confirms. "He'll vote the right way."

"Before we vote, I'd like to know if Drummer wants to say anything in mitigation? Has Hawk got a valid reason to leave?"

I look at Blade, and he stares back at me. I try to think of something, *anything,* I can use in my son's defence, but nothing comes to me. I give my answer to him in one word, "No."

Am I sealing his fate, as I, his father, can't find anything to give validity to his announcement today?

Heart and Mouse are viewing me sorrowfully.

"Anyone got anything they want to say?" Wizard asks. "This is a serious fuckin' situation and I don't want anyone's view to go unheard." I suspect Prez would prefer to be anywhere but here right now. Fuck knows, I had hated sitting in his seat when we were discussing a member's fate. I respect him for not showing emotion. Wiz was a good choice for prez.

Peg waggles his hand. "As ex sergeant-at-arms, his going worries me. He knows where the bodies are buried, knows the state of our armoury. Knows the strengths and weaknesses of everyone sitting around this table."

Hound nods. "That too, concerns me. He's the fuckin' VP for fuck's sake. He knows *everything.*"

"Is there even a decision to be made?" Marvel frowns. "Letting him walk seems too dangerous to me."

"It's Hawk we're talking about." Lady rolls his eyes. "The boy whose diapers we all saw being changed. I can't believe we're even discussing this. He might be leaving the club, but he's still got blood family here. He's not going to betray his dad, his mom or his brother."

Joker grabs Lady's hand and squeezes it as though hanging on to a lifeline. I wonder if he's remembering a time he thought he'd have to leave the club. Not because he wanted to, but because he thought he'd be forced to if he admitted his sexuality.

Truck looks around the table. "I agree with Lady. I trust Hawk to keep his mouth shut."

I try to read the expressions on everyone's faces. Cast looks unsure, but then he probably would. While he's been a member since prospecting beside Hawk, he's only recently returned on a permanent basis having completed his final tour as a Marine. My gaze moves on. Roadkill looks undecided as well. Drifter looks stern, and Jekyll I'm sure is thinking of places he'd rather be, probably like all of us. This is a shock, a situation we've not been presented with before.

Or, perhaps we have, as Shooter reminds us. "We let Hyde go without a beatdown." He shrugs.

All eyes shoot to him, then come to me. "Why?" Wizard asks. "Remind us, Drummer. Hyde left before I patched in."

I glance at Heart. He probably remembers more than me, but I dredge up what comes to mind. "He prospected for eighteen months, mainly because Heart here, and Slick," I pause while men put their hands over their hearts remembering our deceased brother, "had issues with him. He worked hard, got his patch, then found his old lady. He would have given his all to the club, but it didn't come naturally. He wasn't a good fit."

"He was a good man," Heart surprisingly agrees. "This

wasn't his place. We parted on good terms, and he's always been a good friend to the club."

He's still our neighbour. He and Sarah had rebuilt her gramma's house and live on the adjacent land.

"Hawk's a good man too," Lady insists.

Again, it's Heart who speaks, this time to disagree. "Hyde was just a member, not the VP. He hadn't sat around this table long and hadn't much knowledge to take with him. Hawk's been patched in seven years now."

Wizard picks up the gavel and bangs it. "Three options to vote for, brothers. One, we allow Hawk to leave, no retribution." Even I can see objections coming to that. I'll have some myself. "Second, he gets a beatdown and third," he pauses, and his face becomes dark, "we consider it too dangerous to allow him to leave. In that case, he's dispatched to meet Satan."

I let out a shuddering breath, but I can't dispute Wizard's options. If it wasn't my son we were talking about, I'd vote for the third option to protect the club.

"Are we ready to vote?" Prez asks.

No. I want to scream. *I need more time.* If they vote for death, how could I explain it to Sam, or to Zane? Oh, I've already acted as a husband today, sharing more than I should have and tried to prepare her for whatever the outcome is. But how can you truly prime a mother for the possible loss of a son's life? Ignoring the distress in my head, I force my face to remain stoic. I can't allow my emotions to influence this vote.

"How you going to do this, Prez?"

"I want this over with. One vote. The majority have it. All agreed?"

Ayes are said, hands are raised.

He's not calling for a unanimous vote. *Would I have?* Possibly. But it's Wizard in the hot seat.

"Can I make one suggestion?" Throttle asks in a choked

voice, continuing when Wizard raises his chin. "If it's death, it's delivered quickly."

I go cold just thinking about it. But at least it's agreed, a merciful end for my son.

I don't think I've ever been so scared in my life when Wizard starts the vote. My hands sweat, and I find it hard to breathe.

With a pointed glance at the empty seat by his side which should be occupied by his VP, Wizard moves his head a fraction and nods at Throttle.

"Beatdown."

"Dollar?"

"Beatdown."

I start to breathe again, but then when it's his turn, Marvel says, "Satan."

Bullet looks at me, then shakes his head, his brow furrowed in misery. "Satan."

Lady says, "Let him leave," but Joker's for a beatdown.

Wraith mouths sorry to me, then agrees, "Beatdown."

Peg's eyes are full of pain. "Satan."

Blade can't meet my eyes. "Satan."

It's come to me. I can't vote that he gets away scot-free, I wouldn't be serving my club properly. Hardening my heart, I propose, "Beatdown."

Rock's for a beatdown, Heart too.

Mouse stares at me, seeming to need a moment to make up his mind. When he shakes his head and pronounces, "Satan." I can't find it in myself to blame him. He's about protecting information after all.

Shooter hesitates, then votes for death.

Jekyll says, "Oh shit. Fuck it. Satan."

Truck's for lenience, Drifter's for making Hawk hurt.

Roadkill votes for Satan, as does Cast.

Fuck. This is close. Mentally I've been tallying it up. If I'm right, there are nine votes for a beatdown, eight for death, and two to let him out unscathed. Hound and Wizard are yet to vote.

Hound exchanges a chin lift with Peg. "Satan."

There's a sharp intake of breath around the table. Seems I'm not the only one who's been keeping count.

"Fuck," Wizard rasps out, knowing he's got the deciding vote.

I forget how to breathe. It could be seconds or just one minute, but when Prez opens his mouth, I wish he'd give me more time. *I'm not ready.* But who could ever be ready for this? The rest of my life won't be long enough to cope with the consequences if Prez votes to end my son's life.

He picks up the gavel and brings it down once. "Beatdown."

Even from the ones who voted for death, there's a sigh of collective relief.

"That boy of yours," Hound looks down the table at me, "he steps one foot out of line, he says one thing he shouldn't, and I'll be taking him out myself."

I give him a sharp nod. That's just how it should be. Betrayal and there would not be a second chance. Eli wouldn't deserve one.

As Heart's tapping on the tablet, recording our vote for prosperity, Wizard looks directly at me.

"You throw the first punch, Drummer. Then you get out of there." I shake my head and start to object, but he stops me. "No arguments, Drummer. Things are going to happen that no father should see."

The murmuring of agreement around the table stops me disputing that I should be there for my club. For my son.

A beatdown sounds like he's getting an easy ride out, but I know he's not. With tempers running as high as they are? Hawk, or Eli as he'll now forever be, may not survive.

Perhaps a single shot to the head might have been easier.

The table is silent as Eli's called back in. Understandably, he's not directed to a seat, instead instructed to stand at the end of the table.

Wizard stares at him, his gaze almost as steely as mine, then without emotion pronounces, "You've disrespected every man at this table, Eli Felis. There's not one brother that's immune from the pain of being abandoned by their VP. You vowed to respect the club and abide by the regulations when you were patched in. That vow should not be taken lightly. The club has decided to let you leave, but not without punishment. The club has voted for a beatdown."

I'm watching my son carefully, noticing with pride the imperceptible straightening of his shoulders, and that he makes no protest or plea for clemency. But then he is, *was*, the VP. He knows what to expect.

"After which," Wizard continues, "you will no longer be welcome on this compound. Your old lady can stay or go with you as you and she see fit. She will always have a place here, she's club."

I feel as well as hear Wraith's sigh of relief. Eli will be gone, but Wraith's daughter doesn't carry his stain.

Prez stands. "We will continue this… conversation… in the storeroom."

Eli closes his eyes briefly as though preparing himself, then, flanked by Hound and Throttle, he turns and is escorted away.

As I take my place in the group following him, Wraith's hand rests on my back.

"You okay, Brother?"

"No." I tell him the truth. "I feel like my heart's been ripped out of me. I've seen, *done*, some bad fuckin' things in my life, but this by far is the worst. That's my fuckin' son, Wraith. How did it come to this?"

"What the fuck made him do it?" Wraith sounds angry. "Sorry to say this, Drum, but he's one selfish motherfucker. He's leaving, and he'll be taking my little girl away from me."

Olivia may be a grown woman of twenty-five, but she'll always be Wraith's child. "She could stay." I remind him what Wizard had said. "And if she does go, they'll be fine." I try to sound reassuring as I voice what I know is a lie. How the fuck could two Satan's Devils' kids live in the civilian world?

It's he who says the truth back to me. "They have to be. I know my daughter, she'll throw in her lot with her husband, and for Eli? Well, for him there's no way back."

The events of today have blindsided me. It's not often something knocks me off kilter. I want time to slow down. I want hours, days, to process what this all means, but I don't get that, or anything close to it.

It seems only minutes later we arrive at our destination. All too soon Eli, head held high, takes his place in the circle of men.

When Wizard beckons to me, I know there's no way out. No way I can avoid what I have to do. I'm club.

This might be the boy who I saw take his first breath, his first step, taught him to ride his first bike, but he's also a man who's disrespected my club and all that I've stood for my whole life.

Briefly closing my eyes, I put regret behind me, instead summoning up the anger. He's disrespecting and betraying me as well as every other man here. I pull back my punch and let it fly. He bends as air whooshes out of his stomach, and I turn when Wizard taps my shoulder and jerks his head toward the door.

With a heavy heart and dragging steps, I walk out. I'm only halfway through the door when I hear the next fist hitting flesh.

Immediately I know Wizard was right. I couldn't have stayed to watch. At some point I would have broken and begged for mercy for my son.

Neither do I have it in me to go home.

Instead, I enter the clubhouse and order the prospect to

hand me a bottle of whisky and a glass. Then I sit all alone and drink. Lost in my thoughts, wondering where it all went wrong, I lose all sense of time. The whisky which should be numbing does nothing to turn off my brain. My main worries veer between *was it my fault?* And *what am I going to tell Sam?*

"It's done." Wizard plops down in the seat opposite me. "He's alive if that's what you're wondering."

"He bad?"

He shoots me a 'what do you think' look, and nods. "Not many punches were pulled." Picking up the bottle of whisky, he takes a long swig. I don't bother to point out neglecting to use a glass is unhygienic.

When he puts the bottle down, he gives me a look of understanding. "This isn't on you, Drummer. It's all on him. He's a man. He's responsible for his decisions."

But is it? How the fuck hadn't I read the signs? How has it come to this?

CHAPTER FIVE

Eli…

I come to and immediately wish they'd killed me. Every single part of me hurts. Hurts? Fucking understatement, screams in agony more like.

For the moment it's all I can do to try to breathe. Every breath sends pain shooting through me from ribs that are clearly broken. *That was Hound, I think.* I try to catalogue what my injuries might be.

My own dad had gotten me in the stomach first. Then Peg had gone for my jaw, but though I've probably got whiplash, I don't think he broke it. Rock had kicked my legs out from under me. Fuck, my hand. I can't move my fingers on my left hand. *Are they broken?* Did someone stomp on it? If so, was it accidental when I was prone, or deliberate?

Marvel had got me from behind. If I'm not pissing blood for a week, it would surprise me.

There's a deep, sickening ache in my groin. *Thank fuck I was out of it when that was done.* Someone must have kicked me in my junk.

Pain. Physical pain. I welcome it, relish it. It's no more than I deserve.

"I think he's coming around." I hear a female voice. *Is that Amy?*

"Are you sure he's going to be alright?" The anxious voice is that of my wife. *Fuck. I don't want her to worry.* Could it hurt the baby?

"He'll be in pain for a while, but he'll be fine," Amy reassures her. "Just keep your eye on him. He's got some broken ribs, and I'm just a bit worried about his kidneys. You'll have to take him to the hospital if the blood doesn't ease."

"What about the stitches in his face? Will they have to come out?"

I hear a female sigh. "Yeah, they will. Look, I'll check if Wizard's okay with me making a house call."

Why will she have to check? Oh. I'm no longer a member of the club. Of course I can't expect to be treated by the prez's old lady. And where will we even fucking be?

I hadn't thought that far ahead, just knew I had to get out. But I expected to have time and make plans. Surely they're not just going to be throwing out me and my pregnant wife onto the street?

I suppose we could go to a hotel for a time. I've got some money saved; money put aside for the baby. We'll have to dip into that.

I'll have to find a job. Christ, what a mess. Right now, I can't even sit myself up.

"Eli?"

I must have twitched or given some sign indicating I'm not unconscious anymore. Making an effort, I open my eyes. Or, half open one, the other must be swollen completely. But it's enough to see my wife staring at me.

"Eli, you frightened me half to death. How are you feeling?"

Like I've been trampled by a herd of elephants. Which, actually, might not have been as painful. "I'm fine," I lie. I try to smile reassuringly, but I'm sure all I achieve is a grimace. My ears still work, and I hear strange sounds around me. "What's going on?"

"Prospects are packing up our stuff. We're leaving as soon as they're ready."

"Leaving?" *So soon?*

"Yes. We're going to Heart and Crystal's old house. The club still owns it. At least we won't be out on the streets, or not yet." There's more than a hint of censure in her voice. "We can stay there until we find our own place."

When Heart's first wife had been killed, Heart had never wanted to go back to the house they'd shared. The club actually owns it through a shell company, so it couldn't be traced back to us. Over the years we've maintained it and kept it on, it being useful when we needed somewhere for someone to hide. But it's not 'we' anymore. Something that's going to be hard to remember. I don't belong now. I'm my own man, just as I wanted.

My only responsibility from now on is my wife and child. I no longer have men depending on me.

My eyes have closed. I open them again, unfortunately in time to see Liv wiping tears from her eyes, and I have the thought that not all of them, or maybe any, are for me. I'm upending her life, changing everything and taking her away from the life that's been all she's known. I know it's selfish of me, but I can't see any other way out.

"Ha… Eli. Need you to get dressed." It's Rascal, and with the tone of voice he's using he's showing outright disrespect for his VP. I open my mouth—painfully—but then close it as it all comes back to me. I'm not VP anymore, and though he's just a prospect, he is club. I'm not.

"Here, I'll help." Liv tries to put her arm around me as I attempt to sit up.

"For fuck's sake, can you help her?" I call out. "She's pregnant."

"Should have fuckin' thought of that." Now it's Nathan

speaking insolently. Well I can't blame him I suppose. He, Rascal and Butcher are working their asses off for the patch I've turned my back on.

Nevertheless, he does help me. He's also gentler than I deserve, though as I sit up, unable to suppress my groaning, I can understand why. There doesn't seem to be a part of me that's not stitched, bandaged or black and blue. As for my balls… My uninjured hand cups them to try to get some relief, feeling they're twice the size of normal.

When I find out which asshole did that… I'll do nothing. Whoever it was wouldn't give me the time of day, never mind the chance to take a swing at him.

Liv tosses me some sweatpants. I slide them on, grateful my legs at least support me as I go to stand showing there are no broken bones. When she picks up a suitcase that seems far too heavy for her, I realise I should be the one carrying that, but it's all I can do to put one foot in front of the other. I try to give Nathan a grateful nod when he notices her plight and takes it himself.

In recent years, due to the numbers of houses which have been built here at the top, we've paved the track leading up from the bottom of the compound so trucks and cars can be driven up. Today I'm grateful for that, as I don't have to shuffle too far before I'm sliding into the passenger seat of our car, and Liv gets into the driver's seat. Behind us, I notice the prospects are getting into a truck.

I take one last look at the house we designed and equipped together, knowing today is the last time I'll see it as I won't be welcome back here. Then, I glance toward my dad and mom's house, seeing no one coming out to say goodbye.

Guess it's all too raw. Maybe, given time, they'll forgive me.

Mom will, I know that. Dad? I'm not so sure. I've just torn up and stomped on everything he held precious. Like me, he'd been born into the club, lived and breathed it all his life.

The difference being, while he thrived, I've become smothered.

Fuck but my head hurts. Or is my chest worse? When will the ache in my groin stop throbbing? At least the pain takes precedence in my head, overcoming the sense of loss for which I've only got myself to blame. As I ease back my head, I turn slightly, noticing Liv's jaw is set.

She, too, is staring into the rearview mirror, back at the house we've just left.

"We'll be fine," I tell her, trying to sound positive.

"Will we?" She looks more angry than upset as she turns to meet my eyes. "Will we, Eli? I'm not so sure about that."

I owe her an apology for uprooting her life. But she's my wife. It's her role to support me, isn't it? To be by my side? I feel a flare of temper myself. But the pain in my body tells me I've no desire to have an argument right now.

She slows while the gates slide open, automatically triggered by the remote in the car which Mouse will probably immediately disable, then we go through. I don't even turn around to see the home where I've lived all my life disappear behind me.

It's a rough ride down the long track which leads to the main road. However much I try to brace myself, everything hurts when we hit a pothole or bump even though Liv is driving as carefully as she can. I bite my tongue, refraining from asking her to slow down, torn between my suffering and my need to be far away. I'll feel better, at least mentally, once all this is behind me.

Once we hit the road, I can breathe more easily. I try to summon up the excitement I knew I'd feel once I was free and able to start my new life. That I fail and any joy evades me, I put down to my physical injuries. It's hard to look forward when I dread having to get out of the car and again having to balance on my feet.

At last we drive up to a single-storey adobe house, the

yard at the front looking nicely maintained. Well, if it wasn't, the prospects wouldn't be getting patched in—but I suppose from here on in, I'll be doing that myself. The club won't lift a finger to help me.

Liv pulls up the SUV in front of the garage, then gets out.

At least she waits for me, though she doesn't run around and fuss, leaving me to get out and shut the door behind me. I'm exhausted as a result. Parts which hadn't hurt so much on the drive make themselves known now.

She finds the right key—she must have already added to her keyring—opens the front door, and stepping up to the alarm consults a piece of paper she takes from her pocket and inputs the right code. At least this place is secure. It will do as our temporary home until we can find a place we can make ours.

I've not been inside for years, so I refresh my memory now. The front door enters straight into a comfortable living room. There's an outdated television on the wall, and two couches which have definitely seen better days. I also recall it's a three-bedroom house, but one will work fine for now. I'm in no fit state to explore, so I go and lower myself onto the couch, letting out another groan. I think I've uttered more of those than words since I first woke up.

"You can't stay there long," Olivia informs me. I open my one working eye to stare at her.

"Prospects are bringing our couches in. I hate to even think about sitting on that." She points, in disgust, at the sofa I'm sitting on. Yeah, now she's mentioned it, the musty smell reaches even my blocked and probably broken nose. I can feel a spring poking up under my ass. "Heart said to throw anything that was here out."

When the prospects stagger in through the door, I struggle, get myself upright again, then a few moments later sink my backside back onto our own couch from home.

I'm useless, unable to offer to help. But then, that's what

prospects are for. *Not anymore.* After this, I'll be doing every-thing myself. I realise they're not helping me, they're helping *her.* The old VP's daughter still garners respect while I don't. Not anymore.

The decrepit television is taken away, ours installed. Our bed comes in too, along with her bedroom set.

I sit bemused while boxes of kitchen equipment are brought in. Liv directs the prospects as to what should stay, and what should be removed. A loud whirring sound and a blast of cool air shows the air conditioning, at least for now, works.

In comes our fridge, out goes the ancient one. Pots and pans are banged around as she decides whether there's anything here that needs to be taken away.

It wasn't the talk with Throttle, it wasn't the discussion in church, it wasn't even the beatdown I'd received. But when the prospects finally leave and I stare around an unfamiliar house with all the comforts of my own, it's then I realise I've really left everything behind and closed the door on my old life. Now I'm faced with opening a new one and I'm not yet sure which way to turn. *Time for that when I'm feeling stronger.*

"Do you want anything?" Liv asks me tersely.

I think she's angry. But when I take a good look at her face, I realise she's trying hard not to cry.

"Babe…" I start, but get no further than that, as her face tightens.

"No, Eli. Don't say a word. Not one bloody word, okay? This is our life now. We move forward, and I'll try not to look back. You're hurt, I get that, so I won't press you today. But in time you're going to tell me why. Why you left the club. Why you left the only life we have ever known. Why you've taken me away…" Now the sobs start, and she turns so she's facing the opposite wall as if trying to hide them for me. "You are going to tell me, and soon. Because I don't understand, Eli."

Then she runs off. I hear a door bang, and then I hear her wailing from one of the bedrooms.

Oh fuck.

It hits me what a useless piece of shit I am.

In my desperation to get out, to do the thing I had to do, I hadn't considered her. I just dragged her along with me.

CHAPTER SIX

*O*livia...

I cry until there are no tears left.

I threw in my lot with Eli before I said my first word. It had always been him and me against the world. Other people call me Olivia or Ollie, to him I've always been Liv, his girl. Mom and Sam had suggested I stay on the compound, leaving Eli to reap what he'd sown alone, but I couldn't consider that for a moment.

My husband rides, *rode*, with a one-percenter motorcycle club. I always knew I could be a widow one day if he'd had a bad accident on his bike, or if he'd gone up against the wrong enemy. This way of life is not without risk, and it was always a possibility that I would have to live without him. Or 'that way of life', I should now say. It's not mine anymore.

I couldn't have stayed at the club and watched him walk away into the sunset. My place is here, beside him. I'll survive outside the club, I'm just not sure I'll thrive, or whether he will. Right now, I'm not certain he realises exactly how much or what he's given up, or whether there'll ever be any kind of substitute for what he, and I, have turned our backs on.

No, there was never any question about choosing between

the club or my husband. But hell, it's hard. I've no mom or family living close by me. I'm on my own with only an injured man for company. A man who's not in danger of dying on me. A man who brought his hurt on himself. Heaven forgive me, but I can't feel much sympathy.

The baby kicks at my stomach reminding me some things are not going to change. In three months I'll be a mother, and it's up to me to do my best to give this child a happy home. Sometimes I wonder whether Eli even wants a baby. Oh, he says the right words, but I can't be sure.

It's been a whirlwind twenty-four hours. I knew before he spoke to me that something was wrong. Perhaps it's my fault I hadn't spoken to him before, forced him to open up to me. But what woman wants to hear they're not enough for their man anymore? It's because that was what I feared he would say to me that I hadn't pressed him. I never dreamed he was troubled by anything else. Why, oh why, hadn't I questioned him before? Could I have talked him out of the answers he had come to on his own?

If I'd been braver, could I have stopped it?

Why am I wasting my time thinking about it, or apportioning blame? It's happened. Eli's left the club and has taken his punishment. There's no way back, no point in dwelling on it. Forward is the direction I should be looking. However much I want to turn back the clock, I can't. I have to move on.

And moving on isn't going to happen while I'm lying on this bed feeling sorry for myself.

Yeah, baby. I smile as I feel another movement inside me. *We'll make this work. We have to.*

Blotting the last of my tears, I sit up, then stand, then open one of the boxes the prospects brought in. I place clothes in the closet and in the drawers, then put fresh linens on the bed. My stomach growls, reminding me life goes on and I've got to eat. *No more going down to the clubhouse and seeing what's cooking.* Nope. That's going to be all down to me as well.

As I pass by the couch, I see Eli so still, I'm sure he must be sleeping. I continue into the kitchen and look at what food the prospects unpacked. I give a wan smile, seeing my mom's hands in some of my favourite cereal and cookies. The cupboards and fridge seem to be well stocked, but damn, I don't feel like cooking anything. There is one benefit to being in the city, it will be far easier to order food to be delivered here. I settle on ordering in pizza. To hell with what Eli wants.

A phone rings, the unique tone telling me it's mine. First, though, I have to find it. I spy my purse on the worktop and manage to extract it and answer before it rings off.

"Olivia, it's Mom."

I roll my eyes. Kind of guessed that when her name appeared on the screen. "Hi, Mom," I reply, both welcoming her voice and wishing she hadn't called. She reminds me of home, and everything I've lost.

"Just want to call and remind you I'm still here. We're all still here for you, Olivia. You need to come home, then that's what you do."

"I am home," I remind her as well as myself. My home is wherever my husband is.

"Yes, well." I can hear disapproval in her tone. Then with forced brightness she asks, "Are you settled in?"

"The prospects did a good job." I don't add I've spent the time since they've left wallowing in self-pity.

"Yeah, well. If you need anything else done—"

"Mom," I stop her, reminding her of the fact, "we're not club now. We'll have to do everything ourselves."

"Tell her I'm more than capable of doing anything my wife needs." My eyes snap up at Eli's voice. It's hard to tell as his face is so swollen, but it looks like he's glaring.

"Look Mom, I gotta go. Eli's just woken up, he's been resting. I'm going to sort out some dinner for us. I'll come and see you soon, okay?"

I hear her sigh, and there's a pause before she tells me, "Love you, Olivia."

"Love you too, Mom." But our automatic goodbyes were stilted, as if our relationship has shifted as well, as though it's not just physical distance between us. A reminder that my mom's still an old lady and I'm not.

Instead, I'm a wife, my injured husband my responsibility. I stand, tapping my phone against my mouth. "I was going to order pizza. Pepperoni?"

"Yeah." I see him try to move his mouth side to side as if experimenting whether he's going to be able to eat.

"Or do you want something different?"

"Baby food might be good."

I huff a laugh, then wonder whether he's being serious. "Amy gave me some painkillers for you. Do you want to take some?"

Eli's never been one for taking anything before, that he nods and says yes he does, which shows me how much pain he's in. I get some for him, bringing a glass of water for him to wash them down. Then I use the phone and call for pizza.

As the first night of the rest of our lives, it sucks.

We eat. Eli stays sprawled on the couch. Then we watch something neither of us are interested in on television. Sure, we spent time with just each other in our house back on the compound, but I was never bored. Mom was close by, and if I wanted to talk to a girlfriend, there were my sisters, Eliza, Hilda and Zoey, or my pseudo cousins, like Isabel, Amy or Maya to name but a few. Amy was good for baby talk too, her being a nurse and pregnant herself.

I miss the brothers too. The F.O.Gs, as Wizard had named them. Men who'd been in the club for years along with my dad treated me as if I was a favourite niece. The younger ones, they were a laugh, they'd flirt with me to get a rise out of Eli.

My brother-in-law Zane seemed to be in our house as

much as his own, the two brothers catching up with each other.

Now it seems quiet. Too quiet. An evening with nothing to do, punctuated with moans from my husband who's hurting through every fault of his own.

We go to bed early. I toss and turn half the night. In the end, I drag out a couple of clean sheets and use one of the old beds in a spare room as my constant movement is keeping Eli awake too.

The next day is not much of an improvement on the one before. I try to get more stuff put away and organised, while Eli has stiffened up and is incapable of doing much more than moving from the bed to the couch.

Halfway through the morning, Eli's phone rings. The house is small, I can't help but eavesdrop.

"Mom."

I take it that it's Sam on the phone.

"Yeah. I understand… Yeah, I'll be okay… Fuck, Mom. We're good. We'll be fine… No, don't do that. Yeah."

I don't try to pretend I wasn't listening. "Your mom?" I prompt.

He closes his eyes and leans his head back. "She just wanted to make sure we're alright." He lifts his one working eyelid and looks at me. "It's raw, for us and for them. Lots of changes."

"Is she coming to visit?"

"No. I told her not to. She's torn, Liv, between us and the club. We all need time to make the adjustments."

Adjustments? Who's he kidding? My world has been turned upside down.

If my life were a novel or a film, Eli would have bounced back to his normal fit and healthy self in a day or two and become the strong supportive husband I need. In a book, I'd have met the neighbours and made new friends, and would have been happy settling into city life. Eli, having got what he wanted would be happy, and his cheerfulness would have rubbed off on me.

But this is reality, not a dream and instead of being contented with my new lot, I find living is hard to do.

I miss everyone I'd left behind as much, if not more, than I'd done that first night. My loneliness and longing for home gets worse as the days pass. Eli doesn't bounce back fast. We come to accept broken bones take weeks to heal. It doesn't help lift me up when he, too, is as miserable as fuck, frustrated when his broken ribs and fingers prevent him from doing stuff.

I'm scared to return to the compound by myself. Not because I'm worried about the kind of reception I'd get, my phone calls with mom tell me I'd be welcomed with open arms. But I know returning to the place I'll always think of as home will upset me too much, and I might be tempted not to return. From time to time I hear a motorcycle coming up the road outside the house, causing a pang of nostalgia. I hold my breath, but the bike never stops or even slows down. *Nothing to do with us.*

Mom and Sam want to see me, maybe not so much Eli as they've not forgiven him yet. They're old ladies, loyal to their men and their club. For the present, the awkwardness that will be there prevents them visiting, so it's only by phone that we stay in touch.

One evening a knock comes at the door.

"Careful." Eli drags himself to his feet and is by my side when I go to open it. A gun has appeared in his hand and I'm not sure from where—another sign of how my life's changed. On the compound, closed doors never had danger hiding behind them. Before anyone could approach the houses, they had to first come in a gate, and only then if they got past the prospect guarding it. Then they had to walk past the clubhouse, where no stranger would be tolerated lurking about unescorted. They'd be confronted fast and stopped before they ever got close.

If Eli hadn't have warned me, I'd probably have opened the door without a second thought. Instead, I glance toward the monitor by the side of the door and see who it is standing outside. When I recognise him, I don't keep him waiting.

"Zane!" I throw myself at him as soon as the door's opened, and he's able to come in. I choke back the sob at seeing a friendly face.

"Olivia. How are you, babe?" He kisses me on the cheek and briefly hugs me.

"I'm good," I lie brightly, hoping he doesn't see through my untruth. Like when I talk to my mom, I hide my emotions and thoughts. It would be a betrayal for people to know how unhappy I am. I've got to make this work for my husband's sake. However much I might want to, unless I leave Eli, I can't return to my previous life. I'm not yet at a point where I don't think my marriage will work.

"Brother," Eli says warily.

Zane's eyes meet those of his sibling, and dual expressions war for supremacy on his face. Anger and sorrow. Eventually he sighs. "Can I come in and talk?"

"Nothing to talk about," Eli warns him. "My bridges are well and truly burned. Made my decision, and there's no going back on that."

Zane looks up and down his brother's broken body and gives a sad jerk of his head. "Can kinda see that, Brother."

"Come in. Sit down. Can I get you a beer?" I want to keep Zane here. Just seeing a friendly face has raised my spirits.

"Sure, babe. That would be great." Zane takes a seat on one of the chairs, while Eli walks stiffly back to the couch. I bring in beers for both of them, and a can of soda for myself.

"Why are you here?" Eli's shortness seems rude.

Zane ignores the sharpness and instead stares at his brother. "I'm not club, remember. I've no beef with you, Eli.

But I'd like to know why." He wipes a hand over his face. "I don't understand. Fuck, nobody does. Why, Eli, why? All our lives joining the club was the only thing you ever wanted to do. You had no desire for anything else. You even tried to persuade me into the life. You lived and breathed the club. When I heard the news, I couldn't believe it."

Eli shrugs. "Did I really want it, Zane? Or was it Dad forcing me in that direction? You never had the same pressure, you were able to do what the fuck you liked. It was me Dad groomed to follow him."

Zane shakes his head. "That's not how I remember it. Dad treated us both the same. You fell in love with everything the club stood for. I was the one who preferred cages to bikes. I was the one who saw a life that didn't involve patching into the club."

"What would Dad have said if I hadn't had prospected?"

Eli's brother looks confused. "Way I remember it was you didn't need any persuasion. You were always hanging around the club. Working with the bikes, rebuilding Dad and Mom's classics. Truth be told, I felt a little left out. I didn't have much in common with my family."

Eli shrugs. "But you followed your dreams. Got a degree, a good job, and have joined SD Construction. You're a partner at twenty-three. Life's been fuckin' good to you, Zane. You've not missed out."

"And you have?" Zane looks incredulous. "Are you actually my brother, Eli, or has someone else taken your place?"

I've stayed out of the conversation, but I've been listening hard. Zane's just echoing my own thoughts. Lately, Eli does seem to be someone else, someone I don't know and will have to relearn all over again.

"Anyway," Zane takes a drink from his bottle, then wipes his lips, "I've come with a message." He waves his hand toward his injured brother. "Dad and Mom are lost, they don't know what went wrong. They blame themselves and are upset. But they are also angry and confused. Neither know why you didn't go to them. There may have been a different way of working this out other than the club leaving you half-dead."

"I'm my own man," Eli says. "I knew what I was getting myself in for, and it was the fastest way out. Dad would have tried to persuade me to change my mind, and I didn't want to talk. My decision had been made. Sure, Throttle might have brought it up quicker than I expected and forced the issue, but though I'm hurting, I'd never take it back."

"He didn't even talk to me, Zane. I had no idea he wanted to leave the club." I can't keep quiet any longer.

"I knew you'd try and persuade me to stay." Eli's eyes come to me, and I notice they look cold. "You liked your life the way it was. You'd have used every argument in the book to stay on the compound. You might see it as being surrounded by family, but you, too, have been smothered, Liv. You, too, have been railroaded into a life you might not have chosen had you not been born the daughter of the VP."

"Are you saying I was brainwashed?" I snap, annoyed. Does that include my marriage to him? I love Eli, always have.

Zane coughs as though reminding us he's there. "Look, I'm here because Dad feels guilty. Not that you've left the club, but that when I was at college, he paid my tuition fees. He knows you might think you lost out. Truth is, had you chosen that direction, he'd have come up with the cash for you too. So he's putting some dollars in your bank account as he knows it will take a while for you to heal and get back on your feet."

Eli's teeth grind together. "I don't need his help. I can provide for my own wife and child."

Zane looks at him incredulously. "Your fingers on your left hand are fuckin' broken. You've got broken ribs and a broken nose. Christ knows how many other bruises. Not to mention you look like Frankenstein's monster with those stitches on your face. How the fuck are you going to get a job to support your family? You can barely walk."

"Your bedside manner's a bit lacking," Eli observes, his swollen face doing its best to smirk. "Doesn't change facts. I don't want Dad's fuckin' money."

"I do," I butt in. "I'm six months pregnant. I'm happy to try to get a job, but I've had an easy life. All I'm capable of being is a barista or something." I've never had to work in my life. I always knew I was Eli's, and it was enough to be his support. It's not because I'm lazy, but college wasn't for me. Being the old lady of the VP, I was a weak spot. Neither my dad nor Eli had wanted me to spend time off the compound, and I hadn't taken much persuading. If Eli doesn't take this financial help, it will be down to me to support us while he heals, and I've no idea how to start to do that. I've no work experience except knowing how to prepare meals for twenty or so people. Even if that got my foot in the door, what employer wants to take on a woman who in three months will be adding a kid into the mix?

"Listen to Olivia," Zane urges. "She's expecting your fuckin' baby. Are you so little of a man now, you're going to depend on her?"

But I can see Eli's face is set into his stubborn look. I haven't known him since I was a kid not to be able to read him well. His brother, too, recognises his closed-off expression. Zane finishes his beer, stands, then throws the gauntlet down.

"Money's going into your account whether you want it or not. Look at it as a loan if you don't want to accept what you're owed. Me? I think you should take it. Dad's right. He gave me a start in life, seems like he ought to treat both his sons equally."

Zane's made a good point. But I can see arguments ahead as I try to get Eli to spend it. Maybe he will. When he gets fed up with eating ramen noodles that is, which is probably what we'll be down to once the food in the pantry run out.

"I'll see you out." I stand, while Eli makes no effort to rise.

On the doorstep Zane leans in, speaking quietly so Eli can't hear him. "I'm fuckin' worried about him, Ollie, and about you and the kid. I… well, he's acting completely out of character. I never imagined he'd do what he's done, or be like this."

I try to reassure him, or am I reassuring myself? "He'll be better once he's physically well again. You know how he gets Zane, when he can't do the things that he wants. Remember when he fell out of that tree and broke his wrist? He was like a hornet whose nest had been poked until he could use it again."

Fleetingly, a grin crosses his face. "Yeah, I remember." Then he grows serious. "Christ, Olivia. I just hate this. I feel part of me has been ripped away. It's not just him, it's you and the baby."

"We're still here. You're welcome anytime, Zane." I truly mean it. He's got no beef with Eli as he's not a club member. He's family, and I need someone on my side.

"What are you two whispering about?" Eli's annoyed voice sounds from behind me.

I give Zane an apologetic look, but the expression he gives back to me is annoyed. "If you need someone to talk to, Liv, call me. Okay? You need help with anything, I'll be here right away."

As I wrap my arms around him, I nod my head, acknowledging his offer, but hoping I don't need it.

"Tell Mom and Sam I'll come to see them soon."

"You better," he warns me. "They might have lost him, but you're still part of the family, Olivia."

CHAPTER SEVEN

*D*rummer…

The loud clearing of a throat interrupts me. I stand, reach out for a cloth and wipe oil off my hands. I've been doing some maintenance on Sam's Vincent Black Shadow which we've managed to keep going over the years. Christ, is it really more than twenty-six years ago I first saw her broken down by the side of the road? Some days the memory's so fresh it seems like just yesterday.

She'd changed me that day. I'd been a single man one year off my forties, had no intention of making anyone mine, but she'd stepped into my life and stayed as my old lady.

I've never had one moment of regret, until now. Until I hear her quietly weeping in our bed at night, and I'm unable to comfort her. I feel so fucking guilty that she's estranged from her oldest son. Had I really missed the signs and forced him into something he didn't feel for the same way as me? Had I seen a boy I could shape, not a son who had hopes and dreams of his own?

A second soft cough reminds me I'm not alone. I glance over my shoulder, raising my chin when I see who it is. "Prez."

"How's he doing?"

"How the fuck should I know?" I snarl. Wizard knows the score. Eli's turned his back on the club. I, and the club, need time. A hell of a lot of water has got to flow under the bridge before things can start to settle down. Will I ever have a relationship with my son again? Right now, I don't know. Maybe we'll never be able to reconcile our differences, our views on life so far apart.

Wizard just stands, arms folded, a smirk on his face and a raised eyebrow.

I take in a deep breath and let it out angrily. "Okay, so I sent Zane around."

Looking behind him, Wizard sees there's a bench the right height. He moves back a few inches and cocks his hip against it. "And?"

I throw the dirty cloth down. "He's pretty badly beaten."

Wizard huffs a laugh. "Not news, Drum."

I know it's not. Grimacing, I add, "Zane couldn't get a read on him. He thinks it might be because he's hurting, but what is clear, he's left without making any plans."

"That doesn't sound like Eli." Prez frowns. "But we did force the issue, maybe he was waiting until a better time, once he'd got a job and place to live lined up."

That's the thought that's been going around and around my mind. "See, that's what I don't understand. It's why we all voted him in as VP. He never took a step unless he had a direction to head in. He'd been thinking about leaving the club for a while, yet hadn't put anything in place. You must have noticed he wasn't quite with us for the last few months." I glance at him to see him grimace. We all had, but just thought he needed space to get his head around whatever was bothering him. "I think we all were ignoring it. All of us, except for his best friend. It would have come to this whether or not Throttle had confronted him." I go to the fridge I keep in my garage and take out a couple of beers. Opening them, I pass one to Wizard. "Something tells me he'd not have been better prepared even with more time. He was focused on getting away from the club, not about what he'd do once he achieved that objective. Else, at some point over those months, he'd have had options lined up."

"The old Eli would have," Wizard agrees. He takes a drink, then muses, "It started after the wedding."

I shake my head. "Possibly even before that. When Olivia found out she was pregnant, and he knew he'd have to step up and be a family man."

"Are you saying, he doesn't want a baby?"

"Been thinking about it, Wiz. Been talking to Sam. If that was so, he'd have left Olivia behind. Christ knows, Sophie and Sam tried to persuade her."

Wizard sighs. "Ollie's a good woman wanting to stick with her man. It might have been better for her if she'd let him go alone. She didn't ask for any of this. Now she's been taken away from everything she's known. Amy's worried about her."

"All the fuckin' women are."

"And it's not just the old ladies. Wraith can't settle to anything now she's gone, a shepherd without all his flock." Wizard drinks some more of his beer down. "Wanted to ask you something, Drummer. I'm without a fuckin' VP now. Need someone to have my back in case shit goes down."

"Of course you do." I swallow down the pain that that should have been, *had been*, the role of my son. "Any thoughts who you'd want?" It would need to be a club vote, but the man in the hot seat can usually influence who he wants to be his right-hand man.

"No one comes to mind." He grimaces. "Sure, I can name any number of men who'd be ready in time, but none who I think could step up immediately. Obviously there are some who just plain wouldn't want it."

The VP needs to be someone who can run the club if the

prez isn't around. He's got to be someone who can lead and have the respect of the men so when he says jump, we all ask how high. He also needs to know he'll probably never move into the top spot and be content to be second in command.

"Have you thought about moving Wraith back up the table? At least until you can shape someone else."

"Wraith's not in the right mindset right now. We both know that. He's too cut up about Olivia." Wizard scoffs. "Nah, but I have thought of one person. On a temporary basis as you suggest." He pushes away from the workbench. "I don't want to jump and put someone in for the sake of it. You know the risks we take every fuckin' day when we ride. If something happens to me, I've gotta know the VP can handle the club." His mouth curves down. "I thought I had that in Hawk. I was wrong."

It hurts that my son turned out not to be the dependable man I'd always imagined him to be. Bowing my head, my hands toy with my beard.

"All my thoughts circle back to one man, Drum. You."

What the fuck? "Wizard, you must be fuckin' crazy, or my hearing's gone. Thought you said you wanted me to be VP."

"Nothing wrong with your fuckin' ears, old man." He chuckles. "Look, don't dismiss it out of hand. It's not permanent. Just to give me some breathing space while the club mends after losing Hawk. It's affected everyone. I hear the talk. They wonder what's gone wrong when someone like him walks away without glancing back. It's a betrayal that's gonna take strong leadership to keep anyone else from walking away. At the moment we're, *I'm*, weak. We've got to show strength. What better way than for you to step up and be my VP?"

It's the last thing I expected. But even I have to agree, he's got a point. I might be old physically, but I've still got all my faculties about me. My eyes, with the aid of glasses, are as sharp as any man's, and my hand's still steady enough to fire a gun. My brain, well, that's what he wants of me, and apart from forgetting shit like what I came into a room to find, that's as clear as it's ever been.

I know all the men trust me. Wizard and I would make a good team.

I glance at him wryly. "Thought I'd done my time."

He doesn't say a word, he doesn't have to. If my son hadn't made the decision he had, I'd have been allowed to enjoy my retirement.

I've given my life to this club. Everything I have I owe to the Satan's Devils. If my club asks something of me, I have no choice other than to agree. Even if it makes my gut churn to think I'll be sitting in the chair where my son should be.

I put my fingers to my face and pinch the bridge of my nose as I think things through. There's only one thing I can do. Turning around, I offer my hand. "I accept. I'll gladly serve as your VP."

Wizard takes my hand, shakes it, then uses it to pull me forward so he can slap the other against my back. "Better get Sam sewing then." He grins as he lets me go, and, reaching into his pocket, pulls out the VP patch.

I roll my eyes, but take it and raise my chin to him as he leaves. Seems I'm going to have to wait a little longer until I can just while out my days at the back of the pack with the other F.O.Gs.

Then without turning around, I say over my shoulder, "You can come out now."

A rustling sound from the opposite side of the garage, and Sam stands, a wrench in her hand.

"You could have told me to leave."

I raise my shoulders then lower them. "Would have, had he started discussing club business with me."

"You've done the right thing, Drummer." She loosens her hair, brushes it back, then wraps the tie around it again. "I hate the thought of you leading the club into danger again.

Thought now you'd retired, I'd be able to breathe. But you're not one to stand back when the club needs you."

She walks around in front of me and nods down to what I'm still holding in my hand. "You want me to sew that on?"

I was prez when I met her. I sewed that damn patch on myself. I'm more than capable of sorting this one out too. I grin at her. "Think I trust you more with that wrench than I do a needle and thread. Anyway, I'll have to wait until after it's all made formal in church." She smiles. That curve of her lips that's never ceased making me catch my breath. Stepping forward, I curl my hand around the back of her neck, and lower my forehead to touch hers. "Fuckin' love you, Sam."

She relaxes into me as she's done a hundred, a million times before, our bodies attuned to each other. As my cock hardens, I know if I wanted to find out, I'd find her wet.

For once in my life, the needs of my cock take a back seat. "I'm worried about our boy, Sam. Something doesn't seem right."

"I know," she tells me back. "What you said to Wizard, you're right. He just wanted to get away and leave. He had no idea what to do next."

"It's not just him, is it, though?" I stroke my hand up and down her back. "It's Olivia, who we both love like a daughter, and our grandchild. I'm worried as fuck about them all."

"I don't know what to do," she whispers. "I want to go see him, but I don't want to let you down. I know you're still angry with him."

"You're still his mom, whatever he's done, darlin'. If you want to go see him, you can."

She huffs. "Be easier if you told me to stay away. I'm angry with him too. I've spoken to him, he tells me he needs space."

"Perhaps we all do." I run my fingers over her silky hair as I think aloud. "I'd give my eye teeth to know what's going on in his head. What really made him walk away? Did it just build up? Was it my fault?"

"Not just yours, Drum. Mine too."

"Why don't you get Ollie to come here? At least we can find out how he's doing."

"Sophie doesn't think she can handle coming here yet. Oh, Drummer." Her face falls. "Olivia's having a hard time. Sophie hears the longing in her voice and understands. She doesn't want to come back to the club, see the house she was forced to leave, or see her friends she's now apart from."

"We're still her family, Sam."

She's quiet for a moment. "I think I'll leave her to approach us. Sophie's offered to visit her or meet her in town, but Ollie always makes some excuse. But she talks on the phone to Sophie most days, and Sophie updates me. If Eli's rebelling against things that we did, or his interpretation of them anyway, then maybe it's best to give them both some distance to figure things out and where they both want to be, and how to live outside the club."

"Space and time," I agree. "May not be what we want, but it's probably what they need."

"Sophie and I are thinking of postponing our trip to New York."

"That's still a couple of months away, isn't it?" I tilt my head to one side. "You've been planning this forever." They have. They had to work hard to convince us to let them go alone. Sophie had always wanted to take in a Broadway show, and Sam was excited about that too. "Things may have settled by then."

"Drum?" Her question starts with her biting her lip.

"What, darlin'?"

"What if he comes to realise he's made a mistake? What if he wants to rejoin the MC?"

I harden my face and my heart. "No way back, Sam. No fuckin' way. Nothing could be a good enough excuse."

"I hate it," she tells me.

I fucking hate it too.

I think that again when later that day, I make my way down to the clubhouse and into church. Was it really only last week when the vote was taken about Eli? When I'd sat around this table waiting for my son's fate to be agreed? So much has changed in such a short time. Now, unless anyone disagrees, I'm going to be taking his seat.

Fucked up situation for certain. For a moment I stand, letting men file into the meeting room past me, my finger and thumb pressing into the bridge of my nose. I'd noticed my son growing quieter but put it down to friction within his marriage, and nothing for me to interfere in, unless he'd come to me. If I'd pushed him for answers then, would things have turned out differently? Would he still be here and not ostracised from his family?

My delay means I'm last to enter the room. As I take my seat at the end of the table beside Wraith, I take a second to watch the men, seeing them tossing glares toward the empty seat to Prez's left. Wizard was right, they've been knocked off kilter by the loss of their second in command, and he's correct to quickly fill the position. He's also not wrong about me. If I was still prez, I'd jump at the chance to put an experienced man in that chair.

I'm ready to serve my club once again. Now all that remains is to check they still want me.

Wizard bangs the gavel. "I'm going to start with a proposal. I need a VP. Got a man in mind who's agreed to take it temporarily."

"Temporary?" Hound looks surprised. "You're promoting someone who might not make the grade?"

Wizard barks a short laugh. "Nah. I'll cut to the chase. We'll take a vote if it's needed, but I'm proposing Drummer steps up as VP."

For a moment there's a stunned silence. Then a chuckle

from Peg. And, as he starts to slide under the table, Blade puts his head into his hands and says loudly, "Oh for fuck's sake. Thought I'd gotten away from that man being able to order me about."

I snort, and realising old habits die hard, find myself slapping him around the head.

Wizard bangs the gavel again and says sternly, "Now if the kids will shut up and behave, I'm asking if we need to discuss this—"

"No discussion," Throttle interrupts. "We need a strong man in that seat. I second the motion."

"Thirded," Joker puts in, his eyes looking around. "There's not going to be one person against this, Prez. I propose Drummer moves seats and we get on to discussing what else we need to."

"Show of hands," Prez says. "Who's for Drummer moving into the VP seat?" As far as I can tell, the next question is unnecessary. "Anyone against? Okay. That's settled. Drummer. Come up here."

I do, realising I will indeed be getting some sewing practice in later tonight.

It's a standard meeting with nothing particular to discuss. When it draws to a close, I step out and go to the bar, unsurprised to find Blade, Peg, Rock and Mouse waiting for me there.

"Wiz did good," Peg tells me. "Need to show some strength from the top right now."

I have to agree. Particularly as one omission is Wraith. He'd walked out fast when we'd exited church. Not, I'm certain, because he thinks the role should have reverted to him, but because he's worried as fuck about his daughter. Since Eli and Olivia had left, Wraith's been a man lost—one of his chicks is missing from his nest.

CHAPTER EIGHT

$\mathcal{E}$li...

For the first time in my life, I don't know what tomorrow will bring. Less pain, for a start, I predict and hope. Though my broken bones won't heal for another few weeks, my bruises are already starting to fade. Amy came around last night, took the stitches out of the wound on my face, and seemed fairly happy with the way things were going.

Not that it hadn't been awkward, it had. Wizard's wife had come and left. It was clear she didn't know what to say to me and was business-like in her approach—just a nurse with a patient. She had exchanged a few words with Liv, but their conversation was stilted, much left unsaid. Of course, she wouldn't want to share how life was going on at the compound, and as there wasn't much going on in ours, Liv had nothing to say. Then Amy had gone, and I was alone with my wife once again.

Physically, the reasons for not getting off my ass are receding. Mentally, I'm frozen in place. I keep telling myself my inability to think about what I want to do for the rest of my life is down to the injuries I received when I was beat out of the club. I suspect I'm lucky to be alive.

Had I not made plans as I'd expected them to kill me instead?

Possibly. Dead men have no future to plan for.

"Babe? You awake?"

"Yeah. I'll be there in a sec," I call back to Liv, knowing I need to get myself moving. I groan, though not this time so much from the pain, but from the effort of getting up to face the next day of my life.

If it wasn't for Liv, I wouldn't get out of bed. But she's here, she's my wife. *She's my reason for living.*

Isn't she?

Shaking my head to clear that train of thought, I have a quick shower trying not to catch sight of myself in the shower. Then, when I've removed the plastic bag covering my bandaged left hand, grab a pair of jeans out of a drawer, and pick up a t-shirt without caring or even looking to see which one it is.

Liv's got breakfast ready to serve by the time I arrive in the kitchen. She's plating up which means her back is turned toward me. I wonder why I've no reaction at seeing her ass as it moves in the way I used to find enticing when she stretches to lift a pan then puts it back. Is it still that my balls are sore? They seem to have gone back to their normal size. Could it be getting kicked in the 'nads takes it out of a man? Or could it be that my wife just doesn't make me feel horny anymore?

I'm a man. It doesn't take much to get me hard, as my morning wood normally demonstrates. Except, even that hasn't been putting in an appearance recently. Does Olivia simply not turn me on anymore, or is it worse? *She turns me off.* I realise I haven't wanted her for weeks.

Christ. This is the woman I'm tied to for life. The woman who's going to have my kid in just a few short months now.

Back at the club, surrounded by people, it was easier to hide my doubts that I still wanted her to be by my side forever. But now it's just the two of us, I feel trapped, forced to confront things I'd hoped to be able to avoid.

"Here." She turns and places a plate down in front of me, then smooths her hand over her stomach.

I force myself to think of someone else for a moment. Two someones actually. "How are you? Is the baby okay?"

"Fine."

I frown, looking at just the one plate she's placed down. "You not eating?"

"You overslept. I had something an hour ago." She does, however, place her cup of decaf down, and takes the seat opposite me. "Eli, I'm getting concerned. You won't use the money you got from your dad, which means we should both start looking for work." She pauses, and her teeth worry her lip. "I know you need to heal a bit more, but you don't need to physically go out to look for work. Why don't you browse the internet to see what's around?" She pulls her tablet toward her. "I've been looking myself and—"

"You're not getting a job," I growl. "Not in your condition."

"My condition?" Her eyes widen. "I'm pregnant not helpless. Plenty of people work while carrying babies around."

Maybe they do, but they're not my wife. I don't particularly relish the thought of stepping into the civilian world myself. The thought of her working alongside men, and even women, I don't know or trust, makes me angry. Anything could happen to her.

"There's a job at the library, no experience necessary. I thought I might apply."

"Liv," I snarl, "you'd have to carry books around, go up ladders to stack shelves."

"You don't know that. I could at least go along and find out what's involved." Her eyes sharpen. "In fact, I am going. We need to eat, and you need to heal. If you—"

"Fine." I slam my uninjured hand down. "I'll use some of the money Dad put in my account. That will tide us over until I start work."

"We should still minimise what we take from that. We'll need money for when I have this baby."

Fuck it. I hate that she's right. I've been getting away with the excuse I didn't want to buy shit too early and tempt fate, but that vindication is fast running out as time moves on. But I haven't been entirely useless. "I've started putting money aside," I remind her. Well, I did before I walked away from the club.

"That won't be enough. There are the medical costs, let alone all the stuff we haven't even thought about buying yet—"

"Fuckin' hell!" I yell and abruptly stand. I didn't mean to, but I knock my plate off the table, and it smashes onto the floor.

Immediately I kneel and start picking up pieces of broken china, thinking how the shattered plate summarises my life at this point.

She sits and watches, her face at first confused, then her jaw tightens. As I reach for a piece that's slid a distance away, my shirt must ride up.

"What are you going to do about that?"

She's referring to my back-patch tattoo, the one with the devil looking over three glowing-eyed demons which covers all my back from my shoulders to my ass. I'd been so proud when I'd been patched in, the pain of the needle was nothing measured against the pride I felt showing the world I was a true Satan's Devil now.

I hate it.

"Are you allowed to keep it?"

I shake my head and reply tersely, "No, I'll have to get it blacked out."

Her hand covers her mouth. I know exactly what she's thinking. It's going to look horrendous when a tat of that size is covered over. Still, better that than the constant reminder of what I'm not anymore. Once it's gone, I won't be afraid to catch sight of my back in the mirror.

"Can't you turn it into something else? Or get it removed?"

"I doubt it," I tell her. Then as I see the subject has brought tears into her eyes once again, I add, "But I'll see what I can do, okay?" I'll have to do something soon. If I don't, I risk another beatdown or worse if a Devil catches me with it uncovered.

"Are you happy?" she suddenly asks. "Are you getting what you wanted from this new life? Is this what you expected, Eli?"

"Liv," I start, as though speaking to a child. "Of course I can't fuckin' enjoy my new life. I'm hurting. I've got a broken hand and ribs. I'm useless right now. Things will be fine once I'm able to work." They have to be. I can't go on as I am. All I need is a purpose in life that will set me right.

Olivia grabs some paper towel and joins me on my knees. She scoops up the scattered food and then drops it in the garbage can. When she comes back with a damp cloth to wipe the floor, she stares straight into my eyes.

"Is it me?"

I can't force the word no out of my mouth, but I hesitate to say yes. To confirm her worst fears would be to shatter all her hopes and dreams, and the promises that I've made.

A simple one-word answer isn't enough, anyway. It's too complicated to be summed up so easily. Leaning back on my heels, I open the cupboard under the sink. Reaching in, I take out the dustpan and brush and soon have all the remaining shards of china swept up.

"We need to talk," I tell her, not missing the pain that crosses her face. "Come sit with me."

I walk into the living area and take a seat on the couch, this time leaving space for her to sit beside me.

"Liv..." I start, once she's sat down. "We never had a

chance, did we? Put in the same crib from the day I was born."

"You protected me. You were always there, from that very first day."

I breathe in deeply. "We were pushed together. Yes, I know we were genuine friends. But do you ever think what would have happened if there had been more of us around? More the same age?"

She frowns. "But there was. Amy was already there, then Tyler, remember him? Though, of course, he was older and wasn't there long."

"Amy was three years older than us. Noah, Jacob and Isabel, all younger."

"You chose to play with me." She bites her lip. "We were always inseparable. Then our feelings changed, or, they did for me. Are you saying they didn't for you?"

"Of course they did." I stand abruptly, starting to pace, knowing I'm fucking up this conversation and needing to restart it a different way. "You know how my father got his road name, Liv?"

"Everyone knows that." She seems bemused that I've thrown his name into it. "Drummer banged everything in sight. Until he met Sam."

For the first forty years of his life, he'd lived up to his handle. "Have you any idea how many women he must have fucked before he met Mom?" I snap the question at her.

"Enough to know he's lucky he didn't get an STD," she throws back.

I lurch toward her, my good hand grasping the arm of the couch. Leaning my face down I spit out, "How many pussies has my cock been in, Liv?"

She pushes me away and stands. "One." Her eyes flare. "One. Mine. Are you saying I'm not good enough? That you could do better than me?"

The words are wrenched out of me. "How the fuck do I

know? There's only ever been you and me. My first kiss. My first fuck. I'll go to my fuckin' grave not having anything to compare you against."

"What more do you want? Don't you come? Because I don't know how else this got here." Her hands go to her stomach. "Well, tell me? What are you missing? Someone who gives you head? Well, hey. That's me. Just what more do you want? Someone who lets you try new things? Well, that's me too as I remember. Doggy style, shit… Are there more positions you want to try?"

"I don't fuckin' know!" I turn it around on her. "You've only ever known me. What if there are better cocks out there? What if someone can do things you enjoy more? Don't you ever want to find out and see?"

"No!" she screams at me. "I enjoy sex with you. And it's not just sex. I love you, and that makes all the difference to me. We connect when we make love. It's a completion of what we feel for each other."

"It's different for a man," I tell her, coldly. Not actually knowing, but thinking it is. Another pussy would feel different. Tighter? Perhaps, but I can't see how. We are a good fit. Another mouth might allow me to go deeper, a whore might not mind me choking her with my cock. But while I'm with Liv, I'll never find out.

"This is why you left the club?" she starts, incredulously. "You knew you wouldn't be able to get away with fucking someone else while we were there."

I bark a laugh. "You think I couldn't have gotten away with it? The whores would keep their mouths shut if they knew what was good for them, and my brothers were loyal to me. If I'd strayed, you'd never have known."

"Have you?" Her eyes widen with suspicion.

"Isn't this what I'm telling you?" I huff. "No, I have not."

"But you want to find out," she whispers, her eyes filling with tears.

I hate seeing the hurt I've put there, but I don't know how to stop. "Yes. No. I don't fuckin' know," I cry out. "Doesn't it bother you, Liv? That you've only known me."

She moves jerkily across the room as though her body's being controlled like a puppet on strings. "Well I never thought it did."

When she picks up her car keys, I feel a pang go through me. *She's going to leave.* Or, maybe, just run back to the compound and tell my mom what an ass I am.

"Where are you going?" I call out as she opens the door.

She spins, her eyes throwing sparks at me. "Out on the fuckin' prowl. It's what you want, isn't it?"

The door slams behind her before I can react. The car engine starts, roars, then the noise recedes.

Fuck.

CHAPTER NINE

$\mathcal{O}$livia...

I had to get out of there before I said something I would regret, or he said something he'd be unable to take back.

I manage to get into the car and away from the house before the tears start to roll down my cheeks. I'm not even sure if they come from anger or hurt.

I'd thought we were living the fairy tale, ours the love of the century. Both of us virgins when we came together. Sure, we'd fumbled at the start as we tried to figure out what to do — of course we knew the basics—you don't grow up in a sexual environment as we had without learning the mechanics. When we'd tried to put it into practice ourselves, we'd shared a lot of laughs. The first time we'd come together, it was more like fooling around which went a step too far.

Eli had been terrified that Wraith would somehow be able to see I wasn't his innocent daughter anymore, as if it would be written on my forehead, but luckily, Dad had had no idea I'd lost my virginity at the age of eighteen.

Eli had hoped to get lucky for a while. Unbeknownst to me, he'd started to carry condoms around. He'd been prepared and optimistic for months, but he'd waited for me. I knew I was his first as he was mine. It had been obvious we were equally untutored when we got together at last.

I sometimes think Dad had chosen to remain in ignorance. Looking back, I don't see how he couldn't tell things had changed between us. It had been hard to hide my adult love for Eli, so different from that of a child. I think now, he probably knew, but didn't want to confront it.

Neither of us had ever expressed a desire for other partners until today. I'd always loved the thought that I was his one and only and would be for the rest of my life. I honestly don't see how our sex life could be any better, and personally, I wouldn't want the variety or to go with someone else.

I hate him for even thinking it.

I drive, aimlessly, finding I'm heading up toward the famous 'A' that towers over Tucson. Parking my car, I get out and walk, then sit, staring at, but not appreciating the glorious views over the city. It's a clear day, the sun shines down fiercely. I won't be able to stand it for long. But consciousness of my physical discomfort evades me, overpowered by the pain in my mind.

Who is this stranger I'm living with?

The Eli I know and love would never hurt me, even with words. Yet he must have known suggesting I wasn't enough for him sexually would cut me deep down to the bone.

Was he serious?

Could it have been he was just sharing his thoughts with me? Letting me into his state of mind, the ideas that were making him uneasy. Or, is he going to act on it? Is he going to leave me and find another woman instead? Heaven knows he hasn't wanted me lately. Is it because he wants someone else? *Has he already found another woman?* No, I don't think he has. He hasn't been furtive and secretive as though trying to hide an affair from me.

I'm six and a half months pregnant. Surely, he wouldn't

leave me? But he's living in a fantasy world if he thinks I would give him some freedom, turn a blind eye while he put his cock in new pussy, just to find out whether he liked it better.

He's not thinking he could come home with fresh ideas, is he? Well, he'll have to think again if that's what's on his mind. If he stepped out on me, I wouldn't be able to have him back. No number of showers would cleanse him enough for me to ever trust him again.

It would be the end of our marriage.

When did he start changing?

I think back to our wedding. He seemed fine then, if a bit distant, perhaps, the day before. Although us old ladies were kept out of club business, it had been impossible not to pick up things had been touch-and-go. There hadn't been trouble in the club for years, and I remember thinking why did it have to come for us now? In the hours leading up to the ceremony there was even talk of cancelling it.

Then, like the sun reappearing from behind the clouds, smiles had appeared on everyone's faces again.

Lady had married us, having recently been ordained as a Satanist of all things. It had made perfect sense, seeing as we were all Satan's Devils.

That day had been everything I'd dreamed of. I married the man I'd loved all my life surrounded by family, both blood and friends.

I'd been just three months pregnant then, barely showing. But, as my baby bump grew, Eli started pulling away. Imperceptibly at first, then even I had to accept something was wrong.

It's not just that he wants to experience variety, I realise. It's that he doesn't get the hots for me anymore. Have I become too familiar? Have we just burned out? Or is it that I'm pregnant?

"Hey, I don't mean to interrupt, but I don't think it's a

good idea for you to sit out in this heat in your, um, condition."

I look up sharply, not having heard anyone approach. In front of me stands a man with brilliant blue eyes and pale, almost white blond hair. He's tall, over six feet in my estimation, muscled, and tattooed. If he was wearing jeans and leather instead of his shorts and t-shirt, he could pass for a biker.

Is this the kind of man I could go for? It sounds odd, but I've never looked at anyone other than Eli in that way for all my life. I try it out now, staring at him for a moment. He's rugged, but handsome enough, and a muscular build not too dissimilar to Eli. *What would I feel like if this man put his hands on me? What if his lips touched mine? Would his cock swell, and would I like knowing I could affect him?*

"Hey, you okay?" His head tilts and his brow furrows.

I feel my cheeks burn and hope he thinks it's the sun that's caused the reddening of my skin. *What the hell am I doing? Eyeing up a stranger like a piece of meat.* I start to stand, realising I've absolutely no interest in him and was just using him to test whether it's possible to feel horny for a man who wasn't my husband.

Preparing myself for when Eli leaves me.

I shouldn't think like that. I should fight for my man.

"Here, take my hand," he offers when he sees me struggling. "Dust storm is coming over. Best get back to town while you can."

I wave off his help. I'm pregnant not decrepit, but standing see that he's right. A storm is coming and pretty fast. Already the wind is getting up. The very least I should be is safe in my car, and not outside when the thunder and lightning gets going and the rain starts lashing down.

When I'm on my feet, I cast one more worried look at the approaching storm, then throw a brief look of gratitude at the man who warned me. "I best get going. Thank you."

"Gabe. I'm Gabe."

Wondering why he so freely offered his name to me, and determined not to give mine, I hurry to my car.

Moments later, I'm winding my way down the road leading to the bottom, hoping I'll beat the rain. I drive over the washes knowing once the heavy drops start falling, I'll have to slow down and stop. Arizona hasn't got a stupid drivers' law for nothing. It's suicide to cross a wash once they start to fill up. The water can become a torrent within seconds.

Lightning flashes and thunder rumbles, echoing my mood. There's no other man for me but Eli. If he does betray me with another woman, our marriage will be over, and I'll give him no second chance. But I'll never go looking for another man, no one could ever measure up. I'll just die a lonely old lady, living only for my child.

While I don't end up having to wait for a wash to clear, I do have to slow down as the rain is coming down in sheets. I shiver, seeing the temperature has dropped by twenty degrees. It's a regular summer weather occurrence in Tucson, one moment unbearably hot, the next so much cooler. Then the sun comes out, and all the water dries up. I've never known anything different, having lived here all my life. Mom though, I smile, she still complains during monsoon season, having come over from England when she was my age. For a moment, I think about the culture shock she went through, leaving her home in a town not far from London, and ending up in a motorcycle club in the United States. She had to get used to a different style of living. Perhaps history is repeating itself. She learned to love a new way of life, perhaps I should try and integrate into civilian ways. I might find I like it.

But not without Eli. I can't do it by myself.

The problem is, Eli's not only not helping me, he's not helping himself.

Sure, he's hurt and his bones need to heal, but it's he who

wanted this new life. So why isn't he reaching out and grabbing it?

I wish he'd speak to me. I wish he'd explain the real reason why we had to leave the compound. He gets harder to understand every day.

As I get closer to home my slow speed isn't just because of the torrential rain that's falling, it's because I'm reluctant to return. I've no idea what version of my husband will greet me. Or whether he'll even be there.

I resemble a drowned rat after running just the few steps from my car to the house.

Eli throws open the door. "Where the fuck have you been?"

"Out thinking," I spit back at him. "You gave me a lot to think about."

"You should know better than to just head out, Liv. I didn't know where the fuck you were. What if something had happened to you? I don't even have prospects who I can send out to search anymore."

I roll my eyes as I poke him in the chest with my finger. "Firstly, whose fault is that? And secondly, if I really went missing, one call to my dad and the whole club would turn out."

"That's always been your answer for everything. Run to daddy like a little girl."

My eyes roll. "Yeah? Like your dad wouldn't step in to help if you were in trouble?"

"My dad doesn't give a damn if I'm dead or alive." He stands, his chest visibly moving in and out, his cheeks puffed and his whole body tense.

Despite him looking angry rather than hurt, I make an attempt to console him. "He'd come, if you needed him."

"Well I don't fuckin' need him, do I?" he snarls.

I throw up my hands. "I'm going to lie down in the bedroom. There's no talking to you in this mood. Though I will tell you one thing. If," I punctuate my words with another poke to his ribs, even now avoiding those which are broken, "if you ever go off with another woman, even if just to fuel your fantasies, that's us finished. For good. So you better do some fucking thinking what you want. Just one betrayal would be all it would take."

His eyes go wide. "You'd leave me?"

"Damn straight I would."

Then his mouth quirks and I get a brief glimpse of the man I fell in love with as he jokes, "I better cancel the whore I arranged for later then."

But I'm in no mood for levity. Huffing loudly, I walk across the living room and down the hall to our bedroom. Before I can turn into it, I see the bed's been made in the guestroom. I know it's not because we're expecting company.

As if on cue, the baby kicks, reminding me I'm not alone, even if Eli is pulling away. I stand in the hallway, looking from the master bedroom to the guest room, wondering how my life and our marriage has come to this. Separate rooms now. What's next? Separate lives?

Suddenly I feel warmth behind me, a scent which is so familiar to me, I'd know it blindfolded.

He murmurs his explanation. "I toss and turn. I know I keep you awake. Until I'm healed and I can get a good night's sleep, I thought it was best if I move in here. You need your sleep."

"I don't mind." My anger has fled, sorrow chasing it away. "How can we make things work if we're not together, Eli?"

"We're hardly apart," he scoffs. "I'm only going to be spending the nights in the guest room. Now I'm not doing shit for the club, we've got time together during the day. Hell, we might like the break at night. It will stop us getting on each other's nerves."

He'll never get on my nerves. He must be speaking for himself.

"Once you get a job, Eli, you'll be gone during the day. I may too, if I find something for me."

"Told you before, not having you go to work. Hell, I was worried enough when you disappeared today."

I spin around. "Then you shouldn't have pissed me off." Hell, he makes me so angry. "And it was only because you didn't know where I'd gone. You could have picked up the phone and called if you were that worried. We're citizens now, Eli. That means I go out and do citizen shit. Go to the grocery store without an escort, get a job like any woman wanting to support her husband and child."

He growls. "And I told you, you're not supporting me."

"I didn't mean totally, for goodness' sake. We're in this together now, you and me. I want to play my part. Isn't that what civilian women do?"

He doesn't reply. It's his turn to spin on his heels and walk off.

I call out after him, "It's about time you decided exactly what it is you want, Eli." When he pauses, I add, "We're out of the club. We've both got to forge a new way for ourselves."

CHAPTER TEN

*O*livia…

It's been four weeks since we left the club and nothing much has changed.

I haven't returned to the compound, and neither Mom nor Sam have come to the house because I've discouraged them. While I've been speaking to Mom daily on the phone, I've made up every excuse under the sun not to go back to the place I'd probably not want to leave. The reason not to have them visit me, was almost the same. It would be only too easy for them to persuade me to return with them.

I pretend I'm enjoying my new life, but the closest I get to that in actuality is that I endure it.

Heart's house was originally chosen as it has no close neighbours, secluded and out of the way. The only person I tend to speak to in person, other than Eli, is the cashier at the grocery store I go to, and that's only to tell her no, I don't need help out to my car. Oh, there was a woman who asked with interest when my baby was due. But I'd stepped back and eluded her when her hand started to reach out, and I was suspecting she was going to take the liberty of feeling my baby bump the way some people expect to do.

Constantly I pretend to myself everything is well, while knowing it isn't. Eli and I still sleep in separate rooms, and while we haven't revisited the conversation concerning the lack of sexual partners in his life, I remain scared in case we do.

I haven't been successful putting Mom off entirely. My excuses ran out when she sensibly suggested if I wasn't going there, and that she couldn't come here, then meeting up in a coffee shop in Tucson would do.

Meeting face-to-face will tell her everything she wants to know without me uttering a word. I don't have a poker face and know she'll realise things are not right in my world.

Eli doesn't seem to care what I do, as long as he knows where I'm going and why. A habit born of years of the club looking after their old ladies, keeping them protected from enemies. Well, he's not a Satan's Devil anymore, so we've got no one we need to steer clear of. But I've humoured him, explaining I'm going out to meet my mom.

"I'm off now," I tell him. "I'll be a couple of hours."

"I might be out when you get back."

I notice the practice of saying where and who with doesn't extend to him. Or not without me pressing. "Where are you going?"

He raises and lowers his shoulders. "What you're always bugging me to do. Job hunting. Thought I'd try the Harley stores. See if they're hiring."

What Eli doesn't know about Harleys isn't worth knowing, or any make of motorcycle come to that. It's a good idea, so I tell him so, wishing him good luck. His going job hunting is a good sign, isn't it?

I even have a slight spring in my step as I approach the coffee shop where Mom and I are meeting until I enter and spy not only her, but Sam as well. *It's an ambush.*

Mom stands and holds out her arms. I walk straight into

them. We hug, both of us fighting tears, then she holds me at arm's length.

"Bloody hell. You've gotten big."

"Mom!" I bat at her arm. "You're lucky I'm pregnant."

"How are you, Olivia?" Sam's eyes are full of concern.

I suspect she means maternity wise. "Fine. Though I'm getting swollen ankles."

"Your doctor think everything's progressing okay?"

They won't be content with platitudes, so I give them chapter and verse on my latest check-up, having to admit that Eli hadn't come with me.

Sam's mouth thins. "Why not?"

I shrug and lean forward, pausing briefly to thank the waitress who'd brought a soda to me.

"He's busy looking for work." I cross my fingers under the table, knowing it's only today he's started searching for something, and though that's what he'd told me, I'm not entirely convinced that's what he's out doing.

Sam's looking at me carefully. "Is Eli excited about the baby?"

"Of course," I tell them. "He can't wait to meet him."

"It's a boy?" Mom claps delightedly.

"We don't know yet. Eli's convinced it is." Or he used to be. Now I wonder if he cares what he gets.

Sam's regarding me carefully. "How's the baby's room coming along?"

Another bone of contention. I force myself to say brightly, "We haven't started on it yet. Eli thinks it's too soon."

"Olivia, sweetie, you've only got two months. It could even come early. You need to start thinking about what you need."

Mom reaches under the table and delves into her purse. "What do you think about these? Sam and I want to buy them for you."

She's showing me her phone open to a page where there's

a beautiful crib. Then changes the screen and a stroller appears.

To be honest, it would be a weight off my mind if someone else chose them and bought them for me. I doubt if I can get Eli interested enough, nor could we spare the money to buy anything like this. Presents though, I hope he'd accept.

"I like those." Or, at this point, anything will do. At least it won't mean spending dollars we haven't got, or delving deeper into the loan Drummer gave us.

"I'll get them ordered then." Mom looks pleased.

"The girls at the compound want to throw you a baby shower."

My eyes meet Sam's, then I look away. It sounds too normal, and while the idea is attractive, there's one big flaw. "I don't want to come back," I say, hoarsely.

"Well you're going to," Mom says with determination. "You can't stay away forever. Everyone will want to meet the baby when it comes. They're your family, Olivia. Yours and Eli's."

Not Eli's anymore though.

It's as if I've spoken aloud when Sam looks at me sternly. "Look, Ollie. No one likes what went down. The brothers will have bad feelings for some time, no one can deny that. But Eli left. He took his punishment like a man. They'll come around, eventually. But staying away isn't the answer. You should both come back and tough it out. The girls want to see you, everyone does."

"And your sisters." Mom looks annoyed. "I don't know why you say they can't visit you."

It's hard to pretend everything's well when it's not. I decide to come clean. "I don't want to upset Eli."

Sam's sharp. "He's angry with us? Or, do you think he regrets what he did?"

"I don't know, Sam. That's part of the problem. We're not really communicating now, or not talking about the things that matter. On the face of it, he's gotten exactly what he wants, a chance to be a normal man, and not a Satan's Devil. On the other hand, he's not assimilating into civilian life, and doesn't seem to want me to. But," I give a quick smile, "things will be better once he gets a job."

"Fuck, I hate this." Sam might live with Drummer, but it's unusual to hear her swear. "You're two youngsters out on your own. You've got no family to fall back on. I know he brought this on himself, but he's dragged you down too."

"Come back." Mom's face reddens as she shares a glance with Sam. "Come back to the compound. This isn't fair on you."

"I can't leave Eli," I say fast. That's the last thing I want to do. Part of the reason, and what I'm not going to share, is that I'm scared I'll push him into the arms of another woman if I give him an excuse and the opportunity. *But he might anyway. How do I know he's where he said he was going today?*

"You're pregnant, Olivia. You don't need any stress. And reading what you're not saying, that's what Eli's causing you. I love my son, but he made his own bed. It's for him to lie in, not you."

But the more they try to persuade me, the more adamant I become. "I'm not returning. Maybe when the baby's born, he'll feel better. Maybe he's just worried about me. He's still hurting, you know? He's sleeping badly because of the pain, and he doesn't eat well. Once he's healed, he'll be back to himself. Yes," I say, knowing it's me I'm trying to convince as well as them, "once he's healed and the baby's here, we'll be fine."

Sam's eyebrows rise.

"There's a chance, isn't there?" I insist. Either the baby will make things right, or we'll have to accept the life we'd planned together isn't going to work out. The doubt in their eyes makes me add, "I'll promise you this. If, after the baby's here, things are no better, I'll come back. I'll have to, won't I? For the sake of my son or daughter."

Both sets of eyes stare at me, then Sam lightens the mood. "Where have you gotten to with names?"

That I can answer. "Sage for a girl. Not so sure about a boy. Kai, perhaps?"

"Eli like those?"

I nod. I took his indifference when I mentioned them as having no opinion either way.

"So, what's the news from the compound?" I don't really want to hear how life's going on without me. To give them credit, Sam and Mom simply say everything's much as it's always been, and don't go into much detail, other than in one instance.

"Really?" My eyes go to Sam when she tells me. "Drummer's VP?"

She nods. "Temporarily. There was no one else waiting in the wings, so Wizard wants to work on bringing someone up to speed."

"Dad didn't want it?" I'm surprised. As the previous VP, shouldn't he have been first choice?

Mom moves her head from side to side. "Wraith's worrying himself bloody sick about you, Liv. His head is not in the right place."

Suddenly I realise I'm selfish staying away. "Tell him I miss him, okay? Tell him I will visit soon."

We then move on to talking about anything and everything as we used to, making me realise how much I've missed their company. We discuss movies or series we've all watched and books we've read. I made them crack up when I describe a scene in one of my latest books.

Sam's giggling. "And they really thought that's how an MC works?"

I nod vigorously, grinning myself. "And the number of

bodies they left behind. Even Road's track wouldn't be long enough."

Mom says sharply, "And what the bloody hell do you know about Road's track?"

I roll my eyes. "I live, *lived*," I correct, "on the compound, remember?"

Eventually it's obvious the restaurant would prefer us to leave and vacate the table for patrons who might buy something to go with their coffee. We hug and kiss, me hanging onto my mom for an extra few seconds before reluctantly pulling away.

"Let me know when I can come visit," Mom says.

"Me too." Sam's got a look of longing on her face. "Give my love to Eli."

As I promise I will, they turn to head away, being parked in the opposite direction to me. As they start to walk, I hear Mom lean in and say to Sam, "Your son is a bloody wanker."

"He's an asshole," Sam agrees.

I have to smile. You might take the Brit out of Britain, but Mom will always stay true to her roots.

I watch until they disappear, then, extracting my key from my purse, turn to walk to my own car. I bump straight into someone who uses his hands to steady me.

"Hey, imagine meeting you."

I look up. It's the man from a week or so back when I'd been ruminating in the sun that day. "Oh, yeah. What a coincidence." Tucson must be a lot smaller than I thought.

"Gabe," he reminds me. "I'm Gabe."

"Gabe." I nod back. "Well, I must be on my way."

As I continue on, I wonder whether he thought I was rude not to respond with my name. Still, either way, it doesn't matter to me.

Eli's not home when I return. His bike, which had been delivered without fanfare by a prospect a few weeks back, is not in the garage. At least it's electric with a push button gear change and clutch which he can manage with his injured hand. I thought being able to ride again would have cheered him up, but it hadn't.

Still, he's got his independence back which must be a good thing.

Perhaps he got talking with the men in the Harley shop? Bikers never run out of topics I've found. Eli can talk the hind legs off a donkey, as my mom would say, once the conversations turn to motorcycles. *Maybe he's been offered work?* Now that would be a good thing. This drifting, living from day to day, isn't helping.

I tidy and dust. Looking in the fridge, I decide what I might tempt Eli to eat for dinner tonight. Then, I putter in the yard, pulling up a few weeds until the heat of the sun drives me back inside.

It's not just Eli that gets fatigued. Him from lack of sleep at night and his still healing body, and me from carrying extra pounds of baby along with me.

I stretch out on the couch and close my eyes. *Just five minutes.* But as I go back over the conversation I'd had with my mom and mother-in-law, I yawn, and a wave of tiredness comes over me. I'm exhausted from pretending I can go on this way.

CHAPTER ELEVEN

*O*livia…

"Did you have any success?" I plate up some breakfast and take it to the table.

Eli looks down at what I've put in front of him, grimaces, then pushes it away. "No."

"Aren't you going to eat?" I stare at my husband, realising he's starting to lose weight. His cheekbones are more prominent. I wouldn't know what he looks like under his clothes, it's been weeks since I've seen him naked. My man, who had never been self-conscious at all, now only appears fully dressed in front of his wife.

When he doesn't respond, I ask him again. "Any leads on a job? And please, Eli. Just eat something."

"When are you going to stop fuckin' nagging?" he yells. Standing, he paces to the door, grabs his keys from the table on the side, and goes out. Moments later I hear the roar of his bike.

Suddenly I'm not hungry at all.

I will not cry.

Methodically I push away from the table, take my plate to

the bin and brush all the food away. *I'm sorry, baby. Right now, I've lost my appetite.*

I'm determined not to fall apart. I've a little human growing inside me, depending on me. Trouble is, I, in turn, have no one to lean on.

I could go back to the compound.

That would be so easy to do. Is that what Eli would prefer?

Two things stop me. Firstly, I'm a grown woman who shouldn't be running home to her mom and admitting she hadn't been able to make their marriage work. Secondly, perhaps I'd be giving Eli just what he wants, a chance to bring other women home. To explore, using his terminology, what it would feel like to have his cock in a different pussy.

He's been leaving the house more regularly, as if trying to escape. A niggling doubt inside me suggests he's not out job seeking. *Perhaps he's already found someone else?*

Stuffing my hand into my mouth to stop myself screaming in frustration, I realise I've become a suspicious wife. Before I put his clothes in the laundry, I even sniff them, wondering if I'll catch the scent of perfume or soap that's not a brand I use. I check his pockets for receipts for, I don't know, flowers I didn't receive, or meals out I didn't eat.

I'm living with a man I don't trust, and who I don't know. Living with? Cohabitating more like, we don't sleep in the same bed, and I can't remember the last time we kissed or shared a tender touch.

He's not even trying anymore.

My hand starts to reach for my phone. It would be so easy to call Mom and tell her I want to come home. Within the hour, there'd be a prospect here to help me pack. If Eli's not come back, I could just leave him a note.

Would he care?

It's been two weeks since that conversation with my

mother and Sam, and things haven't just not improved, they've gotten worse.

What should we do, baby? I run my hands through my now very thick hair, a benefit of pregnancy. One of the few. I feel like a clumsy elephant. I'm tired all the time, and my ankles are swollen. My back hurts, and it's an effort to get out of the chair. *Six weeks to go.* I'm ready now. Ready to meet my child, but scared what the reaction will be of his dad. He's not asked about the baby for ages, and, lost in his own world, hasn't enquired about my health.

Deliberately, I turn away from my phone. I've known Eli all my life, and the man I now live with is nothing like the boy I grew up with, nothing like the teenager with whom I first fell in love. He's not the man who put this baby inside me, nor the man with whom I exchanged vows.

Once again the thought hits me. *Is he out there breaking them even now?*

Suddenly I pick up my purse. If I stay here, all these thoughts will just keep whirring. Being constantly upset isn't doing the baby any good. I have to go out, somewhere. Just… not back to the compound, not yet. I fear if I went, I'd stay.

I go out to my car with no real purpose. I usually do my grocery shopping on Fridays, it's Wednesday now, but at least restocking my cupboards will be something I can do without much thought.

With a destination and purpose in mind, I leave the house that I still find hard to call home, and direct myself to the store I normally use. It's easy to find a parking spot, and soon I'm pushing a shopping cart around, trying to think of Eli's favourite foods to tempt his appetite. Then I berate myself, that all I seem to do is think about him and his needs, while he doesn't seem to give a damn about mine.

I'm just reaching over to get a box of cereal down, when someone slams into me from behind.

"Oh my God, I'm sorry. I wasn't looking where I was going. Are you okay?" A concerned male voice reaches me.

Automatically my hands have gone protectively to my stomach which had been knocked into the handle of the cart. In truth, it hadn't been that hard, just a shock.

"I'm fine." I swing around, my mouth dropping open.

"I can't apologise enough—"

"It's you," I interrupt him. "What the hell are *you* doing here?"

He shrugs. "I live close by. I always shop here for the necessities."

It's a valid excuse, I suppose. Coincidences do happen after all. If he lives around here, maybe that's why I saw him the other day.

"Hey, I really am sorry. I don't normally run women down." As he winks at me, I study him, realising I was right the first time I met him, Gabe is a handsome man. Sparkling blue eyes seem to draw me in, as he offers, "Look, can I buy you a coffee to say sorry?"

"There's no need."

His smile drops away. "I'd like to make sure you're alright. I did knock into you after all." His brow furrows. "Are you in pain?"

"I'm fine," I tell him. "I'm not hurt at all. Now, I've got shopping to do, and I don't drink caffeine anymore."

"A hot chocolate, or soda then? I've got nothing to do so I'm fine with waiting around. There's a great coffee shop just up the road. Please? It might do you good to get the weight off your feet for a moment."

I know the coffee shop, it's the place I met up with Mom and Sam, and sitting down sounds attractive. But he's a man. I feel it's only fair to warn him. "I'm married."

He chuckles and points to my very rounded stomach. "Kind of guessed there'd be a partner around." He raises his hands. "I'm not hitting on you, if that's what you're worried about, but I haven't been in town long. I'd love nothing more than to sit for a few minutes and chew the fat for a while. And seeing as I keep bumping into you," his mouth quirks, "I suppose, quite literally this time, it seems like fate that we become friends."

As long as he accepts friendship is all that's on offer. Oh, who am I kidding? I'm seven and a half months pregnant—even my husband doesn't get horny for me now. There's little to no risk that a perfect stranger will want to jump my bones.

I don't accept. I can't. Even if it's just an innocent conversation over a drink in the middle of the day, I know Eli wouldn't like me being around a strange man. I open my mouth to turn him down, then a burst of anger hits me. *Fuck Eli. If I'm right, he could be with another woman right now.*

It's that thought which decides me. "If you don't mind waiting while I pick up a few more things, I'll meet you in the coffee shop." I make the decision to abandon any chilled or frozen items, and just stick to produce that can safely be left in the car.

Gabe smiles, my answer pleasing him. "What do you want? I can go ahead and order."

Telling him just a soda, I watch him go off, presumably to complete his own shopping. When he disappears to the next aisle, I pick up the last few items I need. As I'm paying, I'm rethinking my hasty decision, then convince myself it will do no harm. Truth is, I don't want to go home right now, and learning about someone new might take my mind off my own problems.

Having paid and packed my bags, I place them in my car, then drive the short block to the coffee shop he'd named. I park, then go inside. He's got a table by the window, and stands as I approach, pulling out a chair politely so I can sit down. *Nice manners.*

"You know my name, I still don't know yours," he states, pushing my soda toward me.

That's true. "Olivia," I relent at last.

His brilliant blue eyes stare at me. "It's a lovely name. It suits you. So, Olivia." He voices my name like a caress. "Would you like anything to eat? This place does some delicious pastries."

I'm feeling guilty about even just sitting opposite him and don't want to do anything that might commit me to staying longer, so I shake my head and politely decline, even though the cakes do indeed look tempting.

"You say you've only recently moved to Tucson? Where are you from?" I ask, as the silence lasts a little too long.

"Oh, I've been moving around. I go where my job needs me."

"What do you do?" I ask, pretending an interest I don't own.

"I'm in sales." He doesn't expand on what, and I'm not bothered enough to pry.

"You don't work full time," I say though, wondering why he's not in an office at this time of day.

He shrugs. "My people give me leads, I follow them up. Fortuitously there was nothing for me today, so I can spend time with you."

I raise my eyebrow at him and give a quick grin. "Is this how you like to spend your time? Entertaining a pregnant woman?"

He looks down at his coffee cup, and lines appear on his forehead. "My wife was pregnant."

"Was?"

"She was killed. Our baby died with her. A traffic accident."

I cover my mouth with my hand as I try to process that information. "I'm so sorry."

He shrugs my sympathy off. "I must admit, when I see a lady in your condition, it reminds me of what I've lost. I often wonder what she'd have looked like later in her pregnancy. I suppose that's why I approached you that first time, seeing someone like you brings out my protective instincts."

I'm lost for words, but try to summon up something. "How long ago did you lose her?"

"About five years now." This man knows loss, pain is written all over his face, but he pushes it down and manages a smile. "I've done my grieving. Let's talk about you now. Do you know what you're having? Boy or girl?"

I also try to lighten the mood. "We didn't want to know. I think it will be a girl. My husband insists it will be a boy."

"Any preference?"

"As long as it's healthy with ten fingers and ten toes, I don't mind."

"I'll drink to that." He raises his coffee cup, then asks the waitress for a refill. I decline a second soda, still slowly sipping my first.

When the waitress moves off, his smile widens. "You've got a glow about you, Olivia. You really are a beautiful woman."

I look at him sharply, but his words aren't creepy. It looks like he genuinely means it. It's like rain falling into the desert, any compliment welcome after such a long drought. Eli hasn't made me feel attractive for months now.

But I shouldn't be attracting an unknown man. If I were back at the compound, Mouse or Wizard would have made sure to check him out before I was allowed within ten feet of him. But now I can only rely on myself and my instinct.

What should it matter, as long as he's not going to kill or rape me? No vibes he gives off would suggest he's capable of that. He seems genuine, a man who's known such great loss, and someone who's new to the area, and who could do with a friend himself.

He takes over the conversation. Within minutes he's got me chuckling, then laughing out loud as he relates some of his experiences and people he's come across.

In the end, with nothing to go home to except either an empty house or a husband who I feel I'm walking on eggshells around. I do have another drink, and accept his offer of a cake.

When he suggests we exchange numbers so we can meet up again, not trusting in fate to again bring us back together, I barely hesitate. I've actually had fun today. I've felt a lightness I haven't experienced for a very long time. I've smiled and just for a short while, my mind's been taken off the troubles in my life. It would be good to have a friend I can talk to, who's interested in me, and not just himself. Without hesitation, I hand over my phone so he can put his number in, then I text the contact he's programmed in. I notice he's named himself Gabe.

I'm almost reluctant to leave the coffee shop when Gabe makes moves suggesting he's ready to go. But I pull myself together, knowing the pleasant interlude has come to an end.

Eli's home when I arrive. He carries in the shopping when I tell him I've got bags in the car. Whether he knows I've been gone far longer than normal for a shopping trip, he doesn't ask where I've been. In fact, I suspect he barely notices I've been gone.

When I get a text the following Monday asking if I'm free, and would I like to meet for coffee again, I don't hesitate.

Eli's not even out of bed yet, so I simply put my head around his door and tell him I'm going out. He doesn't ask where.

It's somehow freeing talking with Gabe. I quickly relax and just be me. I don't have to watch my words, or wait for a temper to flare. Neither is he indifferent to me. If I wasn't married, I don't think I'm fooling myself to think there might be interest there.

As I sit opposite him laughing, I wonder whether Gabe would be someone I could turn to if I find proof Eli's having an affair.

I'm berating myself as I arrive home to find the house empty. It's only been five months since I stood in front of Lady and said my vows. Am I really thinking I could ever break them? Of course I'm not, it's just that I'm so starved for affection that Gabe is having an effect on me. It's my husband I want and need, but what can I do when he's not there for me?

I sit, with my head in my hands, wondering what's happened to me. What's happened to Eli? To us?

I never thought anything could come between us. Never dreamed I'd be sitting alone in a strange house wondering where my husband is or whether he's being unfaithful. The worst of it is, I don't know what happened to bring us to this. Is it partly my fault? Or all down to him? Are our stars not as aligned as we'd thought? On the compound we always had family around. Had that hidden that we were drifting apart? Are the cracks showing now it's just us?

The jangling tone of my phone startles me. I feel dizzy as I go from prone to standing too fast, but it doesn't stop me automatically reaching for my purse. *It's Eli.*

"Hi. Where are you?" *Are you coming home?*

But instead of Eli, I hear a stranger's voice.

"Um, are you related to Eli Felis?"

Shit. This can't be good. A stranger ringing from Eli's phone.

"I'm his wife," I say fast. "Has he had an accident?"

"No, er..." The voice sounds hesitant. "He's having an episode or something. I don't know whether I should call an ambulance or not. They can get expensive, so I wanted to check with you."

"What do you mean, an episode?" My voice is shrill. "Why would he need an ambulance?"

"He's collapsed, in the gutter. He's not unconscious, but he's crying and rocking, and I can't get him to stop."

"Where are you? I'm coming." Jeez. What could this be?

He gives me the directions, he's outside, where? *A sex*

shop? Then, wasting no time, I slip back into my shoes, then place another call as I run to my car.

"Drummer."

"Drummer, I need, Eli needs help. I don't know what to do."

I might not have spoken to him for months, but he doesn't waste time on small talk. "Olivia, take a deep breath. I'm heading for my bike now. Where are you, are you at home?"

"No. Eli's collapsed," I gasp out as I start the engine. "He, the man who called, he described it as an *episode*, I don't have a clue what that is." I rattle off where he is.

"You go to him, Ollie. I'll be there as soon as I can."

"Shall I bring him home?"

"If he's not hurt and you can get him moving, yeah. Just let me know what you're doing, okay?"

My destination is on the opposite side of Tucson. As I near the address I've been told, I drive past a Harley store. *Could Eli have gone there, or got distracted on his way?*

It's easy to see where I need to be headed. A bike I recognise as his is backed up against the kerb, but it's the people standing around that show me where he is.

"Let me through, I'm his wife," I demand.

My height puts me at a disadvantage, but the desperation in my voice gets their attention, and soon I see Eli lying on the pavement as though he'd been knocked down. But he's, as the man had told me, conscious, and has his head in his hands. He's not simply crying, he's wailing, his body moving to-and-fro.

"Eli?" I approach, letting him know I'm here.

"We've tried talking to him. It didn't work. Here, take this." A man, presumably the one who called me, hands me Eli's phone. "Is he on something?"

I turn and snap at him. "My husband doesn't do drugs."

"Well he might have today, honey. This shit ain't normal," someone points out.

Crouching down by his side, I soften my voice. "Come on, babe. Let's get home."

But he doesn't even look at me.

I try again, and then again, but Eli just keeps rocking. When I take his arm, it's like trying to move a rock, and all the time, he's wailing.

"I still think he needs an ambulance," someone says.

"Fuckin' druggie," someone else says.

I glance around. "Could someone help me get him to my car?"

"Whoa, no." The man closest to me holds up his hands and steps back. "He could get violent. Who the fuck knows what he's capable of?"

I go back to trying to talk to him, but I'm not getting through.

My situation is pitiful. I'm sitting on the edge of the pavement, my husband rocking and wailing and refusing to move. I'm getting more and more distressed as I'm helpless to know what to do, when the most wonderful sound comes up the road, that of motorcycle engines.

As is Drummer's deep voice commanding everyone to, "Stand the fuck back and give him some space."

CHAPTER TWELVE

*D*rummer…

If Ollie's to be believed and there's no reason why I should doubt her, that's my son lying on the ground with nosy fuckers staring down.

"Stand the fuck back and give him some space." I might have stepped down from my role as prez, but my voice hasn't lost any of the snap to it. Within seconds, the crowd's moved a few steps back, eyeing the group of us with suspicion.

As Wraith cuts his engine and Wizard dismounts his bike, some of the crowd even start to lose interest, as citizens often do with Satan's Devils around.

Wraith immediately goes to his daughter, pulling her into his arms, but after a quick hug she pulls away from him, her concern all for the man lying on the ground.

"Eli, Son." I sink to my knees next to him hearing the creak like a pistol shot as my joints protest. "Eli, what is it, Son?"

It's as if I hadn't spoken. Gently I use my hand to turn his head toward me. Eli's eyes are red rimmed and swollen as I search in vain for some flicker of recognition there.

There's a man hovering. "I thought he might need an

ambulance, but his wife said no." He sounds relieved as though there's a male to take charge of everything.

"She's right," I reply shortly. "We've got it from here." Ignoring him, I look at Olivia. "That your car, there?" It's hard to tell with people who continue to mill around, fewer than there were, but still enough to block my line of sight. When she nods, I instruct her, "Go drive it closer."

Wizard tells the people in her way to step back. When Olivia's brought the car alongside him, I stand, then bend and get my hands under one of Eli's shoulders. Wraith takes the other side, and we somehow manoeuvre him into the car. He makes no protest, but doesn't stop crying.

Christ, I feel so totally lost. This is my son, and he's hurting. For the moment all the differences between us are forgotten, and I just want him smiling again, much like when he was a toddler and had fallen off his bike. I felt as helpless at comforting him then as I do now.

"How do you want to do this, VP?" Wizard asks.

I glance at Wraith then come to myself with a start as I realise he's addressing me. "Someone needs to go with her in case he starts trying to get out or something."

"I'll go," Wraith says tightly. He sends a cautious look toward Eli, and I know he wants to accompany them to make sure Eli doesn't start thrashing around and cause them to crash.

"Got the prospects coming. They'll pick up both bikes. I'll wait until they get here."

I thank Wizard, then watch as Wraith slides in beside my son, making sure he's correctly belted in. To be honest, Eli's no problem, he's allowing his arms and legs to be moved without objection, so lost in his head he seems unaware of what's happening. *Has he taken something?* It's the first thing I'll ask when we're back at the house, but for now the important thing is getting him off the street and to a place of safety.

The man who'd been hanging around passes a bag that he'd been holding onto and gives it to Wraith.

"Er, these were his purchases," he tells him.

As Wraith thanks him, I decide he either works in the store or owns it. Whichever way, he's a good man. I doubt Eli would remember if he'd simply gone back inside and put the stock back on the shelves. In my son's current state, I dread to think what he might have chosen out of a sex store.

Wraith closes his door. Wizard taps on the roof as a signal for Olivia to pull away and start driving. The car moves off slowly and carefully, as though she's got a precious burden inside.

Wizard turns to me. "I've spoken to the sex store owner, he seems a good sort. He'll keep an eye on the bikes until the prospects arrive."

That's fine by me. I want to follow that car without delay, to see what my son's like once we've got him home. I'm hoping for an improvement when he's back in familiar surroundings, but worry I'm being optimistic in vain.

Prez starts to walk to our bikes and speaks thoughtfully, "He's having some kind of mental breakdown."

"I'd have said PTSD," I agree. "But I don't recall anything that could have triggered it."

"Me neither," Prez says. "But things could have built up." He swings his leg over his bike. "Before this all blew up, before he left the club, he was talking, saying the right things, until he wasn't. We took his words at face value, when perhaps we should have looked closer. Seeing him like this? Makes me think his leaving could have been a plea for help."

Then he nods at me, circles his hand and we're moving.

As I ride, I think about Wizard's words, casting my mind back to that fateful day when Eli had received his beatdown. My son hadn't seemed his usual self, a bit off, perhaps, quieter than normal, but nothing to put a finger on or worry about up to the point when he startled everyone. Then he seemed to have reasons for what he'd done, or the ones he'd put into words had convinced us. Had I ignored my son shouting for help? Christ. Seeing him today, it's quite possible. But what could have set him off?

Prez indicates right, and I copy him, making the turn by his side, riding in formation as though in a synchronised dance. Not thinking about what I'm doing, all my thoughts on my son instead.

Wizard might have gotten it wrong. Eli's leaving could have been just what he said, he wanted to get out from how he felt the club was suffocating him. Had something else happened in the past six weeks? Olivia might have some answers.

We make up the couple of minutes we'd delayed before leaving and arrive in time to help Wraith get Eli out of the car.

Once he's out, Eli's actions become automatic. He walks methodically, putting one foot in front of the other, stopping as Ollie gets her key out and turns it in the lock, then moving inside. Whether it's because it's familiar or not, Eli walks straight over to the couch and sits on it.

He's stopped those body wracking sobs, but is still giving out a continuous keening sound, as if he's in pain.

Olivia kicks off her shoes then walks over, sinks to her knees in front of him and catching hold of his hands, pulls them down. "Eli, you're home, hush now. It's going to be fine. You're home."

Christ. He might be twenty-five years old, but he looks like a lost little boy. My heart clenches in actual agony. *Have I done this to him? Was it something I missed? Something I should have seen?*

Home, Olivia keeps repeating. But are they? Should they ever have been here at all?

That's my son there. I try to go over to help, but as I approach and speak to him, he pulls his hands away from Ollie and wraps his arms around himself instead. When I move back, I think I see him relax slightly. *Is he scared of me? Or worried that I'm here at all?*

These four walls feel like they're closing in on me, and I need air. I'm useless, not having a clue what to say or what to do. *Does Eli even want me here?* If it had been a cry for help which I'd let go unanswered, I wouldn't blame him for hating me right now.

I step outside idly noticing the ground's already dry after the monsoon had passed by earlier. Now there's not a cloud in the sky. A door opens and shuts behind me.

"I've called and asked Amy to come."

"Thanks, Prez."

"If it's PTSD, it's unlike the normal reactions I've seen."

I know what Wizard means. We're all too used to men cowering at the sound of sudden loud noises, or a panic attack when their fight-or-flight mechanisms try to kick in in totally inappropriate circumstances. A man huddled up in the depths of despair is not something I can recall seeing.

Amy's car draws up, she gets out, hugs Wizard, then nods at the door. "Is he in there?"

I nod. "Yes, with Wraith and Olivia." I go to follow her in.

"No, Drummer. Let's not crowd him. He'll feel over-whelmed with too many people looking on."

She disappears. When Wraith steps out, I think they ought to fit a revolving door on this house.

"Shit, damn and fuck it." Wraith's taken the bag the man gave him outside the store and has opened it up. "I did not need to see that."

Well, Wizard and I have to peer in at the contents after that reaction. In another situation I'd laugh at the contents, but right now I don't know what to think. There's a flogger, handcuffs, and, oh, a butt plug. At least my boy hadn't forgotten the lube, but I don't point that out to Olivia's father.

"We don't know," Wizard addresses Wraith quite seriously, "whether that's for him or her. Could be Olivia's the one in charge in the bedroom."

As Wraith relaxes a little at Wizard's words, I stiffen. My son wouldn't allow his old lady to flog him. Not if he's in his right mind. Which, I remind myself, he may very well not be.

"Er, what do you think I should do with this?"

"Give it to Olivia?"

Wraith's eyes go wide.

"For fuck's sake, I'll take it inside in a moment." Wizard takes the bag. "Can't see what you're getting all hot and bothered about."

I remember that Amy used to frequent BDSM clubs and wonder about her and Prez's relationship behind closed doors. Wizard seemed completely laid back about the contents in that bag. Mind you, he hasn't got skin in this game, that's not his son or daughter in there.

Wiz tries to get me discussing some club business while Wraith stands with folded arms staring at the door which has actually stayed closed for a while. Basically, we're passing time until Amy comes out and delivers her verdict.

I'm starting to feel more and more anxious, as there's nothing but quiet from inside, but eventually the door opens, and the prez's old lady steps out.

"Okay," she smiles at Wizard, then looks at me then Wraith with a serious expression, "I did a rotation on a psych ward and attended some lectures. I'm no expert, but I've spoken to Olivia at depth. In the old days it would have been named a nervous or mental breakdown, but as a medical term, it hasn't been used for a long time, but we've still really nothing to replace it with. Basically, it's when someone has difficulty functioning in the everyday world."

"Is he going to be okay?" I ask.

At the same time Wraith enquires, "Is there any risk to Olivia, could he harm her?"

"I think so," she responds to me. "But he needs help to do

so. And no, Wraith, I'm pretty certain he's not going to harm Olivia other than worry the hell out of her."

"How did you come to that diagnosis?" Wizard asks, sounding interested. "Has this just happened today, or was his leaving the compound part of it?"

She starts to tick things off her fingers. "First, the cause and how to address it will need to be explored, but Liv says he's been irrationally irritable and definitely depressed. Mood swings for certain, and she's not quite sure what triggers them. Second, he doesn't want to do anything. She says if he's trying to get a job, it's only a half-hearted attempt at best. As if he's scared of being in situations he can't control. He's forgetful and not sleeping well. He's also not eating as much as he did. Certainly a lack of appetite is another symptom. Liv said he seems intolerant of her being with him at times, and," she pauses and looks at me, then Wraith, "he's lost interest in sex. That started months back, and Olivia first put it down to his being worried about harming the baby. But everything adds up. This has been building for months, and it's just all come to a head."

"So what do we do?"

Amy smiles again at her husband. "Really, he needs to be on a psych ward, but I can't convince Liv that he's unpredictable right now and could be a danger to himself. Whatever she thinks, he will need careful watching. Suicide is all too common when people reach this point. I think he'll need antidepressants, at least temporarily. We need to prevent another episode like today. Cognitive behaviour therapy will be essential. This has gone far beyond any 'pull yourself together' chat."

"I don't want him in a fuckin' hospital," I tell her firmly.

"I don't want him alone here with Olivia. She's seven and a half months pregnant. Even if he doesn't hurt her, she couldn't prevent his hurting himself." Wraith is as adamant as I am myself.

Wizard's staring at us lazily, then shakes his head. "Not leaving them here," he tells us as if he wonders why we ever thought we would. "He's coming home."

Both mine and Wraith's eyes look at him sharply. It's me who puts it into words. "You bring him back to the compound without explanation, he's likely to get a bullet through his head from the first brother who sees him. I'll stay here. Hell, when Sam gets back, she won't be able to stay away. That's her baby hurting." Damn bad timing. Sam and Sophie are away on their break in New York at the moment.

The door is open, and I realise Olivia has been standing there, half keeping an eye on Eli, and half listening to us. She looks like she's trying to catch up with the conversation. "Wizard, thank you. But we don't know why he's in this state." She glances toward Wraith. "Dad, I'd like nothing better than to come back, but what if the compound's the worst place he could be? What if it doesn't help, but hinders any recovery?"

"Olivia's got a point." Amy sides with Eli's wife. "This isn't something which has blown up overnight. Until we know where Eli's head is at, we don't know what would help him best."

Wraith looks at me and raises his chin. "We'll both stay."

"Dad, no." Olivia's looking dismayed. "Firstly, we haven't got room. We've only got two proper-sized rooms and—"

"My old bedroom." Amy smiles. "Not that I remember much about it. Is it still painted pink?"

Wizard's arm goes around her, and he kisses the top of her head. A couple of years before Mouse had brought him and his sister, Mariana, to the compound, Amy's mom, Crystal, had died, and Heart had never returned to this house. Amy's room had been untouched for years.

"I think someone must have redecorated at some point." Olivia's frowning. "It's not pink anymore. But it doesn't matter what colour it is, it's not got a bed in there now, just an old couch. Apart from that, I don't want Eli overwhelmed by too many people being here."

"You are not staying alone with him. You can't watch him twenty-four hours a day." Wraith's not backing down. "What if he gets violent?"

Olivia's eyes widen. "He'd never hurt me."

"I'd have said I'd never find him crying in the gutter," I tell her. "He's unwell, Olivia. Who knows what he could do? He could harm himself, or you." Summoning up more words to impress the risk on her, I add, "If he was determined to harm himself, how could you stop him? He's much stronger than you."

This time, I've gotten through to her.

Amy looks from me to her, then pulls down Wizard's head and mumbles something I can't hear.

"We need to get Sam and Sophie back," Wraith tells me.

Yeah. Bad timing. But their trip had been planned for months. I hit the heel of my hand against my head, it had been me that had encouraged them to go.

"Leave them be," I tell him. "They'll be back in a couple of days. We can manage until then." Though truth be told, I'd prefer Sam with me.

Wizard nods up and down once, then turns to me. "You stay, Drummer. Wraith, I think you should come back to the compound. Olivia's right about not having too many people around. Amy's going to speak to a doctor she knows who works in the psych ward at the same hospital as her. See if she can get him to make a home visit. But," he turns to Olivia, "if he says Eli needs to be admitted to the hospital for his own safety, that's what we need to do. Getting him back on his feet is top of our fuckin' agenda."

CHAPTER THIRTEEN

*O*livia…

"Dr de Souza isn't working at the hospital today, so he can come straight away." Amy's frowning, her lips pressed tightly together. "I've explained the situation. Like me, he'd prefer Eli be admitted so he can be properly assessed."

She doesn't insist on it though. Satan's Devils like to deal with their problems themselves, never trusting strangers to look after one of their own. I'm torn. Eli's behaviour has scared me, and I want him to have professional help, but also, I want him close to me.

Wizard lazily raises an eyebrow toward his wife. "Should I be worried you've got the personal cell of one of the doctors you work with?"

She rolls her eyes. "He was helping me with some data for a report."

"So the doctor's coming here, now?" I interrupt, wanting help for Eli as fast as possible. I cast a look behind me, seeing through the open doorway that Eli hasn't moved from his position on the couch. But he's not relaxed, far from it. His hand is going to his temple, then back to his lap.

His hands open and shut repeatedly, and his leg is bouncing.

"He is," Amy reassures me.

"Are you alright?" Dad looks concerned. "Olivia, you're shaking. Come here."

"No, I'm fine," I lie, wanting nothing more than to go into his outstretched arms, but accepting the comfort I knew all those years while growing up would make me give into those tears I've been holding back. I've got to be strong now, for Eli.

"Here," Amy puts her arm around me, "let's get you inside. I'll share one of your decafs with you."

I give a weak smile. "Would give anything to have a tequila instead."

"Me too," she confides with a sigh.

We step through the door, and I walk toward Eli. "Love," I crouch down in front of him, "can I get you anything? Would you like something to drink? Eat?"

He doesn't respond, but continues rocking, back and forth, then again and again. It's like he didn't hear me at all.

Amy puts her hand on my arm. "The doctor will be here soon. Eli will be okay. He needs help, and we're going to make sure he gets it."

I continue into the kitchen and put the coffee on, pleased Amy's here and knows what she's talking about. Her confidence that Eli will recover is reassuring. I stare out the window. *Why hadn't I noticed the signs?* As Amy had been talking to me, asking questions about Eli's appetite, his moods and how he's been sleeping, things started to add up. This isn't something that's come on him recently. It's been building for months. Puzzle pieces adding together and forming a picture which shows that Eli's become overwhelmed with life and isn't coping.

"Here, I'll take those." Amy takes the cups out of my hands which are shaking. She puts them down, then wraps her hands around mine. "Christ, Ollie, you're freezing."

I shouldn't be. The air conditioning is cooling, not set to arctic.

"You've had a shock today. Seeing Eli like that."

I shrug it off. "It's not me anyone should be worrying about."

She goes to speak, but then tilts her head as the sound of a car drawing up outside reaches us and clearly changes what she was about to say. "That will be Rob."

I allow Amy to take the lead. Well, she knows the man and medical etiquette as well. Aware of the men still hovering around outside, Dr de Souza suggests we get Eli into the bedroom so he can talk to him in private.

Dad, Drummer and Wizard come back inside.

"Are you going to tell everyone what happened?" I bite my lip waiting for the reply. I'm sure Eli won't want people to know the state he was in when I'd found him.

"Nah, baby," Dad reassures me. "No one knows we were coming here, and we'll tell the brothers only when and if there's a need for them to know."

Drummer stands and shrugs out of his cut. He looks around. "You got a closet I can hang this in?"

"Yes, but why?" Unless he's in a cage or relaxing at home, it's strange to see Drummer not wearing his worn leather vest.

"Because I'm here as his dad, not as a Satan's Devil," he explains. "It might be easier for him to talk to me if he sees that." He turns to Wizard. "I'm sorry, Prez. I'll step back as VP if I have to. Eli comes first for now."

Wizard makes a dismissive gesture with his hand. "Take as long as you need, Drum. Now, I don't think I can do much more here. I'll get back to the compound. Drummer, Olivia, let me know if you need me, okay?" When I indicate I'll do so, while being unable to think of anything he could do to help, he turns to his wife. "Amy?"

"I'll just wait for Rob to come out, then I'll come home unless Olivia still needs me."

"I'm staying to talk to the doctor," Dad says. "I'm still not happy leaving you here."

"But Wizard is right, Dad." I try to persuade him. "I don't even know whether he'll want Drummer here."

"He probably won't," Wizard suggests wisely. "But you're not staying here on your own. After this?" He waves in the direction of the bedroom and I know he's referring to Eli's breakdown earlier. "He's too unpredictable for you to be left alone."

Dad shakes his head.

"I'm his father," Drummer reminds him again. "Whether or not he wants me, Wraith, I'll be here."

"And I'm her dad." He points at me.

"You're club, Dad," I remind him. "I don't think that helps. I'm not the one sick." I narrow my eyes, letting him know if he tells me I'm pregnant again, I'll probably hit him.

He gets my message and shuts up.

When I'm certain he's not going to object again, I turn to Eli's dad. "You calling Sam, Drum?"

His lips press together, then he answers, "I have to, don't I? Eli's her son. She's going to be so fuckin' worried, Olivia."

Sam and Mom have been looking forward to this trip forever. They've got tickets to a top Broadway show. I hate that their time away will be ruined.

Small talk dies as no one has anything productive to say. An hour or more passes, then Dr de Souza appears. He nods toward Amy, then at me. Then shakes his head at my dad and Drum.

"What's the verdict?" Drummer gets in before me.

"Patient confidentiality."

I bristle. "I'm his wife. I need to know—"

The doctor gives a short laugh. "No, I don't mean I can't talk about what's going on with him, it means, he won't speak to me. Every time I asked him about what could have triggered him, what went on in the last few months, he throws one term at me. *Club business.*" He shakes his head. "It's not unusual for someone to be reticent about sharing at this stage, but I've not heard that term before."

As Dad snorts and shakes his head, the doctor tilts his head toward a chair. When I nod, he sits. Elegantly he crosses one leg over the other, and steeples his hands under his chin. "He is very agitated, and it's undeniable he's reached a mental crisis today. I've given him a sedative to help him relax. I'm also going to prescribe a short course of antidepressants."

"Is he going to get better, Doc?" Drummer asks, adding, "I'm his father."

The doctor considers his words carefully. "I have every hope that he will make a full recovery. But he does need to open up. The issue is getting him to the place where he'll talk so we can see what the root of his problems are."

"And if he starts to talk? How long until he's better?" I ask.

"Hard to say. People recover at their own pace. Could be a month, could be three, could be less, could be more. Could be he needs support long term." The doctor's hands come down to rest on his thighs. "He wouldn't, or in his mind, couldn't, provide any details to me. One thing's for certain, he's become overwhelmed, unable to cope with life. Before I can give a prognosis, I need to know more about what's happened to him, whether what he doesn't believe he can handle can be changed, or whether he's got to learn to accept things as they are. What were the triggers? Not just today. From what Amy said, this has been creeping up for a long time. I noticed he's recently been injured, but he wouldn't explain how he got that way, so I'm unable to say whether that was a trigger or not."

"What do you suggest, Doc? How do we proceed from

here?" I notice Drummer avoids any explanation or offers the information Eli was beaten out of the club. But then, I suppose, Eli's problems started long before that.

Dr de Souza presses his lips together. "We've got to get him talking. Sometimes it seems too hard, too painful. Sometimes it takes a while to get to the bottom of what kicked the crisis off. I, or one of my colleagues will need to see him and get him to open up. I'll get some sessions set up at the hospital."

"Would it help if I came with him?" I ask.

"Or me?" Drummer offers. "If he keeps saying 'club business', I can tell him when it's not."

Dr de Souza nods. "It could well be useful if you sat in on his sessions if Eli's happy with you being there. In the meantime, he shouldn't be left alone."

"You think he's a risk to himself?"

"You've got to understand he is in a world of mental pain right now and isn't thinking straight," Dr de Souza explains. "That's why I'd prefer him on a ward so we can watch over him."

"We'll do that," Drummer says firmly.

The doctor stands, his expression showing he doesn't like it, but has to accept the decision. "I'll set up his appointments and let you know about them. In the meantime, try to get him talking. If he won't talk to me, see if you," his eyes go to Drummer, then land on me, "can get him to explain when he first started feeling like he couldn't cope."

Amy also gets to her feet. "I'll see you out," she says.

She follows the doctor through the door. When she doesn't immediately return, I suspect she's talking about medical stuff with him, or thanking him for coming, the manners which, in my concern for Eli, I forgot.

"I'll talk to him," Drummer states firmly as his hands toy with his beard.

"He hasn't been speaking to me," I point out. "What makes you think he might talk to you?"

Drummer catches my eye. "I can talk to him on different levels. I'm his dad, I know everything about my son. I was also his prez, there's nothing about the club he can't talk about with me."

"Whoa." I hold up my hand. "He's not even a member of the club anymore. He walked away and talking about it might be the last thing he needs. From what he's said, he never wanted the position as VP."

"That's what he said," Drummer agrees. "But there doesn't seem to be anything on the outside that he wants."

"There's more to it." Dad jerks his chin toward Eli's father. "And we need to find out what if we're going to help him."

"Was it me?" I run my hands over my stomach. "Was it my getting pregnant?" My eyes fill with tears which I'm determined not to shed.

The door had opened while I was talking, and Amy clearly overheard.

"Did Eli want children?" she asks, coming to sit beside me.

I nod. "Yes. Definitely. We might have pre-empted things a little…" Dad snorts, and I toss him a glare. "But Eli was over the moon at first."

Drummer ignores him. "We've got to get to the bottom of what's driven Eli to where he is now, as where he's at isn't a good place for any man. He's got no club for support, no job and a wife who's having his baby. I doubt things worked out how he planned."

"He didn't plan," I say. That's the point isn't it? Now I think he just wanted to get away, with no thought about what would happen after that. "What happens if he won't talk to me, or to you, Drummer?"

Dad sits forward and bows his head. After a moment he looks up. "Least you can do, Drummer, is explain the club would be happy with him talking to the doctor. If you tell him you'll go with him, he can be confident any secrets shared will be those you're happy for him to give away."

"What about me?" I waspishly ask. "I'm his wife."

Both Dad and Drummer turn their heads my way and say at the same time, "Club business."

"What should I do, how can I help him?" I try to push my annoyance at not being involved down, realising it's not just hearing what they don't want me to, it's that Eli has always been programmed never to talk about the club to me. That way old ladies are protected. Though it's maddening at times, it does make sense. My suspicion is that he's using club business as an excuse not to talk at all. But I suppose there could be something he's done for the club that's playing on his mind. How can I help, though, if I don't know what's wrong?

"Be his wife, Olivia. He'll need you," Amy says, understanding my position. "He'll need to be kept calm. Encourage him to rest or just watch TV. That's the best you can do for him right now. Show him you're there for him."

And no more badgering about him getting a job, or reminding him of his responsibilities, I suppose. For a moment I wonder whether he would be better off on a psych ward with people who know what they're doing around him. But I keep that to myself. Drummer would never go for that. He wants to be in control of the situation.

"Rob left a script for his medication."

"I'll go get it." Dad stands.

When he leaves, I go to sit with my husband. Eli's resting, a sleep induced by whatever the doctor had given him. I just watch, wondering where and how it all went wrong, and whether there's really a chance we can get through this.

Does it help knowing Eli's not been pushing me away because he doesn't want me, but because he's ill? No, I decide, it does not. I might be the cause of his problems.

Dad returns with the medication, then leaves, saying he'll

be back in the morning. Drummer relieves me from my sentry position, telling me I need rest myself.

But in my bed, I turn my face into the pillow to stop Drummer hearing me cry. All I can see is my husband rocking and wailing in that gutter and remember feeling so helpless when there was nothing I could do for him.

I don't feel much better now.

CHAPTER FOURTEEN

*E*li...

I've just woken with my mouth feeling dry, and my bladder full, but I lie still trying to remember just how badly I've fucked up.

Yesterday I did something so stupid I groan just thinking about it. My memory is hazy, which is a blessing. I can recall waking with the thoughts that I was an immense failure, and how that is affecting my wife and I couldn't shake them. My uppermost concern was that I didn't want sex.

I'd toyed with the idea that I'd become bored with Liv, that maybe I was born to be like my father, unsatisfied unless I was fucking everything in sight. Unlike him, I'd only experienced one pussy. My memory is that hadn't left me unsatisfied, so why don't I want her anymore? Why doesn't the sight of her make me hard? Why have I no desire to see her under her clothes? Is it that she's pregnant? Is it me, or her?

Yesterday I'd seriously thought about going into town and finding a whore and seeing what, if anything, I'd been missing, but the thought hadn't made my dick do anything other than lie limp against my thigh. But still I rode into town, thinking maybe if I see someone I like, my bike and my leathers—now looking naked without the club patches—would be enough to get me a ride of a different type. At the very least it would prove whether my cock was still working.

It was a half-hearted idea, and one which I found I couldn't follow through. Oh, I'd seen a few pretty girls, but none that made my cock stir.

It's me, not her, I'd thought as I rode. Here I was, a twenty-five-year-old man in my prime, and I couldn't get it up anymore. I'd ridden aimlessly, eventually coming across an adult store. I'd stopped. What spurred me on, I don't understand, but suddenly I was focused on going inside. *Maybe adding toys into our sex life would bring back the spark?*

But the more I walked around looking at stuff stocked on the shelves and hanging on the walls, the lower I'd become. *Nothing was turning me on. Handcuffs?* Nah. The thought of restraining Liv, not exciting at all. *Ass play?* Nah, though I used to like it as I recall. *Vibrators? Gag?* Hell no, I liked what she could do with her mouth and those little sounds she'd make while I was fucking her. Or, at least, I had.

When I realised I was getting odd looks, I began to pick up some items without really thinking what they were, how I'd feel using them or whether they'd give Liv pleasure.

I'd paid. At least I was functioning sufficiently to do that.

That's the last thing I remember. I think I blacked out. I'd been only vaguely conscious of people arriving. My dad and Olivia's had been a surprise. The journey back to this house—I can't call it home, it doesn't yet feel like that—is a blur. I didn't analyse why Drummer and Wraith had turned up—part of me wondered whether I was dreaming.

All I remember thinking is that I can't go on like this.

Is eating a bullet the answer?

I can't leave Liv alone.

No, I can't do that. Not when she's having my kid.

How the fuck will I be a father?

The feelings of being a failure I had woken with began to

overwhelm me. The thought of speaking to anyone, too much. My head feels like it's imploding. This life is like a carnival ride and I want to get off, but the roller coaster keeps moving, and no one will make it stop.

I vaguely remember Amy trying to talk to me, but I was unable to answer so I let Liv speak on my behalf. Then there was a man asking questions, but his voice droned on, and I gave him the response that usually shuts people up. He'd given me a shot, and I became woozy and sleepy.

For the first time in months, powered by medication, I slept all night.

What worries me is that my memories of the day before are so clouded, I don't think I was in control of what I did. *What if I hurt Olivia? What if I hurt my kid?*

I can't summon the energy to face the day ahead. I've no explanations to offer if anyone asks me. I'd gotten rid of that man—he was a doctor, wasn't he?—by coming up with some club business excuse, but honestly, it was an instinctive response. I can't have anyone probing. I've been trained from birth not to share with outsiders anything about the club. And my life's tied up in it as much as anyone's could be. Even though I'm no longer a member, I won't betray my family.

I'd like to lie hiding under the bedcovers forever, but my need to piss is all-consuming. Unless I wet the bed like a kid, I'm going to have to move, and going to the bathroom means I might run into Liv.

I open my eyes, stretching automatically, yawning and simultaneously farting.

"Fuck, some things never change."

Abruptly I turn my head, my eyes glaring on the man chuckling. It's my dad, and I wonder why he's here, and why he's amused and not still angry with me for shitting on everything he's ever lived for. But some things take precedence over satisfying my curiosity.

I sit up, feeling groggy as though I've got a hangover. "I need to piss."

Ignoring his presence, I slide out of bed naked as the day I was born. Grabbing a pair of boxers, I step into them as I go out into the hallway, and make my way to the family bathroom a few strides away.

I sigh with relief as my discomfort is eased. While I'm emptying my bladder, I stare at my reflection in the mirror. I barely recognise myself nowadays, even my eyes look dead.

I look away, then frown. I've been brought up to keep my eyes open, to notice little discrepancies which might make the difference between life and death. Something out of place might mean a stranger's been where they shouldn't have, so I immediately see something's missing.

We normally use the en-suite adjacent to the master bedroom, but that's just got a shower. In here is a bath which Liv likes to take advantage of, so she duplicates some of her stuff, including the razor she uses to keep her legs smooth. It's not in its normal place.

Slipping my cock back into my boxers, I flush, wash my hands, then open the medicine cabinet. *Her spare razor blades are also missing.*

Frowning, an explanation comes to me. I begin to suspect, were I to go looking, my knife and gun would also not be where I normally keep them.

Do they think I might harm myself?

Wasn't that exactly what I'd been thinking earlier? That this life has become too hard. That this pain, these feelings of inadequacy might lead me in that direction. Is there really any other way out? If I can't live with myself is it right to ask Liv to do so? If I was out of the way, she could move on and be happy. She deserves so much more. She doesn't deserve me. Not when all I do is hurt her. And if I succeeded in pushing her away, there'd be nothing left for me. Another woman could never take her place.

"You alright in there, boy?"

Christ. Those words, that tone, shoot me right back to when life was easier, to when I was just a kid. When carrying the weight of the world on my shoulders was something not yet familiar. For a moment I wish I could return to that time and do things differently to change the direction my life had taken.

For an answer, I open the door and glare.

The pain, the despair and fear in my father's usually stern eyes has me reconsidering my anger, and replacing it with sorrow instead. He's just one more person I've let down and made hurt.

"You want to eat?"

I shake my head. "I'm going back to bed."

"Nah," he contradicts. "You're going to get dressed, eat, then we've got to get to the hospital. You've got an appointment with the doctor today."

"I'm not seeing a shrink," I tell him. "Talking doesn't help." I couldn't find the words to speak to anyone.

Dad takes a deep breath and lets it out through his nose. "We need to do something, Eli. You can't go on like this."

That's for certain. I stay silent, not answering, not really knowing what to say. I've gone so deep, I can't see how I can dig myself out. Perhaps a permanent escape is the only way.

"Please, Eli. Go get dressed."

I push past him, go back to the spare room I'm using, and slide onto the bed and bury myself under the covers. I hear some rustling, but turn on my side, ignoring him. Something drops onto the bed.

"Get fuckin' dressed."

Again, I don't respond.

"Drummer," another voice comes, patient, not angry. "He should take one of these."

I feel the bed dip as someone sits on it. The familiar feminine scent which reaches me tells me exactly who it is.

"Eli, babe. You need to take this tablet," Liv says patiently.

Take a tablet. Okay. If it shuts them up and makes them go away, I don't give a fuck what's in it. *Cyanide, I hope.* I half sit, pick up the glass of water from the bedside table, and take the capsule she's holding out, placing it in my mouth and swallowing it. I then lie back down.

"Babe. You've got to go see the doctor." When I remain silent, she tries again. "Please, Eli? For me? Just try?"

"Not going anywhere," I mumble.

"Drummer?" she asks softly.

"Eli," Dad snaps. "Get some clothes on, or I'll drag you out of here undressed. I don't give a damn as long as we get you to that doctor."

I'd like to see him try. Perhaps when I was a kid he could manage it. Not now, I'm as tall as he is and younger. *Maybe he should attempt it? I could lash out, hit him, hit something.*

"You can't enjoy feeling like this," Liv says imploringly. "Please Eli. The doctor will be able to help."

But as I can't see how anyone could, I continue to ignore them.

After a while, I hear footsteps, then a murmuring of voices, but more distant, and I can't work out what they're saying.

I close my eyes and try to think of nothing at all.

I must drift back off to sleep. Sometime later, I hear people talking.

Fuck. Has Drummer summoned reinforcements? For a moment I worry about being dragged out and driven to the hospital wearing nothing more than boxers. I realise I don't give a fuck. I'll be going to the psych ward after all, maybe it would be fitting.

"Well fuck," a deep voice sounds. "Thought next time I saw you I'd beat the life out of you, but you're in such a sorry state I reckon you're doing it to yourself."

"Go ahead, Joker. I don't give a fuck."

Why's on earth is he here? I wouldn't have expected him to be Drummer's first choice to help drag me out of bed, but then again, maybe he was the only man available.

"Always expected it was something more when you walked out." I hear a chair creak as Joker lowers his bones into it. "Should have fuckin' guessed it was something like this."

If he's here to drag me out of bed, why doesn't he just get on with it. "What do you want?"

Opening just one eye, I notice Joker's settled himself in. I turn over and show him my back, but it doesn't put him off as he begins, "See, you won't remember this. You grew up seeing me and Lady together. Like everyone, you didn't give a shit and accepted our relationship. But it wasn't always like that." He pauses, as though pulling his words together. "I had bible-strict parents, Eli. To say they didn't accept I was gay by nature and not by choice is an understatement. Made me believe I was wrong…"

Wait a moment. I don't fuck Liv because I can't get it up. I haven't magically changed into wanting men. Is that what they think is wrong with me? Quickly I think back, knowing there's been no time I could have indicated that. Not that there's anything wrong in any one being with whoever they want, but I prefer women.

I've got to correct his misassumption. I roll over and face him. "I'm not gay, so you're barking up the wrong alley there."

Joker chuckles. I notice he's made himself comfortable. He's leaning back with his hands linked behind his head, and his legs are outstretched and crossed at the ankles.

"Never thought for one minute that you are." He taps his nose. "Gaydar tells me you're not."

"Then why…?"

"Why am I here?" He nods. "Drummer knows some of the shit that I went through. He knows I got help and asked me to explain how the one thing you don't want to do might be the very thing that needs doing."

"You got counselling?" I guess.

"Eventually, yes. Not until I made Lady's life miserable and constantly pushed him away, worried as fuck we'd be kicked out of the club with a beatdown, or worse, if it ever came out. I suppressed my desires, ignoring the very heart of me…" Joker pauses and a look of pain flits across his face. "If Lady hadn't stuck by me, hadn't forced me to stop living a lie, hadn't gotten me help when I needed it… Well, let's just say I'd be six feet under by now. Trying to live as something you're not is unbearable. I think if Lady had truly left me, yeah, I'd have taken the easy way out."

Something he says has resonated with me. *Isn't that what I've been doing, living a lie?*

"So, counselling, talking to someone, made me see I wasn't perverted and dirty. That it was perfectly fine to live as I wanted to do. Showed me I was as normal as the next man and deserved happiness in my life. It helped, Eli. So, your dad wanted me to talk to you, explain it's worth giving it a try."

"He wanted me to speak to you," I swallow, not having realised everyone had seen it, "because I've been living a lie?" Somehow it makes it worse that they'd seen through my pretence.

Joker holds up his hands. "Hey, man. I was here to persuade you to talk to someone, not counsel you myself." He chuckles softly. "Don't think I'm cut out for that."

"I can't talk to a doctor, and you know why. What if I spill shit I shouldn't be talking about?"

"So this is about club business? Something to do with the club took you down?"

"Yes… no… maybe."

Joker rolls his eyes. When they come back to level at me, they sparkle. His mirth is infectious, and despite myself, my lips curve upward fractionally. "Well, if that ain't confusing, I don't know what is." Now he draws back his legs until they're bent under him and brings his hands down. "You're ready to talk, but not to a doctor?"

I frown. *Am I?* I couldn't talk to Dad, not to explain how I'd let him down. I couldn't speak to Liv or Mom or my brother. Not Wraith as he's Liv's dad, and not Peg or Blade, they were uncles to me growing up. Joker though. He's always been there, but we've not been close. Club brothers, yes, but if I wanted a confidant, I wouldn't have sought him out. He's distant enough to perhaps be objective.

In some ways his story resonates with me. His parents wanted him to be something he wasn't, but he was true to himself and got out.

"I'll talk to you, Joker. If you've got time."

He shakes his head, stares down at his hands, then, finally, looks up. "If you want someone to listen, I'm here for you. If you want me to give you answers, I can't help. I'm a sounding board only. If you've got that, then yeah, I've got time."

CHAPTER FIFTEEN

*E*li...

I plump up the pillows behind me and sit myself up. Drawing up my legs and clasping my hands around them, I wonder where to start. I decide the beginning is always a good place. If I start to bore Joker, he can always leave.

"My earliest memory is playing with toy motorbikes under the kitchen table with Liv."

Joker chuckles. "You were inseparable. She was sunshine, light and laughter, and you were the serious kid. If anyone made her cry, they had you to answer to."

"Maya pulled her hair one day," I remember.

"Yeah," he glares at me, "you made my daughter cry." His face relaxes as that memory fades. "You were so protective from the word go. I've known you since the day you were born, watched you grow into a replica of your Dad. I remember thinking you were a little Drummer back when you took your first step. You even had the steely glare going on."

"Everyone thought I was going to grow up like Drummer." I take a breath, thinking back. "Dad's father, my grandfather, had created the club. Dad became VP, then became prez. People used to tell me I was just like him and would grow up to do what he had done."

Joker eyes me thoughtfully. "Can't tell you you're wrong. Of course, every man in the club has to prove himself, but it was an assumption we'd made. You were always club, it would appear, from the day you were born. You showed the same traits as Drummer. You started off fiercely protective of Olivia, then all the kids. Then, as you grew, of the club. No man ever doubted you were a Satan's Devil to the core, and I, and everyone, had no difficulty trusting and following you."

"And you were wrong." I flex my fingers only just healing, some residual stiffness still there. I let them all down when I'd left the club.

He stares at me with his brow creased and eyes narrowed. "I'd say we were not. But you see it differently." He gestures and says, "Go on."

"I knew Dad wanted me in the club. I was his firstborn. Even before I walked or talked, he had my future planned out, and I was happy enough to slip into it. Nothing made me feel better than making my dad proud, and nothing made him prouder than when I proved I was everything he wanted in a son. I couldn't disappoint him, so I went out of my way to make him happy. Offer me two toys, I'd always take the motorbike, even if I was tempted by Liv's dolls."

"She liked bikes too," Joker remarks.

She did. But that's not the point. "I grew into what Dad wanted. A son who would follow him into the club. I did everything to show that one day I might even be able to lead it, just like he'd done."

Joker blows air out. "So what I said resonated. That you felt pressured to be something you weren't?"

I shrug. "I wouldn't put it so strongly. I wasn't pressured to go against my nature, I just didn't have a chance to find out what I wanted for myself."

"But Zane, he never showed the slightest interest in the club." Joker frowns. "He didn't feel the same pressure you did."

I open my hands in a 'so what' manner. "Dad already had the son he wanted. Zane was never interested in the club." It's strange looking back to how we were as kids. "He preferred playing with trucks."

"And fuckin' Legos. That kid was always building shit."

I suppose I've got that to look forward to. Treading on those tiny plastic bricks. If I'm still around when my kid's born of course, if Liv hasn't thrown me out, or if... I shake my head to clear it.

"It's not all Dad," I tell him, biting my lip. "You know Mom rebuilt that Vincent Black Shadow of hers? She started working on it when she was sixteen. Already, by then, she was a damn good mechanic. She was never interested in dolls or clothes, just bikes. She liked it when I followed in her footsteps. I could identify wrenches before I could even write."

"And you wanted to make her happy?"

"Doesn't any kid?" I say sharply. "Your mom tells you how clever you are, and you feel on top of the world. It reinforces the behaviour."

Joker taps his fingers together. "I never thought of you as an unhappy kid."

"Are you kidding? I had a mom and dad who thought the sun shone out of my ass. Of course I was happy."

"Did you really want to play with dolls?" he suddenly asks, and it sounds serious.

"No. Or I don't think so. Thing is, I didn't get the chance. Closest I got was putting a naked Barbie on the back of Action Man's motorcycle."

Joker snorts. "I remember. We all thought you'd grow up like Drummer."

"That's another thing." I'd chuckled, but fleetingly. "I couldn't be like him, I never had the chance. It felt like everyone assumed Liv and I would be together, that we were it for life. I never looked elsewhere." I raise my head and stare at him. "You know how Drummer got his name. Me? I've only known one woman."

"And she doesn't satisfy you?"

"I don't know. How could I when I don't know anything different?"

"Eli." Joker actually sounds annoyed. "I was there, okay? Don't rewrite history. Sure, you grew up as best friends, and I agree we all thought it would be cute if you ended up together, but no one put any pressure on you. In fact, Wraith did all he could to encourage Olivia to have options. As did Sophie."

Again, I let my eyes rest on him while my thoughts go back. Suddenly I'm back home with Mom questioning me as to whether there were any cute girls in high school. I remembered thinking the question odd—I had Olivia, why would I look anywhere else? Liv was more than any of them could be. She was my friend, my confidant. I lived for the day when I could make her mine. I hadn't bothered to look elsewhere at all, I hadn't wanted to.

Perhaps I'm biased looking back. They hadn't tried to push us together, nor pulled us apart which would have made us more determined. Things were let to run their natural course, and Liv and I had stayed together.

"Tell me about the club," Joker starts. "We're always hard on prospects. We were harder on you, that I have to admit. Drummer couldn't give you any preferential treatment, and for the sake of Cast who prospected at the same time, we had to give you both shit jobs. I know for a fact we asked more of you so Cast wouldn't have a chance to complain."

"He told me once he was glad he wasn't the prez's son," I agree.

"But you stayed and put up with it. You could have

walked away at that point. What I saw was a man who was prepared to give everything to the club."

I had. I'd barely seen Liv for the whole of those twelve months. But that's who I am. When I want something, I go for it. "I wanted to please Dad. He wanted me patched in." My shoulders rise and fall.

"What did Sam want?"

"She accepted the inevitable. She always knew I was born to go into the club."

"But there was no pressure?"

In fact, thinking back, she had asked if this was what I'd really wanted. I, of course, had assured her it was. As an answer, I shake my head.

Joker grimaces, then taps at his chin. "See, I'm having difficulty with this. The way we test prospects is to find them out. If you hadn't convinced us becoming a member was everything to you, you wouldn't have been patched in, never mind who your father was. I can't believe that you had us fooled or were that good an actor. The man I saw gave his all to be accepted into the club. Got the unanimous vote required with no pressure from Drummer."

"But that's what I wanted. Can't you see?" I add, impatiently. "I couldn't fail. Couldn't let down my dad, or me. By then I was committed, I had to succeed. There was nothing else I was capable of."

"So you patched in. Sat around the table, a full member like me." Joker's hand scratches his face, and his brow creases. "That problem with Archangel, you were the one to sort that out. You came up with the plans on how to handle it. Fuckin' good ones as well, worked like a charm. Not only then, you showed good judgement, but time after time. You've got a good head on your shoulders, and you're a good man to have at your side in a fight. You proved yourself not just as a member, but as a man we could all trust. When Wizard proposed you as VP, I for one couldn't think of a better choice." He breaks off abruptly, then stares at me. "How could you have accepted the VP spot if you didn't want to be in the fuckin' club? You could have said something. No one forced you into that post."

"How could I?" I cry out. "It was the pinnacle of what Dad wanted, for me to step into his shoes. To become VP just like he had back in my grandfather's day. I'd just turned twenty-five, Joker. Too fuckin' young to have that responsibility."

His hand slashes through the air. "Age is just a number. It's experience that counts, and seven years riding with the Devils puts men in more challenging situations than most have in the whole of their lives. We already looked up to you, Eli. Making you VP just formalised that."

"My whole life," I cry out, "plotted and planned from the day I was born. I'd had no choice, Joker. I don't know who I am. *I* got Liv pregnant, I'll admit my part in that. I was VP for the club, responsible for men's lives, and responsible for my wife and the child who's coming along. I was going to fail them, one way or another. Fail the club, fail my wife, fail my kid…" My voice trails off as I start to sob, getting out my final thoughts before I break down. "Everyone was depending on me. I couldn't afford to make a mistake. I started to question every decision. I got to the place where I couldn't even think. Give me a choice, and I couldn't choose. Do that, and someone might die, do this, and it might be someone else. That day… My wedding day, and we thought Archangel was coming for us? I wanted to marry Liv with everything that was in me, but I had to think of my club. Should I cancel the wedding? Should we let it go ahead? Should we send the women away?"

"It wasn't just your decision," Joker states. "At the end of the day, it was all of ours, and Wizard would have the final word."

"But what if I'd made a suggestion and you'd all voted yes? What if it had been the wrong one?"

"Then we'd all have been responsible for agreeing with what you said."

My voice rises. "I couldn't play with people's lives anymore. I had to leave the club. I couldn't put anyone at risk. But being outside is no better, I can't support my wife. Can't even see a way I could bring up a kid."

My head drops into my hands as I realise for the first time, I've told someone my innermost thoughts and fears. That I've admitted my whole life's been a sham, and that the man they thought they knew isn't who I really am.

The tears start to fall all over again. If I was faced with trouble, I wouldn't be able to decide on the correct way to turn. I'm a fraud, and I have been all my life.

Suddenly the bed dips, and the way it does shows me it's not my wife. It's a man. *Joker?* But he wouldn't wrap his arms around me and pull me close. He doesn't have a smell that reminds me of everything good about my childhood. No, it's Drummer, the man who gave me life.

Somewhere in my subconscious I realise he must have been listening all along. It's both a burden and relief that he heard me get everything off my chest. I don't blame him. He couldn't help trying to mould me into a reflection of himself, it's probably what I'd try to do with my own son.

He rocks me as though I'm a child being comforted after falling off his bike, or breaking a favourite toy. He says nothing, just allows me to weep. His only movement is to reach for the box of man-sized tissues someone must have brought in.

It's only when my tears dry and I start to come back to myself that he uses words. "Son, I'd go out and buy you a fuckin' Barbie doll right now if I thought that would help."

A combination between a sob and a laugh is startled out of my mouth.

CHAPTER SIXTEEN

Drummer…

"Sam."

"What's up, Drum? Do you need me to come home?"

Just the way I'd said her name alerted her, showing how well she knows me.

"Yeah. You, and Sophie. I'm sorry to cut your trip short, but we need you both back here." I take a deep breath and then explain what's happened with Eli, and, apparently, the part we both played.

Like she knows me, I know her. I can tell she's trying to hide her own distress. Of course her first reaction would be to reassure me. "It's not your fault, Drummer. Eli's not thinking clearly. You never pushed him into anything. He wanted to be a mini-you from the time he was born."

"He copied me to please me."

"He's not thinking straight right now. He's ill, Drum. Sure, he copied you, but that was because he'd inherited so much of your personality."

I don't know whether that's true. I walk to the window, looking out on the front yard which could do with some maintenance now the prospects don't come around anymore.

It's clear Eli hasn't made it a priority. As for Olivia, she can barely see her feet now, let alone mow grass. Idly I think I need to send someone around.

Sam's voice continues in my ears. "Sophie's here. She's been speaking to Wraith. Mouse is booking us on the first flight home."

"I'm sorry," I repeat. "I'm out of my depth, Sam. Eli needs you, I need you." Truth be told, I worry any time she's away from me, but our old ladies had been planning this time away for so long, I wish I didn't have to ask her to come home. But I'll be fucked if I know how to make this right. My son needs his other parent as well.

"Of course he does. But Drum? Please stop beating yourself up. It sounds to me that Eli's been overthinking things. Sure, he's telling a version of accounts which fit, but they're not what we remember, and somewhere in between probably lies the truth."

There's the woman I know and love, often speaking sense which grounds me. "I miss you, Sam. I need you. I love you." There was a time when I never thought I'd find a woman I wanted forever until I found Sam.

"I love you too, Drummer. I'll be back soon. We'll make things right for Eli." The confidence that things can turn back around bolsters me.

Having her and Sophie home will be for the best. Wraith and I are men of action, dealing with fear that exists in a man's head is way beyond our comprehension.

Olivia and I had been at our wit's end when Eli had again refused to go to see Dr de Souza. Sure, I'd threatened to physically drag him there, but my son is just like me. Being forced to do something would mean he would dig his heels further in and, like a horse being taken to water, he would have refused to cooperate.

I'd been wracking my brains, trying to think how I could get him to understand talking would help. Apart from just making him stubborn, taking a man dressed only in boxer briefs to the hospital was probably a sure way to get him committed.

For some reason, Joker had come into my mind, and I remembered how much psychotherapy had helped him back when he and Lady came out to the club. Of course, by the time they'd told us, most of us had already guessed. But Joker had lived with the fear he would have to give up either the club or the man he loved. The help he got showed him he could have both.

Joker might have been able to persuade Eli to seek help, that was all I'd wanted from him, but he'd done more. He'd shared some of his own pain which had driven Eli to open up.

Fuck, but that had been hard to hear. Listening to Eli speak as he spewed it all out, it sounded like everything I'd ever done for my son had been a mistake.

I'd selected Wraith as my VP when he'd been just a couple of years older than Eli was now. Age doesn't mean much, it's a man's character that means more. I'd been proud as fuck when Wizard, with no input from me, selected Eli as his right-hand man. Back as just a member at the time, I had every confidence in my son. Hell, if I thought he wasn't capable of doing the job, I'd have spoken up. As VP he'd be leading me and the brothers into and out of danger. If there was any doubt of his ability, even if I had applied any influence, he wouldn't have gotten the votes.

But now he's lost confidence in himself. Had we read him wrong? Was what we'd thought we'd seen in him not really there? I can't understand. It doesn't make sense. But to see my strong son brought down to his knees is devastating.

"He's sleeping."

I turn to watch Olivia approach, noticing how her eyes glisten. "Sam and your mom are on their way back."

She nods to show she's already heard, from Wraith I

expect. "How did I not see things were so badly wrong, Drummer? Why didn't I get him help before?"

"Don't beat yourself up. Eli had left the club. Things were bound to be different in the citizen world. You both had to adjust."

"He's been saying some nasty stuff to me," she admits. "Suggesting I'm not enough for him. That perhaps he wants something else."

"That's his illness talking," I tell her, sharply. "And, he is ill. He's going to get better with our help."

"I'm expecting a baby in a month. What am I going to do?"

Yeah, I'd sound distraught, too, if I were in her place. She's got her own health and that of the child she's incubating to consider. She should be everyone's focus, but now she's got the extra worry of caring for Eli as well. She's not going to abandon him. I know her too well to think otherwise.

I purse my lips and look at her carefully. "I think you both should come back to the club."

"That means everyone will need to know that Eli's not right. Otherwise…"

Otherwise he'll never be allowed to come back. She's right. He'd risk a beatdown on sight. "I can go back later and pave the way."

She thinks for a moment.

I give her the time, but hell, there's no shame in admitting someone's got a problem inside their head. Something they couldn't help in the same way as it wouldn't be their fault catching the flu. If I know my brothers, they'll all have Eli's back. I suspect in some ways they'll be relieved that it wasn't the Hawk we knew and loved who walked out, that he hadn't been himself when he'd made the decisions he had. But like me, hell, some will wonder why we hadn't realised and carry the burden of guilt themselves.

When she speaks, it's not to agree. Instead she shrugs, as

though putting any decision off. "I'll go get some dinner started. Dad said he'd be here soon."

I raise my chin at her as she goes into the kitchen, distracted by my thoughts. I'd spoken with Eli, tried to reassure him that he'd never be a disappointment to me, that I'd be behind him in whatever he wanted from life. I couldn't make promises I couldn't keep, but I'd do everything I fucking could to make sure he could come back to the club if that's what he wanted, though right now, that's the last thing he wants.

I was the prez of the Satan's Devils, I'm used to leading men, making decisions which involved life or death. I've never before felt at such a loss as to what's the right thing to do, as this involves my flesh and blood. My son.

Whether it's the tablets that Eli's swallowed down, or whether talking has taken it out of him today, he's still asleep when Wraith arrives. Knowing Olivia won't be alone, and knowing, despite his antics with a shotgun the day he discovered Eli had gotten his daughter pregnant, I know Wraith loves Eli like he would his own kid. I'm comfortable heading off for a time.

I don't need to explain Wizard will be expecting an update, so I get on my bike and ride back to the compound having to admit I'm glad to be going home. I'm pleased as fuck that later tonight, I'll have my wife back in my arms. I need her to help me make sense of all that's being going on.

Parking outside the clubhouse, I step inside and head straight for the bar. Butcher's got my favourite whisky in his hand as I approach. Guess I look like I'm in need of a shot.

"Prez around?"

The prospect jerks his head toward the pool table. "Over there, having a word with Hound."

Wizard happens to look across. When he sees me watching him, he raises his hand and holds up his forefinger. I turn back to the bar, leaving him to finish up his business with the sergeant-at-arms, and take a moment to myself.

Suddenly I lurch forward, almost splashing my precious whisky over the bar. Almost. Peg's lucky. If I had, he'd have had my fist in his face.

"How's it going, old-timer?" As I turn around, he catches sight of my face. "Fuck. I haven't seen an expression like that since we went up against the Herreras."

"How's Eli?" Joker's come up on my other side.

"Eli? What the fuck's up with him? Thought he was the one whose name should never be mentioned." As Rock makes the sign of the cross, Joker gives him a smack around the head.

"There are things you don't know," Joker snarls.

Peg's standing with his eyebrow raised. I'm trying to formulate some reply when Wizard comes across.

"Ready to tell everyone yet?"

Prez seems to think we'll bring this straight out into the open. As I wonder, am I ready to what accounts to baring my soul? My brow creases as I realise I trust all these men with my life, with that of my old lady, with those of my sons. If I'd fucked up, they might as well know about it. The best place for Eli is back with people around him, undoubtably the best solution for Olivia as well.

One of them turned his back on the club. That he wasn't in his right mind when he did so, that he had reasons for acting the way he had done, makes me certain they won't let him down when he needs them now. I'm more concerned of the hurt I'll be bringing to them. If I know anything of the men I ride alongside, it's that they'll all be questioning themselves like I am.

I give Wizard the chin lift he's been waiting for. He wastes no time.

"Butcher. Call everyone in. Church in an hour."

"You going to fill us F.O.Gs in?" Peg asks.

"I don't want to go through this more than once, Peg. Sam and Sophie are coming back early from New York. I've got to make arrangements to get them picked up." With that, I finish my whisky, decline another glass, then go to find a prospect to issue my instructions to.

I go up to my house and crash for what time I have. Sitting with Eli last night meant I hadn't gotten much sleep and I'm in much need of catching forty winks.

As soon as my phone chimes with the alarm I'd set, I'm wide awake. Years of being prez had honed my skills so I could go from being dead to the world to being ready for anything in seconds. After splashing cold water on my face and changing into a fresh t-shirt, I'm ready to go. Or, as ready as I'll ever be. How do you explain your son has reached the end of his tether? That he's been brought so low, there's no further he can go.

Straightening my shoulders, I make Eli a promise. We'll carry his load while he's unable to. We'll make sure Olivia has everything she needs as well.

Men are already milling into the meeting Wizard called. I follow behind, almost diverting to my place I'd adopted at the bottom end of the table when I'd handed the mantle of prez over, but remember in time and still feeling out of place, I take my seat to the left of Wizard. It reminds me of the time decades back when I'd been my father's VP. Of course, the club was in a different location then, and the table with the Satan's Devil's insignia proudly carved into it had been destroyed when the cops had invaded. When I took over the club and we'd moved here, everything was new including the chairs we're sitting on and the table we're sat around. It was a badly needed fresh start. Ancient history now of course.

The sound of the gavel banging brings me back to the present.

Prez nods toward the two empty chairs. "We've two members absent with permission. Wraith, for reasons which will become clear, and Lady who's making a delivery in Phoenix."

Joker raises his hand. "Lady has made me his proxy in case any vote comes up."

"What about Wraith?" Peg asks. "You holding your hand up for him, VP?"

"Let's leave that for now." Prez's stare, rivalling mine back in the day, silences further discussion.

Of course, everyone will be chomping at the bit to find out what they've been called in to discuss at this impromptu meeting today. It normally spells trouble, and most men are tense, anxious to hear what Wizard has to say.

Prez doesn't keep them waiting. "I'm going to hand over to the VP to explain why I've called you all here. If a vote needs to be taken, then Drummer, for reasons which will become clear, will not be party to that. He'll update you, answer questions, then make himself scarce. He will not be party to the discussion we might need to have."

I raise my chin toward Prez. It's as it should be. Brothers should be free to discuss matters freely without worrying about hurting my feelings, and my vote is a given.

Clearing my throat, my prepared speech goes out the window. "Eli's suffering. He needs to come back to the compound and have family around him."

There's a stunned silence. If they had any expectation of what they were about to hear, it certainly wasn't that.

"What the fuck?" Marvel starts. "He's fuckin' suffering? Our VP walked out on the club and now you want him to come back? What, your boy doesn't like it on the outside?" he sneers. "Finding citizen life a bit hard?"

Wizard bangs the gavel loudly. "Will you fuckin' do as I asked? Hear Drummer out and ask questions for clarification only while he's here."

I give Wizard a chin lift to show my appreciation, then take a deep breath. "A year back, I stepped down as president, and Wizard stepped up. We voted in new officers. Though he didn't show it, it blindsided Eli to be given the VP patch, but he accepted it and the responsibility that went along with it. Seven months ago, Eli found out his wife-to-be was pregnant. Think the kid must have forgotten to glove up, as it wasn't planned or expected, though Olivia was already his old lady. Five months ago, Eli and the prez had their wedding. It was touch-and-go whether it would go ahead at the time, or whether instead there would be a firefight with Archangel." I pause and look around. Some look interested to see where I'm going with this, some, like Marvel, already look closed off.

I tap my head. "Who knows how the fuckin' brain works? What's certain is that Eli's has turned against him. Where did it start? Who the fuck knows? When he was first voted in as a VP? Or before that, when we gave him his patch? Maybe it was when we tested him more than any other prospect during that year when he had to prove himself." I slam my fist down on the table. "*I* fuckin' know I was right. He was my son, but more than that, he was the man I wanted riding at my back."

A chorus of 'that was then, this is now' and 'Eli's not that fuckin' man anymore' come from all around. Derisive comments that show how badly my son's bridges were burned. As I let the wave of comments brush over me I realise, it doesn't matter how much I want it, Eli may never be able to come home.

CHAPTER SEVENTEEN

*D*rummer…

Wizard bangs the gavel loudly, and then again until everyone shuts up. "Brothers, I know there's a fuckton of bad feelings, but I need you to think back further than a couple of months, before Eli walked away from the club. Without letting what's happened since taint your views, can any man here raise their hand and say they disagree with Drummer? Did you feel under pressure to raise your hand and say aye when I proposed Eli as my VP? From where I'm sitting, every vote that was taken was a free one and each had to be unanimous. But if anyone had doubts and just followed the pack, I'd be interested to hear you say it."

"Can't say that," Rock inputs. "That's why his departure hit us so hard. How could we have read the man wrongly?" He gestures toward me. "If you've got an explanation, Drummer, I, for one, want to hear it."

There are nods and growls of agreement.

I catch sight of Joker staring at me. He gives a slight inclination of his head, a silent offer of support should I need it.

I grimace slightly. "I want you to think about Eli, because

fuck knows that's what I've been doing. Think of the carefree little boy most of you remember him to be…"

"What?" Peg scoffs, grinning widely. "That kid was never carefree. He was always a mini-you, Drummer. From the day he entered the world he had your scowl dead to rights."

I glare at the ex-sergeant-at-arms. "Eli officially prospected when he was eighteen. Can't say that was when he started living and breathing the club, as far as I saw, he always had. But that was when he came on the books. Then he was patched in. As I said, getting on for a year back, he became VP."

"No need to go over it again, Drummer." Cast sounds bored.

I shrug. "Somewhere, somehow, he started to change, changes I didn't see happening."

"None of us did," Wizard puts in. "Not all on you, Brother."

I notice Joker lifting his chin as I continue, "Eli didn't leave the club because he wanted to or because he preferred life on the citizen side."

"Then why did he fuckin' leave?" Hound asks impatiently.

I inhale deeply. "Because he didn't want to let any man around this table down. He didn't want to expose our old ladies, or children to danger. He didn't want to do anything that might cost lives."

A silence settles as everyone stares at me.

Mouse's eyes, especially, seem to bore into mine. "He was going to betray us? Was he under pressure?"

Pressure is right, but not from an external source. I address Mouse's first point. "He wouldn't betray us, knowingly," I tell them fast. "But inadvertently, he thought he might. He was so cut up with making the right decisions, he thought he could lead us wrong. He lost confidence in his judgement, Brother. Hell," I know my eyes feel wet, so totally unlike me, "he's reached the place where he doesn't know what time of day is right to brush his fuckin' teeth."

"He's bad, brothers." Seeing my plight, Joker takes over from me. "I've seen him, spoken to him, so if you can't take it from Drummer, take it from me. He needs help. He wasn't talking to Drummer, to Olivia or anyone. Everything came to a head when Eli collapsed in the street. It was only then Olivia contacted Drummer, who in turn called me in as I had had therapy and knew what Eli didn't believe, that it could help. Well, I went to speak to him, and he recognised something in me, and opened up. He's as lost as any man could be." He glances at me, notices my distress and continues, "He's hit rock bottom, brothers. He's out on his own with no support."

"He's got his wife. He chose to leave," Marvel throws in.

"Olivia is close to giving birth. Eli's state of mind means he's questioning his marriage, whether he's good enough for her. He's about closed himself off completely."

"Wraith there, with him?" Jekyll suggests incisively.

"Yes," Wizard confirms. "Eli can't be left alone." He wipes his hand over his face. "I've seen him, brothers. My assessment is he's a danger to himself, if not unintentionally to someone else."

"He getting professional help?"

I pick up Peg's question and run with it. "He's been prescribed antidepressants, but refuses to see the therapist right now."

Shooter blows out air noisily.

Drifter glances at him, then says firmly, "He needs to come home. That's what you're saying, isn't it, VP?"

"He's not sitting around this table—"

"Not suggesting that, Marvel. But here, on the compound where we can all take shifts."

"Suicide watch, you mean?" Heart looks upset.

He's not as distressed as me hearing him put it so

succinctly, but he's right. Left to his own devices, Eli might think his permanent absence is best for the world.

"So we're going to vote on whether we allow him back?"

"He left with a beatdown and that was that—"

"Marvel," Wizard growls, stopping the man speaking further. He stares at each of the members who all hold their tongues. "VP, this is where we ask you to step out."

Knowing it is, I stand. The men need to talk freely, and I don't need to be here to listen to shit which I may be tempted to follow up with my fists.

I can't blame them for not leaping in with their offers of help. Eli betrayed the club in the worst possible way when he took off the cut bearing our colours. He'd disrespected our way of life and everything the club stands for.

Surely, if they could do the same thing as I've done, look back over the past year or even more with the benefit of hindsight, they'd too pick up on little signs, things that perhaps we'd missed.

I don't blame Olivia for not realising how serious things with Eli had gotten. For a start, she's pregnant and her mind is rightfully focused on her own health and that of her unborn child, and secondly, at first sight, his problems were of his own making, caused by him insisting they both had to leave the club.

I sit at a table in the clubroom, empty except for a couple of whores waiting around until church is over, and the prospect standing behind the bar. No one interrupts me. I've not touched a sweet butt since Sam entered my life, and prospects know to leave me alone.

Slight changes in Eli's language come into my head. Subjects on which my son had previously been decisive had started to be answered more vaguely instead with an *I'm not certain,* or an *I'm not sure.* Why hadn't that registered with me then? Looking back, I'd put it down to him thinking more with the added responsibility of being second in command, being extra thoughtful and considerate. It had never occurred to me he'd been doubting and questioning himself.

The door opens and reveals the person I want to see most. I stand and greet her halfway.

"Sam." The first genuine smile I've worn for hours comes to my face.

"I've missed you, Drummer."

"Me too, darlin'. Me too." This is where she belongs, in my arms and by my side.

Though it seems she's not going to be there long. "Nathan collected us from the airport. He dropped me here and then went to take Sophie straight down to Eli and Olivia's house. I've just come back to get my bike before heading down there myself. Have there been any developments?"

I jerk my head in a backward direction. "They're voting now on whether Eli can come home."

"If he doesn't, I'm moving in with them. Ollie will need someone, and she's in no condition to be there for Eli."

"I'll be there too." I'm starting to think Eli's house will get pretty crowded, as Sophie and Wraith will want to be close by as well. Best all-around if they can come back. I've done all I can do to engineer that result, it's up to the brothers now.

"Are you coming later?" she asks.

"Yeah, just let me finish up here." I'm hoping I'll be going back with good news, but I'm not entirely optimistic. "You need me to bring anything with me?"

"I'll text you. If Wraith and Sophie are staying, there won't be much room, but if we are needed, I'll want an overnight bag." She doesn't question whether I'll be there with her. She knows that I will.

Leaning forward, I kiss her. "Just let me know."

She prods me in the chest. "Stop worrying, Drummer. I know you. It was nothing you or I did, okay? Or even if it was, we can't go back and change it. All we can do is deal with the cards we've been dealt. We will help Eli. He's not alone anymore."

My lips curve. Sam's been my rock over the past two and a half decades more than she'll ever know. Always managing to find a way to show me how to come back when I stray from the path and get lost. She's right. The past is written in stone, it's the future we can influence.

"Fuck, I love you, woman."

She responds in the same way, then, with one quick kiss she's gone.

I beckon to Butcher. "Rascal's on bar duty—"

He grins as he interrupts me. "You want me to follow Sam wherever she's going?"

He's right. I do. Can't have my old lady riding alone at night, even if it is just down into Tucson. Sam, well, she's not going to take a cage when it's a nice night. Fully understanding, I wouldn't ask her to.

Butcher goes, Rascal comes in. Time ticks by. Tommy shuffles in slowly, using a stick to help him along. His legs seem to worsen daily now, and soon we'll need to encourage him to use his mobility scooter inside the clubhouse instead of parking it outside with the rest of the bikes. It's one which is shaped like a Harley, and even as worried as I am, I half smile as I recall his pleasure when we presented him with it.

Wearing the prospect cut he was given twenty years ago, Tommy slowly makes his way past. He gives me a salute, rubbing his tummy with his free hand. "Prez. Tommy hungry."

Doesn't matter how many times we tell him Wiz now has that title, Tommy hangs onto an idea once he's got hold of it. I raise my chin to acknowledge he's going to raid the kitchen.

"Prez want something?"

"Nah, I'm good, Prospect."

Tommy grins as I give him his title which never seems to grow old.

Then he's gone, and I'm left alone with my thoughts once more.

Is it a good sign church hasn't yet ended? Are they arguing on Eli's behalf or against? My fingers tap impatiently on the table as I try to remember if I've ever before been excluded from saying aye or nay to a proposal. The answer is negative, I have not. But then, nothing has ever been so personal before.

After far too long, I hear the sound of heavy soles meeting the wooden floor. I resist the urge to turn and try to read the expressions my brothers are wearing, knowing Wizard won't keep me hanging around for long.

Indeed, a tap on my shoulder gets my head twisting. When he meets my eyes, Wizard's head jerks back in the direction of his office.

I stand, keeping my head down wanting to hear it from him first, and follow him.

Closing the door behind me, I watch him take the seat that was, for so many years, mine, and at his gesture, take a chair in front of his desk.

"Just give it to me, Prez."

Wizard puts his hands on the top of the desk and clasps them together. "What you missed was an update from Mouse. He's been tracking the feds who we believe are assigned to tracing the whereabouts of Archangel. Word is, they're circling around Phoenix."

My eyebrows rise. "That means they think he's there, too." I frown. "What's in fuckin' Phoenix? Last we heard, he was near the border. Thought he'd gone over into Mexico myself."

"You know what the feds are like." He avoids a direct answer to my question. "They follow leads, and may not have much concrete to go on. We know they want Archangel as he escaped from prison and caused the death of his guards. He's a number one priority for them. One sniff and they'll be all over it."

"But they might be wrong."

Wizard shrugs. "Might be there's a bunch of those mother-fuckers who call themselves the Real Americans getting themselves organised which the feds find of interest. Archangel might be there or not, who the fuck knows? Might have the wrong state, the wrong fuckin' country."

"Or they might have gotten the sniff of a trail and are closing in. Meanwhile, Archangel's holing up in another town." My eyes fix on him.

His nod and response shows he's on the same wavelength. "Phoenix is only a two-hour ride away."

I don't need that reminder. *Too fucking close.* But why's he telling me this now? "Eli?" I prompt him.

"The brothers want no distractions. Satan's Devils were responsible for Archangel going down." He rubs at the bridge of his nose. "If Archangel has discovered that information, then it's only a matter of time before he tries to get his revenge. With rumours of him possibly closing in, the club's focus needs to be on protecting ours and our own."

"And Eli's a distraction? Prez," I don't give him a chance to speak, "if Eli's off compound and there's danger coming, then I need to be with my son. I'd give my life for any of my family, blood or club. But Eli to me is both."

"I hear you." He gestures with his hands. "Wraith won't want Olivia out of his sight, and she won't leave Eli."

"So what do we do?" I wonder aloud. I hadn't realised how much I'd hoped this was just a formality, and that I'd be able to bring Eli back to the compound. Now it seems Wraith and I will be protecting our offspring on our own.

Wizard cocks his brow at me. "We bring them home."

"Yes, but…" As the unexpected words reach my ears, I have trouble comprehending them. "We, what?"

He grins widely. "You know how the brothers are. They all want to have their say, then someone needs to argue a point and they go back and forth. I just had to give them time to come around to the view I've held since I saw Eli in the gutter outside that fuckin' sex shop. Your son is a man in need of family, friends and support. Throttle spoke up after you left us. He catalogued what had made him approach Eli that day. While we might not have noticed, Throttle had. He saw Eli changing, becoming a different man. Said he wished like fuck he'd handled it differently, but I think that's the view of most of us."

"But you said no distractions."

"Distractions like having one of us and their old lady living apart from the club." Wizard looks grim. "What better way of hurting us than taking the son of the ex-prez and the daughter of the ex-VP, both men who are still valued members?"

"You think they're targets?" I don't know why I hadn't thought of that.

"I think anyone connected with the club could be an object of interest to Archangel. We're not going on lockdown exactly, but you know the drill. No riding alone, and old ladies to be escorted wherever they go."

What Wizard has said is chilling. The Real Americans are white supremacists, stirring up trouble wherever they go and Archangel had been their leader. They're known for their hot-headed violence and have been known to dabble in both drugs and sex trafficking. The feds had been chasing their tails trying to pin something that would stick on Archangel. Everyone knew how dirty he was, but officially they couldn't prove it. Mouse had found the evidence to convict him, funnily enough for an unrelated crime but one which would lead to hard time. All we had to do was leave it out in the open for the feds to find. When he went down, leaderless, the groups following him had drifted apart, themselves becoming the targets. We live in hope that he hasn't regrouped and found out who was responsible. If he has, I don't want to think about what he'd think would be just retaliation.

"All we can do is be prepared, Drummer. We protect our own. And one thing I can assure you, when all was said and done, they said that included Eli."

"Even Marvel?"

"Even Marvel."

I smirk. That man's been a thorn in my side ever since he patched over from San Diego. He'd argue just for the sake of it, but when it comes down to it, ends up on the right side. If truth be told, he makes us as least consider alternatives.

I breathe out as relief floods through me. My son won't be alone anymore.

CHAPTER EIGHTEEN

*O*livia…

"I think you ought to see the therapist," I tell Eli as I'm folding his clothes.

"Well I don't. I spoke to Joker, then to Dad. You heard everything and don't pretend you didn't, Liv."

"I only eavesdropped because you wouldn't speak to me." I take a couple of deep breaths, reminding myself he's ill and I must resist the urge to snap at him.

"Put them back in the drawers." He's been watching what I'm doing. "We're not going anywhere."

Drummer had appeared last night and told me the best news ever. Eli and I could go home. Back to the house we designed together, back among the people we know. Eli's reaction to the good news hadn't been what I had expected. Instead of being pleased, he'd said no.

"Come on, Eli. You must know this is the right thing. You won't even have to do anything. The prospects are coming to move the furniture—"

"I'm staying here," he insists, and the look he sends me is challenging.

I'm starting to prefer it when he ignored me completely. I roll my eyes and bite my tongue.

My back hurts, the baby kept kicking all through the night before, waking me every time I dozed. I'm tired, irritable, and finding it hard to hold on to my patience. I know all my thoughts should be for my husband and the horrors in his head he's carrying around, but it's the worst possible time. I'm worried about having this baby as well as about him, and I'm worrying about worrying. What if my tension harms the baby?

"Well I'm going home," I tell him.

He regards me for a moment, then sighs. "It's for the best, Liv. I can't be what you need. I can't see I'm ever going to feel right again. You go, I'll stay here. It's the right thing for everyone."

I open my mouth to respond, when a deep male voice interrupts, "Brother. Get up." Something's taken out of the pile of clothing I'm holding and thrown onto the bed. "Put those jeans on."

"Get out of here, Hound!" Eli yells.

"Not happening," another voice rasps. It's Throttle. "You've got places to go."

"I'm not moving back to the compound."

"Nope. Drummer's got the appointment you refused to go to yesterday moved to today. Hound and I are coming with you."

"I don't want to go."

"I don't give a fuckin' damn," Throttle snaps. "But I doubt you really want to lie here feeling low. We're going to get you fuckin' sorted, Brother. And that starts with you making an effort to help yourself."

"Get dressed," Hound commands again, in a voice he must have picked up in the Marines. It almost makes me want to check to see if I'm wearing enough clothes.

Eli stares, and just when I'm certain he'll tell them to fuck off again, he huffs, and reaches for the jeans on the bed.

Throttle turns me so he can rifle through the bundles of clothes in my arms, picks out a t-shirt and it joins the pants Eli's starting to pull on. None of us offer him privacy. He's my husband, and well, they're men.

Hound bends and picks up Eli's boots, and I come to my senses, doing my part and finding him some socks.

Eli staggers slightly when he gets to his feet. He touches his head. "I don't think I can ride. It's the medication—"

"We've brought a cage," Hound replies.

"You really coming with me?"

"Just to the hospital. Up to you whether you want us inside. Drummer's meeting us there just in case you want him with you." Throttle turns to me. "Sam and your mom and dad are staying with you. Unless…?"

I shake my head, knowing Eli wouldn't want me to go. If I insist, he could refuse, and hell, if it gets him on the road to helping himself, I won't do anything to stop that. If he's going to talk to his therapist, he should be able to do so openly, even if what he says would upset me, his wife.

As Eli's frogmarched out of the house, Sam comes up beside me. "He's going to be fine," she says firmly. "He'll get through this."

I'm not sure whether she's trying to convince me or herself. I can only hope his therapy session sets him on the right path. I'm not foolish enough to think he'll be miraculously cured, and know he will have some way to go. Once out the other side, will he be a changed man? Or will our marriage be over, as he won't want me as his wife?

Wraith opens the door, and two prospects step inside. It's Nathan and Rascal. I give them a nod, then turn to Mom who's come up beside Sam.

"Do you think this is right?"

"What are you talking about?" Dad overhears and comes over.

I try to put my doubts into words. "Eli thinks he's been railroaded all of his life. Herded in the direction that his dad wanted him to go." I give Sam an apologetic look. I wave my hand toward the two men who've entered. "If we pack up and make it a fait accompli yet again, isn't that just confirming he's not in control of his life?"

"It's best that you come back to the compound," Dad states. "There are things going on which you don't know. It's nothing for you to worry about, but we're just being cautious."

I was brought up as the VP's daughter, so I don't bother asking Dad what he's talking about.

"Wraith," Mom challenges him with a growl. "We need more than that."

"Sophie, my love, I've said enough."

She glares, but his mouth remains firmly shut.

"Club business." Sam rolls her eyes. "All I could get out of Drummer was that there's only a teensy-weensy risk of something coming at the club, but being overbearing and protective as usual, they want everyone close."

"Another day won't hurt, will it?" I turn back to Dad. "If I, or you or Drummer can get Eli to understand the risk, then he'll be calmer about returning."

Sam's looking at me thoughtfully then addresses herself to Dad. "I think you and Drum should share with Eli what you can't with us. Even as he is now, he won't want Olivia in any danger."

I grin. That's the way to play it. Trust a mother to know her son. Even if he isn't thinking straight at the moment, I'm sure he'll still want to protect me. Of course I'll refuse to go back home by myself.

Dad stares at Sam, then walks off, taking his phone out of his cut as he does.

After a few moments he returns, his call finished and looking unhappy as if he's received the answer he didn't want. "Drummer doesn't like it, but can see it makes sense. We'll play it your way, Olivia. But if the risk level rises, or Eli holds out too long, we'll fuckin' kidnap him. Not having you in danger. Not for any damn thing."

Sam looks toward me, then at Dad. "So, someone's got to be staying tonight. I'm happy to do that with Drum, but we'll need a change of underwear at the least."

"I'll keep you company if you're going back to the compound," Mom offers.

Dad sighs heavily for a moment, then looks up to the ceiling. "Alright," he growls, reluctantly giving in. Then turns around and yells, "Prospects!" At which, Nathan and Rascal come running. "Change of plan. Leave that shit where it is. Follow Sam and Sophie to the compound, then escort them back here."

With air kisses for me, and a full-on kiss between Mom and Dad, the two women and prospects leave.

It's just me and Dad now.

I realise my plans for the day have been turned upside down. Mentally I run through the tasks I need to do, then, *damn these pregnancy hormones*, I remember I've left some clothes at the dry cleaners I'd forgotten to collect.

Luckily, now I can leave the packing, I've plenty of time to go out and get it before Eli comes back. I delve down into my purse and check the ticket is at least where I remember it is, in my wallet. Then I take out my keys and call out where I'm going.

"Hey, Olivia. Hold up. You're not going anywhere on your own. I'll come with you."

"Dad." I roll my eyes. This is one thing I haven't missed, being followed or escorted all the time. "Look, I'm just going over to the mall. I won't be long. And we're out of coffee, so I'll pick some up."

"Not letting—"

"I've lived here for weeks and nothing's happened, Dad." I start to get annoyed. "If things are so dangerous, why weren't you worried two days ago, last week, last month?" My eyebrows rise as I challenge him. "I've lived here for two months and have gone everywhere on my own. What's happened now to change that?" As he seems lost for an answer, I continue, "What would have happened if Eli hadn't broken down? I'll tell you what." I'm getting into my stride now. "We wouldn't be going back to the compound, the club has washed its hands of us. We'd never have even known there was danger coming to the club because it wouldn't concern us." It seems ridiculous to me. I've gotten used to having some freedom. What's changed in two days?

"Olivia—"

"I'm going, Dad. And you're not coming with me."

Leaving him open mouthed, I pick up my keys and leave the house.

I drive the short distance to collect the clothes that have now been cleaned, then, on the way back to my car, I get a text. I take my phone out of my purse, swearing quietly as I'm sure it's my dad checking up.

Gabe: I was hoping to see you as I'm being transferred again. Any chance we could meet for a coffee? I'd like to say goodbye in person.

Well that's strange, another one of those coincidences. I smile to myself. Seems to happen a lot with him. I think for a moment. If he hadn't said it was to say goodbye, I'd have brushed him off. It doesn't seem right to meet another man, however innocently, with everything going on with Eli. But to share a coffee, or in my case a soda, one last time? To talk about something else and stop worrying about my husband for just a moment?

Before I can have second thoughts, I tap out a reply.

Olivia: I'm actually close right now if you want to meet at the normal place. I can't stay long though.

Gabe: Perfect.

I'm actually glad to have a chance to say goodbye. From my father's reaction just now, once I'm back on the compound, I'll have no freedom to meet anyone for coffee, or not without having a shadow with me.

I don't, however, want my dad to worry. Once again, I send a text.

Olivia: Just meeting a friend for coffee. Won't be long. x

Dad: You should come straight home.

My eyes roll as I hear his voice in my head, replaying it as though I've gone back fifteen years in time. I'm a grown woman, I can do what I like. Eli won't be back from the therapist for some time, and now I want to meet Gabe for what will be the last time and close this chapter in my life.

Olivia: I won't be long. x

Putting my phone on to silent, I slip it back into my purse, unsurprised when it vibrates again. It will only be Dad telling me to go straight back. I ignore it and drive the short distance between the store and the coffee shop.

Gabe is sitting in his normal place by the window, and a soda is already waiting for me, along with a cake that he knows I enjoyed the last time we were here.

"Hey, how you been?" He stands to greet me, his features forming a welcoming smile.

I rub my stomach which seems to stretch further every day. "As good as can be."

"You're glowing."

Ignoring his compliment, I ask a question myself as I sit down, "So what's this about you leaving?"

He grimaces. "Yeah. I'm leaving today. It's what happens in my line of work. You have to go wherever the leads take you."

"You don't get much choice in it then?" I sympathise.

"No, not really. Tucson's not a good place for me to be anymore."

"You still going to be in Arizona?" *Mmm mmm* I think to myself, taking a bite of the delicious cake.

He watches me eating, then shakes his head. "No, I'll be leaving the state. So this, sweet Olivia, is the last time we'll meet like this."

"That's a shame." I take another bite, moaning as the sweetness hits my taste buds. As it happens I won't be around either. But I don't bother to tell him that. It would lead to questions about where I'd be living, and I don't really want to go into details about my family being bikers.

"It is what it is." He shrugs. "And you'll soon have your hands full with the baby."

I nod, and smile, thinking how good it will be living close to Sam and Mom once again while in the last stages of my pregnancy.

"How long have you got to go?" He seems to be making polite conversation.

Before I answer, I take another bite, chew, then swallow. "Just another four weeks. I must admit I can't wait to meet him or her now." I finish my cake, then lick my fingers clean of the icing. "What?" I ask, as he's staring at me with a distinctive curve to his lips.

"I'm just glad you're enjoying your cake."

"I am." I yawn loudly, covering my mouth with my hand. "Oh, sorry." I feel my cheeks redden.

"Pregnancy makes you tired, or that's what my wife always used to say."

I remember he lost her, so cover his hand with mine. "I'm sorry."

He turns his hand over and his fingers grip mine tightly. He mumbles something, but I don't catch it.

I'm feeling a bit strange. Lightheaded. Maybe too much sugar has gone straight to my head.

"I think I better go." I try to stand and stumble.

"Is she okay?" I vaguely register a female voice asking.

"She's fine," Gabe replies for me. "Just got up too quickly. I'll take her home."

He's holding my hand, painfully tightly. His arm is around my waist.

Something's not right.

"This isn't my car," I complain as he opens a door and starts pushing me inside. I try to resist, but my limbs feel like jelly, and my swollen stomach weighs me down. I drop into the seat as my legs refuse to support me. The door bangs shut loudly.

Immediately, he's around the driver's side, sliding in behind the wheel.

With what's left of my senses, I try to open the door, but he's already locked them centrally, and in my increasingly befuddled state, I can't find the button to override that.

He's drugged me.

"What have you given me?" I manage to rasp, my fear for the baby forcing my words out.

He doesn't answer, just starts to pull out of the parking lot.

I try to stay conscious, to watch where we're going, trying to pick up clues of where he might be taking me, but my eyelids keep lowering as if by themselves. Eventually, it's too much effort to lift them again, and I succumb to the darkness.

CHAPTER NINETEEN

*E*li...

I could have killed Hound and Throttle when they dragged me out of the house this morning. All I'd wanted to do was wallow in my own misery, perfectly content to spend the whole day doing exactly that.

What actually got me moving wasn't the orders that Hound had barked at me, but the knowledge that they were there in my bedroom in the first place. Even stranger, they'd made no mention of my leaving the club, and the word *Brother* had come from their lips.

I'd felt I'd reached my lowest point and had no idea how to climb back out of the mire. Their appearance gave me a glimmer of hope that there might be a way back. Not to the club, I didn't want that, but perhaps a way out of this grave I feel like I'm living in. If they'd put themselves out for me, maybe it was up to me to try.

I had absolutely no faith in the doctor I was going to see. How could talking about my problems help? There's no magic wand to fix me, but if Hound and Throttle want me to go through the motions, I'll give it a go.

At the hospital, Dad's already waiting. He offers to come

in with me, but I'm a fucking man, aren't I? Surely I don't need a parent holding my hand. Straightening my shoulders, I follow the instructions I'm given as to where I should go.

I'm surprised when first I'm given a full physical with blood taken. It's only then that the doctor starts on the therapy. He's not the same man who came to the house, but I'm here, so I may as well cooperate.

First, he asks me a list of questions, and gives the instruction to answer truthfully. Here, within these four walls, I'm assured of confidentiality and nothing but total honesty will help me in any way. I do make a mental note to steer away from club business, but decide I'll tell him everything else.

No, I don't take drugs. Never have, never will. Sure, I use cannabis from time to time, but not every day. Doesn't everyone?

I don't smoke. Drink? *Is he having a laugh?* I'm a biker for fuck's sake. Or I was.

Have I suffered trauma? Well, yes, but that's something I can't admit to. While he's assured me he won't share anything I say, there's always the possibility that knowing I've killed and tortured people and buried bodies where they'll never be found might send him running straight to the cops. I know he's probing to see if I could be suffering post-traumatic stress, and honestly, nothing I've done has had that effect on me. I'm not haunted by the faces of dead men in my dreams. Anyone I dispatched to meet Satan deserved to die. I don't dwell on the time a bullet came too close to me, nor the time I was rammed by a truck causing me to lose control of my bike. When we mete out our own form of justice on those who had wronged us or ours, it got adrenaline rising, not fear. I live, *had lived*, for those times.

Health issues? Nah, my health is good.

How's the relationship with your wife? What relationship? I can't be bothered to work at it anymore.

How often have you felt down, or depressed? That you had no control over the world? Every fucking day, Doc. Every fucking day for months.

We go through my sleep patterns, my appetite, my energy. Then comes the big one.

Have you ever thought of suicide?

If I don't reply honestly, he won't be able to help. I shrug and admit it seems like it could be the answer.

He doesn't react, just nods, and taps at his keyboard making notes. We talk about whether anyone else in my family has ever suffered depression or stress. I almost laugh. Drummer? He's always in total control, and so is my mom. We talk through the events of the past few years, concentrating on the last twelve months. He seems particularly interested that I was voted in as VP, though I'm careful not to say all that entails. I concentrate on telling him how I take overall responsibility for the running of our businesses, and the general well-being of the club. And that, if Wizard is away, step in and act as the president. My long-term relationship with Liv is picked apart, how we moved from friends to lovers, then to being wed. His eyebrows rise slightly when I add she's expecting a baby in a month.

Finally he pushes away his keyboard and takes off his glasses, swinging them gently. "Barring nothing untoward turning up in your bloodwork, I think what we're looking at is clinical depression brought on by the stress of sudden life changes. You've had a lot thrown at you over the past year."

Raising my eyes, I look toward him as he gives what I'm suffering from a name. *Clinical depression.* I'd half expected a pull-myself-together lecture, to be told I'm a man and my lot's much the same as any man carries. That I'm wallowing in self-pity and to pull myself together, to suck up what's been thrown at me by life.

"I don't know myself anymore," I admit. "I feel inadequate. My club trusts me, and I'm not sure I'm worthy of that. I could," *lead a man to his death,* "make a decision that ruins us financially." He waves at me to go on. "My wife is depending on me to be there for her and the baby, but I'm worried I'll fuck up."

He doesn't tell me all men worry when they're expecting a child imminently. Instead he taps out a few more notes.

"Why has this happened to me?" I suddenly cry out. "I don't understand."

He gives me his full attention. "Depression is far more common than you would expect. I suspect you always have been self-aware and self-critical. Stress can build up when there are a series of events that bring it to a head. Maybe none of the events by themselves are particularly serious, but they can add together and put you on a downward spiral. It's nothing to be ashamed of, and something we can help you overcome. Asking for help, coming here today, is an important first step."

I was forced to come, but I don't tell him that.

He's given me a diagnosis. I'm no longer floundering wondering what's wrong. I don't want to live the rest of my life like this, if I do, it's likely to be short. I may have needed persuasion to speak to someone, but now I have, perhaps I owe it to everyone, Liv in particular, and even myself, to continue to get help.

"How can I fight this?" As soon as the words leave my mouth, I realise I want to fight my demons. Right now I know I've got a battle ahead, and though I'm not sure I can win it, I'll give it my best shot.

A half-smile appears on his face. "Continue taking the antidepressants—"

"They do nothing but make me sleep."

He dismisses my objection. "They take time, two weeks or more to have an effect. It's important to keep taking them regularly. I can reduce your current dosage if they make you too fatigued."

I hate the thought of being doped up, but I also hate feeling the way I do now. I'm more interested when he suggests CBT —Cognitive Behaviour Therapy. At first I shrugged it off until he explains what it is. We'll pinpoint my negative thoughts, feelings and behaviours, and work on changing my response. I can even do the course online. He's right, I've always been critical of myself, starting from when I was a child. I would think before acting, part of the reason I was made VP, but also the reason I failed. Maybe if I can learn not to take it to extremes, I'll be able to manage my own expectations better.

He encourages me to stop doing what I'm most guilty of, shutting people out. Maybe Hound and Throttle appearing today show I've a whole wealth of support that I'd thought I'd left behind. Maybe moving back to the compound would help, confronting my fears rather than running away. *If someone doesn't kill me on sight.*

When he mentions exercise, I smile. I'm sure Peg would help me get back into shape. The corners of my mouth quickly turn down. *Am I ready to go through an intensive training programme with Peg in the gym?* Well, it's one way of killing yourself.

Surprisingly, I leave the doctor's office with more positive thoughts. The biggest takeaway being he was confident that I'd come out the other side okay. That these feelings I have are not going to stay with me for life. That I'll have confidence in myself again one day. That I can be man enough to be a dad to my kid.

Hound's head tilts to the side when he sees me. Then he smiles and his arm goes around my shoulder, slapping me on my back. "You're walking taller, Brother."

Drummer stands from the seat where he's been waiting. His steely eyes settle on me. I frown, unable to read the expression on his face as he steps closer.

"Fuckin' proud of you, Son," he tells me, his voice cracking. When I crease my brow, he explains, "You've taken the first step."

I'm thinking hard as we walk through the hospital corridors, making our way outside to the parking lot. Dad goes to his bike telling us he'll meet us back at the house. I follow the others to the truck. When we get there, I finally speak.

"Throttle, Hound—I owe you an apology."

"You don't owe us fuck," Hound growls. "You want us to get all lovey dovey and apologise for the beating you took? You want to spend your time reliving all the old slights and rehashing them again and again? Or does the future start now?" He waves at the building to our rear. "In there, with your therapist, you can talk about what went down, but with us? All we need to know is how we can help and what you need to get through this."

"While I agree with the sergeant-at-arms," Throttle begins, "Brother, I'm here if you do want a sounding board to talk about where things went wrong."

It's my state of mind, but tears well up in my eyes as everything I'd thought I'd willingly left behind hits me right in the face. *How did I think I could do without my Satan's Devils' family beside me?*

I didn't tell them because I was ashamed, guilty that I was letting them down, even if it was only in my head. Their forgiveness and ability to start over fresh makes me chagrined and regretful I didn't speak to them before.

"Come on, let's get you home."

Home sounds good. But it's not Heart's old house that I want to return to. Suddenly I make a decision. "Forget what I said earlier. I want to move back to the compound."

Throttle fist pumps the air. "Now that's fuckin' music to my ears, Brother."

He prods my back and pushes me into the car.

I rest back against the headrest with my eyes closed on the short drive, going back over what the therapist said. One thing had struck me, that I'm far from alone in getting depressed. Depression, it would seem, is suffered by many, far more than people think. But, as I've discovered, when you're deep in the depths, it's not something you want to talk about or admit.

Maybe the first step to recovery is acknowledging something is wrong, disclosing how you're suffering and asking for help.

I'm a man. I've been brought up in an environment where men are strong, decisive, and leap into action. They are not weak, hesitant, or scared to make a move in case it's the wrong one. The imbalance between what I thought I should be, and what I was, had all but destroyed me. It's time to discover who I am, but not out on my own in the citizen world. No, I need to be among my family with my brothers around me.

Arriving home, I notice that Olivia's car isn't there. I'm disappointed. I wanted to talk to her, to tell her I've put my foot on the first rung of the ladder to recovery. That I'll do my fucking best to be a good husband to her, and that if I fall back, it won't be for want of trying.

I want her. My wife. Not completely, not just yet. Another thing the doc had explained was that the erectile dysfunction was due to what's been going on with me, not because of her.

Her pregnancy has just made her more beautiful to me, but I'd convinced myself I didn't deserve her. I had been pushing her away as I thought it would be better for her if she'd leave, all the while knowing that if she had left my life, well, that would have had me eating that bullet for sure.

The door opens. Dad's already there, standing, hesitant, his sharp eyes examining me. He waves me inside.

I stand for a moment, looking around the house that had never felt like home to me. "I'm coming back to the compound," I tell him. Then I take a deep breath, pushing my feelings of inadequacy down, and the shame of how much I've disappointed him. I add just three words. "I'll get there."

Understanding me completely, he raises his chin. "I know you will, Son."

"Eli?"

I go to my mom, pulling her into my chest. "I'm coming home," I tell her.

"Well that's bloody good news," Sophie calls, having overheard.

"I'm calling the prospects back," Hound informs.

"Where's Liv?"

Wraith appears. He doesn't look happy. "She went to pick up some dry cleaning. Then I got a text saying she was going to have coffee with a friend."

I frown. A friend? I didn't know she'd made any while she'd been here, but then, she could have told me, and so wrapped up in myself, I might not have taken it in. I'm sure she'll come home if I call her, trouble is, I don't even know where my phone is. Last time I know I had it was when I went out the day I had my breakdown. "Can you text her, Wraith? Ask her to come back." Now I've made my decision, I don't want to hang around.

"I'll call her," her father agrees, and takes out his phone, tapping at the keys. He raises it to his ear with a small smile, but then his features slowly rearrange themselves into a frown. "No answer," he observes unnecessarily. He tries again. Then, looking down, taps at the keypad.

"Her location is showing as The Coffee Cup." Wraith looks up then down again. "She's probably got her phone on silent or something. She ignored my fuckin' text telling her to come back." He tries for a third time to place the call, then shakes his head. "It's going straight to voicemail."

"For fuck's sake," Dad snarls. "Weren't you worried about that?"

"No I fuckin' wasn't. She was in one of her snits. Christ,

Drummer. She's been away from the compound for months. She's gotten used to doing what she wants."

"What friend is she seeing? You got her number?"

"I didn't get an answer to that."

Throttle sighs. "Want me to go and hurry her up? Two women gossiping? It could go on for hours."

"The prospects will be here soon. Probably need her to tell us what they need to pack up." Hound gives me a sideways glance, but I just nod. To be honest, I didn't take much notice of what's ours and what was here when we arrived.

"Yeah, thanks, Throttle."

When Wraith agrees, the enforcer holds out his hand to Hound who passes him the keys to the truck.

I make my way to the couch and settle down to wait. I sigh, feeling exhausted. The effect of the tablets and the draining discussion with the therapist have knocked the shit out of me.

A hand touches my shoulder. "How are you feeling?" Mom sits down beside me.

"Wrung out," I admit. It's true, I feel I've been put through the wringer today. I'm trying hard to hold on to my positive thoughts, but the darkness keeps threatening to take me under again. An inner voice I'm trying to fight back is trying to tell me it's fate. It would be far easier not to disturb Liv's day, go back to bed and delay the move... forever? *Is it the right thing to do? Am I sure?*

"It's going to be okay," she tells me softly. "Take it day by day, Eli. We know what we're dealing with now."

Dad's pacing. I half listen as he speaks to Wraith. "Why didn't you go with Olivia?"

Wraith sighs. "I should have, but Olivia got in one of her moods and made a good point. What was the difference between today and the past two months?" He pauses. "She made me feel fuckin' guilty. If Eli hadn't collapsed, we wouldn't have thought about protecting her." Wraith waves his hands aimlessly. "I was still trying to come up with a good enough response when she walked out."

I smile. Yeah, that sounds like Liv. Once she throws shit like that at you, it's hard to argue with her good sense.

"You're going to get there." Mom's still talking to me. Her voice is soothing. For a while she just lets me sit and relax. I'm disturbed when Dad answers his phone.

"Jesus H Christ!" he shouts at the top of his voice. "Are you fuckin' sure?"

"What's up?" Wraith's voice is full of concern.

"Olivia's car is at the coffee shop. No sign of Olivia. He questioned the waitress who said she left with a friend—she's been there with *him* before. She said Olivia looked faint and that her companion had to help her outside. She thought it was to do with her being pregnant."

A man? I feel the blood drain from my face. *Is she leaving me? Have I been successful and pushed her away?*

"Maybe it is," Mom states, standing and taking hold of Sophie's hand. "She's eight months pregnant. The baby could be coming early. He could have taken her to the hospital."

Wraith's checking his phone. Then he places a call. "Throttle. Her phone is still showing… Yeah, ask the waitress. I'll hold… Yeah?... You sure?... Yeah. Call me back." He ends the call. "Her phone's not been handed in. Throttle's looking for it outside. It's there, somewhere."

My eyes flick between them all, my brain focusing again on one word. *Him.* A man. She's been seeing a man behind my fucking back. She's been doing what I suggested I'd do to her. But it's her who's taken the next step. Why would she leave her phone? She must know that's how she'd be traced.

"She's left me." The words come out of my mouth. "It was all a lie. She didn't want to come back to the compound, so she's left with someone else." Suddenly her betrayal, which was what I encouraged after all, doesn't seem as bad as the thing that hits me most. "What if I never see her again? My baby!" The final words leave me in a wail.

I did this. I chased her away.

"Fuck!" Dad's voice seems to come from far away. "Take it straight back to the compound and give it to Mouse. See what he can come up with. We're heading back now."

Suddenly I'm pulled to my feet. Hands come around my shoulders and shake me. "Stop it, Eli. Stop it now. You think you pushed Olivia away? You fuckin' think she'd have left you without a word? That is not the Olivia I know. You wallowing in self-fuckin'-pity right now isn't helping anyone. We need to find her!"

Find. Her. Dad's words, the expression he wears, feels like a slap to my face.

"She might be at the hospital," Sophie cries out. "This may be nothing to worry about."

Wraith's there, holding her to him. "We'll fuckin' check. Drummer, we'll go by the hospital she's registered at. She'll have headed there if the baby was coming."

Drummer nods, then shakes his head. "If that were the case, she'd have gotten a message to you."

"Not if she dropped her phone," Mom offers reasonably. "There's a chance, Drummer. If the baby's started to come early, or something's wrong, she could have lost hold of it."

Either she's left me, or… "The baby's coming early. She'll be at the hospital." I shake my head, willing myself to think she left of her own volition.

Wraith swears as his eyes flick to me, then he holds Sophie close, hugging her before releasing her. "Sam could be right, we'll get to the hospital and check it out. Wherever she is, we'll fuckin' find her, Soph. I swear it to you. We'll find her."

The hospital. It's the only acceptable explanation.

CHAPTER TWENTY

*D*rummer…

I'd felt a glimmer of hope when Eli had come out from seeing the doctor. There was a slight difference in his bearing which suggested while he'd hit his lowest point, there was a chance he was going to pull himself out of the hole he'd gotten himself into. Clearly he couldn't do it without encouragement and help, but now with the whole club rooting for him, I believe there's a good chance he'll pull through.

Then, my temporary rise in my spirits had come crashing back to the ground when we discovered Olivia was missing.

Any man not in an MC wouldn't have immediately thought the worst. The waitress's explanation that she thought the baby might have started to come would have been the one most likely and probably accepted by the majority of the civilian population. But I am not a normal man, and I don't clutch at innocent explanations. I also dismissed the thought that she'd been having a secret liaison, and that rather than return and be confined to the compound, she'd decided to throw in her lot with another man. That wasn't the Olivia I knew, nor the woman worrying herself sick about the state of Eli, the woman who'd been crying in her bed these past few nights.

No. Someone's taken her.

I'm angry she'd made it easy. If I'd been here, I'd never have let her go off alone. I'm fucking furious at Wraith, fighting not to let that ire show as I know he's blaming himself for so badly fucking up. She must have twisted him around her little finger as daughters are wont to do. Damn everything to hell and back. I'm enraged for her sake, she's like a daughter to me, and for my son's. That she's missing isn't going to help his recovery at all.

Wraith and Sophie have gone on what both he and I know will be a wasted trip to the hospital to check if she's there. I know deep down in my gut they won't find her there. Throttle had swung around and come back to the house to pick Eli and Hound up and are currently driving ahead of Sam and me. We're following on our bikes, riding in perfect unison, knowing every move the other will make after all these years.

I'd lost Sam once, before I'd admitted what I'd felt for her. She'd been taken by a sex trafficking ring. I can still taste the fear that had consumed me when she'd disappeared. That means I know exactly what my son will be going through once he loses hope there's an innocent explanation for this. Would it be kinder to allow him to think she could have walked out of his life under her own volition than have been taken by someone who may want to hurt her?

She knew the man. I remember Throttle's words. The waitress had said she'd been in with him a time or two before.

I didn't get where I was in the MC without examining every angle. Although I immediately dismissed it, I do need to consider whether Eli was right. Could I be wrong? Could she have been so starved of affection, and having caught someone's eye, decided to leave her husband? No, that wouldn't be the girl I've known all her life. Especially not now when Eli is at his lowest. Anyway, Olivia would more likely confront Eli before doing something underhanded.

If I rule out that she's gone to the hospital, or that she's left Eli for another man, it means she's been abducted, and not by a stranger, by a man who obviously targeted and deliberately befriended her.

If so, this was pre-planned. It's not like she was snatched off the street. I don't know when or how they'd first hooked up together. Christ. My hand slams on the handlebars, as I realise all the gaps in my knowledge.

Who would take the time to gain her trust and get to know her? Perhaps more importantly why? She's attractive and, when not carrying an almost due baby inside her, is slender with a fine figure. Now she's matronly, and not someone you'd immediately think ripe for trafficking. Unless it's to fulfil a twisted fetish. In that case, why wait weeks to take her?

When Eli and Olivia had left the compound, to the club they were Satan's Devils no longer. But what if we were the only ones to think that? Could we have an enemy who took the chance Olivia being who she was, the daughter of the old VP, a girl born and bred in the club, remained important to us? They'd be right. She's still ours, ours by blood and by being part of the MC family. We'd just made it easy for someone to use her against the club.

But who? Who would take her?

Right now, I don't have an answer.

She'd looked faint, Throttle had told us. Could she have been drugged? If she didn't leave with him voluntarily, it sounds likely. But what would that mean for her, and for the baby?

Sam and I both indicate at exactly the same time, then turn down the track that leads to the compound. As soon as my bike's parked in its spot, I nod at Sam and fly into the clubhouse, going to the office of the man who should be the most help.

Throttle follows me inside. He passes me Olivia's phone, which I in turn pass to Mouse.

"You found it just lying by her car?" he queries, making me realise Throttle's already warned him what we need done. When the enforcer nods, he adds, "Like it was going to be easily found?"

Throttle's head bobs up and down again.

I switch my attention toward the man with my daughter-in-law's phone in his hand. His mouth is pursed as he links it up to something, then does some magic to obviously break the code that lets him get to the data. Fuck knows how he works that shit, but it takes him no time at all until his mouth curves in the right direction.

At that moment the door bangs open behind me. "What the fuck, Drummer?" Wizard comes in and rushes around the desk, but he asks for no further explanation. "Whatcha got, Mouse?" Then he meets my eyes over the desk and shakes his head. "Wraith's called. No sign of her at the hospital. She certainly hasn't gone to the maternity ward."

"Can you check the emergency rooms? If she passed out, he might not know where to take her." I'm clutching at straws. Everything points to her having been kidnapped. But Wizard nods and pulls Mouse's spare laptop toward him.

"Right," Mouse starts, "she was texted this morning." As he examines the screen, he tilts his head to one side and his eyes narrow. His face screws up as if he's thinking, then his tanned complexion pales. "Jesus Christ," he breathes out.

Wizard, now looking over his shoulder, stills. "What are you looking at?"

"The phone was found where we could find it." Mouse repeats what he'd been told. "It could have been dropped…"

"But you think it's a message?" Wizard's eyes sharpen as he reads the texts. His brow furrows. "A code?"

I'm trying to hold back my frustration. "What do the messages say?"

"I'm not bothered about the actual words," Mouse says.

"What the fuck is it?" I growl out impatiently. "You found anything? I want to know now."

Mouse takes back the phone and scrolls up and down a message chain, then his eyes rise, meeting mine. "Looks like Olivia's met this man a few times."

Yes, that's what the waitress had implied. I don't much like it, but Eli's been being an ass to her. Doesn't excuse her for betraying him, but finding her is the most important thing now. She's a daughter of the club and we're not going to abandon her.

"It's fairly innocent shit," Mouse says. "Looks like they only met for coffee a few times, nothing to suggest they were in a liaison but..." As his voice trails off, he rests his gaze on me, then continues, "It's not what she was meeting him for, it's the name of the man she was meeting."

"Oh, fuck," Prez breathes out.

"What the hell are you talking about?" I lay my fist on the table. "Who the fuck was she seeing?"

"His name is Gabe." I'm faced with two men who are used to dealing with information, seeing by the look on their faces they're adding two and two together in a type of math I can't understand. The name doesn't register. Until Mouse expands, "I'm guessing it's short for Gabriel."

"Fucker's playing with us." Wizard slams his hand down on the desktop.

My gut churns. "Mouse?" I ask cautiously, hoping the answer to the sum I've come up with isn't right.

Seems that it is when Mouse jerks his chin upward. "Unless it's one hell of a coincidence, and I think it's not, it's

Archangel Gabriel. He wants us to fuckin' know it's him who's got her."

Turning, I slam my fist into the wall.

"I should have put two and two together." Throttle speaks through a tensed jaw. "Didn't get much of a description, but the waitress said this Gabe had white blond hair and was a tall, muscular motherfucker."

Wizard waves him off. "You weren't thinking of matching a man from his description at the time, Throttle. Don't beat yourself up. We wouldn't have done differently if we'd known earlier. We can confirm it properly when we get the CCTV footage from the coffee shop, but I'd say there's not too much doubt with what you've just said and the handle he's using. Drummer. I think it's best we assume fuckin' Archangel's got Olivia now, and I've fuck all idea what he's going to do with her."

"Give me the phone." I hold out my hand. "I'm going to fuckin' talk to him."

Prez shakes his head. "Not without us thinking this through." He closes his eyes as if he's thinking. "Eli and Ollie were out on their own. He doesn't know the club is involved, unless Olivia told him. If there's a chance he doesn't yet know, I want to keep him in the dark."

A chance. A slim one. "He's playing with us," Throttle observes.

Mouse waves to Wizard, holding out his hand. "Let me examine that, Prez."

"Can he trace the phone?" I remember Wraith could from his own.

"That's what I'm going to find out." Mouse looks tense.

It could make a difference if Archangel knows of our involvement. Wizard is right. If there's a chance we can stay in the background, we might have a better chance. If he believes there's only a man who's not in his right mind trying to find her, then he might fuck up.

I rake my fingers through my hair, questions chasing each other around in my head. *Why take Olivia? And, should I tell Eli exactly who we think has got her?* What will it do to him for him to know it's our worst enemy? *Let him believe she ran off with another lover? Would that be kinder?* At least he wouldn't have to worry about her not being alive.

No. He might think it right now, but no man deserves to believe he's been left for another. I beckon for the unlocked phone which Mouse reluctantly hands over. I read the messages for myself. Mouse was right. Nothing more there than to think they met for anything other than coffee. Mouse impatiently reaches for the phone again, and I surrender it back.

Thinking about it, Olivia went from being surrounded by people, both men and women, to living an isolated life with a man who gave her no attention and wanted none from her. She was lonely and would have been ripe to be picked by a friendly voice. Everyone here had known she was Eli's from back when they were kids. No one's ever seriously flirted with her. She's not learned to be wary around strange men, and is likely to have treated him just like she would a woman who approached her.

"What you thinking, VP?"

"This Gabe targeted Olivia. Fuck knows how. It was planned."

"How, we can only guess at, but we do know why. To hit us where it fuckin' hurts." Prez whistles out air through his teeth. "I asked Butcher to round up everyone for church. We need to locate her and fast. Jeez, Drummer, I hate to think what he might be doing to her." Fuck. Archangel could use her to hurt us in so many ways. Disappear her so we never know what happened to her? Leave her dead body where it could be found? None of the reasons why he'd want her are good ones.

Prez continues, "Mouse, you stay here and search for any leads that could help us."

A sharp rise and dip of his head and the half Native American shows his agreement.

"What do you want to do about Eli, Prez?" I ask him, being undecided myself. Would knowing what's happened to Olivia destroy him completely? Or is that just as likely to happen if he eventually finds he's been left out of the loop? I have no idea what a man in his state can deal with.

Wizard thinks for a moment, clearly considering my question carefully. Then he voices my own thoughts. "Things have happened fast. Do we make or break Eli by getting him involved in this?"

If Eli's head was screwed on right, I know there'd be only one way to look at it. I realise I don't have any option but to treat him like the man he was. "Involve him," I decide when the decisions passed back to me. "How the fuck would you feel if it were Amy? I know how I'd be going crazy if it had been Sam who disappeared. Can't keep him out of it, Wizard."

Prez's hand grasps my shoulder. "You think he can handle it?"

Shaking my head, I reply, "I've got fuck all idea, Prez, but that we should give him the chance is my gut feel."

He nods. "Okay, Drummer. He's your son. I'll defer to you on this one. Eli joins us in church." He then opens the door and disappears out of it, Throttle close on his heels.

I pause a moment. Mouse reaches for his joint, picks up a lighter and applies the flame to it. "We'll get her back." As he speaks, his intense dark eyes compel me to believe he'll do what he can, but if he's right, we're dealing with a man who hasn't got an ounce of compassion within him. We might not have much time.

"Find her fast, Mouse."

I leave and head to the meeting room as brothers are filing

in for church. Making my way to the top end of the table, I receive slaps on the back, or serious nods, that simple gesture conveying sympathy, support and promises of retribution to whoever's taken one of our own. I'm not surprised in a situation like this, word has already gotten around. Hound meets my eyes from the opposite side of the table and gives me a nod, an acknowledgement he has already filled people in on what's gone down. It saves time, I'm down with it.

Three chairs remain empty as everyone takes their place. That of Wizard, Wraith, and my normal seat at the end of the table.

A minute passes, then two. Then one more. Glances are sent my way, but I shake my head. This is Wizard's show now, he should be here to lead it.

Eventually the door opens. Prez steps in.

Looking grim, he goes quickly to his place at the head of the table. Instead of banging the gavel, he raps the wood, an unnecessary gesture as attention is already on him.

"Olivia's missing."

"Any info on who's got her?" As Peg snaps his question, I realise no one else knows yet.

Wizard pauses, then says, "We think Archangel's got her."

The reactions are about what you'd expect, and it takes a moment for everyone to settle. This time Prez does need to use the gavel.

"We've brought Eli back to the compound." There's not much comment. That had been agreed to previously. However, Prez's next statement isn't accepted so easily. "I'm bringing him in on this discussion."

Hound again raises his chin my way.

"What the fuck, Prez?" Marvel groans, putting his head in his hands. "You think that's a good idea seeing as how we all feel about him? Enough to agree to having him close, but having him seated around this fuckin' table?"

Before I can open my mouth, Hound's voice thunders,

"Do I need to remind you, Eli had gotten to the point when he couldn't mentally cope. It wasn't his fault, nor a conscious decision. Now his wife's gone. I agree, he deserves to be part of getting her back."

Marvel's face looks thunderous. "If he hadn't taken her off the compound, she wouldn't be in Archangel's hands. I don't see how I can forgive him, not for this, Prez. He should have stayed, explained—"

"He didn't fuckin' know what was wrong with him. Hell, even if there was something wrong." It's Joker who aims his comments to Marvel now. "You don't wake up feeling different one day. It creeps up gradually, until you can't distinguish who you are anymore, or remember a time you thought differently." He pauses and makes sure he's got everyone's attention. "Eli got it stuck in his head that he was going to let everyone down. Rather than risk someone dying on his watch, he walked away. Fuckin' feelings he couldn't put into words overrode any rational side of his brain thinking clearly."

"We could have killed him." Lady turns to his partner. I remember he was one voting for leniency and wonder now whether he recognised something at the time from having watched Joker spiralling.

Joker nods grimly. "Sometimes death seems the only way out." He pauses to let that sink in. "Eli got to a place where there didn't seem a way out. He wasn't thinking rationally. Perhaps we weren't either. We didn't ask questions."

Hound is nodding as Joker speaks, when he finishes, he takes over. "I've seen Eli, spoken to him. From a sergeant-at-arms point of view, Eli saw himself as a danger to this club, so chose to leave it. He wasn't thinking of himself, he wasn't being a fuckin' selfish bastard. He was protecting us the only way he thought he could."

"But the upshot is Olivia was left exposed and has been taken." Shooter looks confused. "If Eli's so lost in his head, shouldn't we be finding her for him? What fuckin' help can he be? He could be a hindrance."

"We can't leave him out of it!" I roar. "If I'd seen his distress, spoken to him earlier, all this might have been prevented. Let's not repeat the same fuckin' mistakes."

"I don't understand why he didn't talk to you, Drum. Or you, Throttle." Shooter sits back, folding his arms.

Prez rolls his eyes. "That bitch you went with, before you hooked up with Charlotte? You almost lost yourself in the bottle when she walked away."

Shooter goes bright red. Yeah, he ran on alcohol fumes for a while. Known for being a sharpshooter, he nearly fucked up when he missed a critical shot. Luckily Heart was there and took it for him instead. We all knew what was wrong, asshole hadn't admitted it until Blade, surprisingly, had put it together and confronted him. We'd stepped up and given him Satan's Devils' therapy—told him to get his head out of his ass, pull himself together, and go fuck a whore. Worked, as I seem to remember. The point is, he hadn't asked for help.

"We're men," Lady puts in. He ignores the snorts. "We bottle things up. Eli was feeling shit, but didn't know the reason. As Joker deduced, his own brain turned against him."

Marvel, to give him his due, looks thoughtful. "I ain't got an old lady. Never have, never will. Partly because I don't want to have anything that I could lose. Except my bike. That would fuckin' kill me if I lost that." He gives a weak grin, then looks serious again. "I know you think I'm hard and unfeeling, but I fuckin' love this club. Hate anything that threatens it. If Eli thought he could lead us wrong, well, perhaps it was right for him to step out. Now he's lost his old lady." He glances up to see if we're still with him. When he sees we are, he carries on, "Losing her and the baby will fuckin' destroy him. No way he'd recover from that. Not knowing what's going on could drag him down too. Now you've explained, I can't see how we can keep him out of it."

"You suggesting we bring him in on our discussions?" Wizard asks. "Or just keep him updated?"

As Marvel thinks of his own answer, Throttle supplies his own. "Eli doesn't trust himself, but I still do. Whether he knows it or not, he could have something to contribute. Olivia's his life, always has been. He needs to have a chance to shape how we get her back."

I notice he's being positive and not saying if. It's the only way we'll survive this. It's not just Eli who would be destroyed if we lost her forever, it would be each and every member of this club. That's the reason Archangel took her. He knew how to get us where it would most hurt. He'd have gotten the same result if he had taken any one of our old ladies, we just made it too fucking easy for him to take her.

At that moment, the door opens and in steps Wraith. I'm not surprised by the desolate look on his face as he drops into a chair and his head falls into his hands. Peg's arm rests on his shoulder, but no one offers words of sympathy. There's nothing you can say to a man whose daughter is missing.

Prez raises an eyebrow toward him. When Wraith looks up, he catches his eye, and tells us, "Sophie's a fuckin' mess." His own dishevelled appearance suggests he is as well. "Sam's trying to comfort her."

"Eli outside? He know you couldn't find her?"

"Yes, and yes." His eyes meet mine. "That shut down mood he's been in? Well, he's swung the other way now. The prospects are having a hard time holding him." Wraith shakes his head. "I've seen him the past few days, Drummer. Seen him at his worst. Now he's got a need for action, and it's tearing him up. He's just taken a swing for Nathan, desperate to go and look for her himself, even without a clue where to start."

"Get him in here, Wraith," Prez demands. "Can't have him running off as a loose cannon.

"I'll go," Joker offers, and then stands and disappears out

of the door. Only seconds later it reopens, and Eli pushes past him to get in.

I notice Eli sits next to Wraith, but doesn't look at him. I'm still angry with the man myself. I'd never have let Olivia go off alone whatever her arguments had been. But I don't say a word. One look at the man shows he's suffering enough without anyone pointing his fuck-up out.

Eli, himself, looks agitated. His hands fidget, his body almost seems to be twitching as though it's too great an effort to keep himself still. I suspect he's avoided taking another of his antidepressants this morning.

Prez bangs the gavel. "Eli. You're here as a guest not a member." He breaks off and looks pointedly at Marvel, before he resumes, "Olivia's missing and we're going to help get her back. What you don't yet know is that we've got good reason to believe she's been taken by Archangel."

Eli looks like he's stopped breathing. His hands fist, his knuckles go white. Instead of the constant movement, he looks like he's frozen.

This is it, I think silently, watching him carefully. This is the point where he loses it completely, or resurrects the man I know is still inside.

"Breathe," Marvel says from beside him. "Fuckin' breathe, Brother. You're not on your own now. Need your head in the game to get her back."

I think we're all surprised it's Marvel who speaks to him. Then again, you never know which way that man will jump. That it is the one most likely to have confronted him seems to pull Eli up.

He does indeed take a couple of deep breaths, visibly struggling to pull himself together, then addresses Prez. "Why…" His voice cracks and he tries again, "Why do you think that?" His voice becomes a little firmer. "What evidence have you got?"

Prez nods my way. I take over.

"A man calling himself Gabe appears to have befriended Olivia." As a pair of distressed eyes in particular come my way, I elaborate, "It's sounds like an innocent friendship. It's not the first time they had coffee together. Though from the message thread on her phone, they've only been in contact for a few weeks and only ever met at the coffee shop."

CHAPTER TWENTY-ONE

*E*li...

Liv's gone.

When I'd first heard, my immediate thought was that she had left me. I couldn't blame her, I'd pushed her away. But Liv would have faced me, told me, not left without explanation, if only to tell me what an ass I'd been. Then, I expected the baby was coming early, and hell, that was such a scary thought, I just filed it away. *I'm not ready.* I'd left it to Wraith and Sophie to go to the hospital, unable to cope I'm ashamed to say.

When she hadn't been found, well, that was the point it had gotten through the mists in my brain. *Liv was missing.*

For the first time in months, thinking of someone other than myself breaks into the depths of despair and self-loathing that I've been drowning in. Just a crack in the walls I've been hiding behind. I feel I'm stumbling my way through a thick fog, knowing I've two options facing me. I could take the easy way out, stay here immersed in my pain and misery, or I could start looking for a way out. A way to contribute to finding my wife.

Believing I was still on my own, that no one would help a

lost son of the Satan's Devils, my first impulse had been to ride around the streets of Tucson, just trying to find a trace of where she might have gone.

The prospects had to physically restrain me. I became more and more agitated that I was helpless, held back from doing anything at all.

Then Joker had come out to collect me and had brought me into the space I'd never thought to enter again—the hallowed meeting room where the Satan's Devils hold church. It seems strange to sit here without the comforting weight of my leather cut on my shoulders. For a start, I don't understand why I'm here. I do notice Drummer's sitting in the VP's seat, the place that so recently was mine, and once again, I'm relegated to a position lower down the table beside Wraith.

When I listened to the chilling rendition that they think Archangel has Liv, I froze. My brain screaming, *I can't do this.* I could walk back into that fog and disappear behind those walls I'd built for myself. *Nothing can hurt me there as I don't care.*

"Breathe," Marvel says from the other side of me. "Fuckin' breathe, Brother. You're not on your own now. Need your head in the game to get her back."

Need me? What good am I to anyone? I swore to love and protect her. I can't give up on her now. *They think Archangel has her. Why would they think that?*

So I ask, and get an answer I suspect I was primed to hear.

Oh, Drummer made it sound innocent, a friendship growing between two people who had conversation over a coffee together. But what exactly would Olivia had shared with him? That she's married to an asshole who barely speaks to her, who's expressed a desire to find someone else, who doesn't act like he wants the baby? Archangel must have been laughing his fucking ass off as he listened to her.

I'd made it easy by rejecting her.

Or was she so starved of affection she'd take it from anyone? Even from the man who was our worst enemy.

She didn't know.

I'm hurt, raw, as though cut open and bleeding. But now's not the time to retreat to my safe place. What Liv didn't know didn't save her, it hurt her.

With red-rimmed eyes, I stare around the table, then, raise the fingers on my right hand. A familiar gesture, attracting attention, conveying I want to speak. Prez nods his head.

"Stable door, horse gone and all that. But I propose a fuckin' change." My voice sounds, feels stronger than it has for ages. "We keep old ladies out of club business for good fuckin' reason. But when we've got an enemy coming for the club, old ladies ought to be warned, ought to know what to look out for. Olivia hadn't a clue who she was fuckin' sitting down with. If she had, she'd have run a mile from this Gabe."

"Seconded," Wraith says.

"Agreed," Peg says.

"Happy with letting them see a picture of someone, but with no information attached. Just a watch out for and beware," Prez agrees. He stares at me. "Amy works off compound. She could have been fooled just like Olivia."

"Now we've bolted the fuckin' stable door, how are we going to get Hawk's old lady back?"

Marvel's referred to me as Hawk. I shrug. *It's just habit.*

"It's my fault," I admit, sending an apology to Wraith. I'd been blaming him for letting her go out alone, but hadn't that been what she'd been doing for weeks? It all comes down to one thing. "I took her off compound." Should have known I'd fuck up.

"Not your fault!" the new VP snarls. "You left the club, Eli. We even helped you out. To us you weren't fuckin' club anymore. Problem is, Archangel didn't get the memo."

"He knew better than us." Wizard stares at me. "You were still ours, always would be. You're club. Our reaction to him taking Olivia proves that. He couldn't have fuckin' hurt us more if he'd taken my old lady."

Heart growls, presumably at the thought his daughter, Amy, could have been taken.

I stare at them as an idea starts to take shape. With a rise and lowering of my shoulders, I shrug off all the excuses. It's moving forward I've got to concentrate on. And that starts by, "I'm going back to the house," I announce. My words are immediately misunderstood.

"Fuck!" Peg snarls. "You can't do this by yourself, Eli, and we're not asking you to. You need the club and you've got us, Brother. We just invited you to sit around this table, now you're throwing that in our fuckin' faces?"

I grin, evilly. An expression I know look's eerily like my dad's, and my eyes become cold as steel as the plan in my head begins to take shape. The mist parts as I begin to think clearer. "Not throwing anything back, Peg. I know I need your help and appreciate it, and can assure you, I'll be fuckin' using it. But as you said, we've left the club. It's only Archangel who thinks there's still a connection. What if we show him there's not? What if I go it alone, trying to find Liv?"

Most of the brothers are looking confused. Throttle, though, he's on my wavelength. He barks a laugh. "I can see where you're coming from. We don't give a damn about Eli and Liv," he states. "Club goes on as normal. As far as anyone outside of this room knows, they've made their bed, they lie in it. Archangel wants to hit us where it hurts, well, we show this way doesn't work."

Wizard isn't slow to catch up. "So we look like we're going on as normal—"

"And like the proverbial swan, paddle as fuckin' fast as we can under the water," Dad finishes for him, also having caught up.

Blade sticks his knife into the tabletop, hard enough to

make Wizard wince and glare. Undeterred, the ex-enforcer starts talking. "Could buy us some time if we don't react the way Archangel expects us to. Problem. Archangel knew Olivia had gone out today. He must have had eyes on her. What if he's been watching the house? If he has, he'll have seen Devils going in and out of Eli's house, and what's more, Eli's here now. How are we going to explain that?"

Wizard has a comeback immediately. "Eli is Drummer's son, Olivia, Wraith's daughter. Just because Eli's out of the club, his parents will still likely be concerned. As for Eli being here now, well, he's come to ask the club for help, and we'll send him away with his tail between his legs."

"No." Dad's eyes gleam. "If Eli's going where I think he is, Archangel's got to believe we've circled the wagons leaving both Eli and Liv on the outside."

"What about Hound and Throttle?" Wraith asks. "They went to the house. Fuck, if he's been watching, he'll know he's being played."

I get back into the game. "Let's think about what Archangel knows and doesn't know. Two men today turned up in a cage, they weren't on bikes wearing colours. Even if he's got eyes on our house, Satan's Devils don't have a who's who on any website so he's unlikely to know Throttle and Hound are part of the club. They've never met face-to-face."

"Unlikely, but it is not impossible."

The door opens and Mouse steps in. I swivel around in my chair. Mouse nods at Prez, then holds up Liv's phone. "He's installed a tracking app. That's how he knew where she was."

"How?" I say, fast.

"Invisible code in a text he sent to her." Mouse goes to his normal chair. "Very sophisticated and took me a moment to find."

"When? When they first met?"

Mouse shakes his head. "No. That's the sophistication, long before she listed him as a contact. He must have found her number somehow and sent a text telling her she'd have the chance to win a few thousand dollars for completing a survey. You know the sort of scamming shit that gets sent through. She opened the text, deleted it, but the damage was done. After that he could trace wherever her phone went, and would have rightly assumed she'd take it everywhere with her."

For the first time in months I feel a kernel of something I recognise as excitement. "So he didn't need eyes on the house." My plan will work.

"What are you thinking, Eli?" Prez asks.

"I take Liv's phone and as I said, return to the house. He'll have traced the phone here, so I'll let him know I came here for help, and you refused me. I'll let him know I'm on my own." I grimace, knowing if Archangel thinks he's lost his hold over the club, he might just kill Olivia, anyway. But there's a chance he'll hold off, if sending her back in pieces isn't going to get the results that he wants, and the only person who'll meltdown is me.

"That's all well and good," Peg frowns, "but surely he's not going to believe we're just going to sit back and take the loss of one of our own?"

"Fuckin' right we're not," Wraith growls. "And it's not going to come to that. Eli, with all due respect—"

"You can't rely on me?" I challenge, but wearily. He's seen me at my worst, I don't blame him.

"Eli won't be on his own." Prez stares down the table. "Physically, yes, but we'll be doing what we can in the background. At the moment we're in the dark, and Archangel thinks he's got the better of us. We have no idea where he's holding her, or what he plans to do with her."

My gut rolls, but somehow I keep myself under control. "At the moment, I don't know it's Archangel I'll be calling, do I? I'm a desperate man ringing every contact in her phone, trying to find out if anyone has seen her. I'll address him as

Gabe. I'm hoping it will give him pause for thought and us enough time to locate Liv and bring her home."

"When Eli makes contact, I can try and find his location." Mouse's eyes gleam.

Wraith's staring at me, then he turns his head and looks at the opposite end of the table. "Prez. This isn't going to stop us doing all we can. If Eli can play his part convincingly, it could buy us some space or give us a location. *If* Eli can pull it off. *If* he can convince him the club doesn't give a fuck… Lots of ifs…" When he pauses and looks at me again, I try my best to look like a man who can play the part assigned to him without falling apart. I have to. There's too much at stake.

Wraith resume, "It will annoy him if he's sitting back gloating, thinking we know exactly who's got my daughter. He'll think he's sent us a plain and clear signal he knows we were responsible for sending him down."

Peg looks thoughtful. "He'll know we've got that message, but he's shown his hand with nothing to bargain with, if we can convince him we're not concerned about getting Olivia back."

"He'll be angry," Rock inputs, his brow furrowing. "What's to say he won't harm Ollie and then move on to another plan?"

Prez gives me hard look. "Archangel's cold. A narcissist with no conscience. He'll accept without question that we can cut Olivia out of our hearts and thoughts. It's the way he works, and what brought him down in the end."

Wraith slams down his hand. "And that there's the hole in your thinking, Eli, Prez. Archangel's the devil incarnate. If Olivia isn't useful to him, he'll dispose of her."

I hear Wraith, but I've taken that into consideration. I clear my throat loudly. "I'll leave, go home. I'll contact him, let him know I'm not getting support. I'll act…" I break off, knowing I won't be acting at all, "as if I'm a broken man. I'll tell him I came to you, begged you for support, and that you turned me down. Now we... you're forewarned." I change it at the last minute, remembering I'm not part of the club anymore. "You go on lockdown. What he's done is made it harder for himself. By taking Liv, he's put you on guard."

"What are you fuckin' talking about?" Wraith snarls. "This plan will only work if we're actively trying to hunt him down. We're not going to hide out on the compound."

Mouse waves his hand. "We will be working to find him. I'm planning on hacking into any CCTV footage we can find to try to track where he was heading when he left the coffee shop with Olivia. When Eli calls him, I can ping his phone. I'll put feelers out on the dark web, see if anyone knows where he might be. We won't stop searching, Wraith. Fuckin' assure you of that."

"We'll leave no stone unturned," Prez says. He's an even better computer wizard. It's how he got his name.

"What about the feds?" Rock puts in. "Last time we got the information to them that allowed them to pick him up and take him in." I nod. It's a good point. Feds don't like missing a prisoner who's escaped from the penitentiary, and definitely not one who's killed their guards. "We could let them know he's in Tucson."

"Or was," Hounds points out. "We don't know where he is now."

"He can't leave a trace," Wizard says. "Even chartering a flight would be hard for a wanted man like him. I'd place good money that he's not taken her far, or at least is within driving distance."

"He'll stay close." Shooter frowns. I realise I don't want to hear his reasoning that Archangel might be wanting to send her back in pieces or leave her body somewhere it could be found.

"How does he know it was us who ratted him out?" I wonder aloud.

"Good point, Eli. Again, Mouse and I will see what we can find out."

I'm wracking my brains on what to do next. "Speak to Raptor, Wizard." He's the president of the local Wretched Soulz, having taken over from Chaz some years back. "They've got a price on Archangel's head. They want him as badly as us."

"Another good point," Wizard repeats. "I'll do that. Raptor will be very interested to know he's back in town. They'll get searching as well, you can bank on that."

"I can set up a meet," Dad proposes. Prez nods.

"I want to go back with Eli," Wraith offers.

I feel uneasy and tense, but for the first time in months, I'm not focused on my inner self. "No," I say, before Prez can respond. "We can't rule out Archangel's got eyes on the house. I need to be on my own." I'm starting to get twitchy, fed up with talking. "Can I go now? Sooner I get the ball rolling, sooner we can get my wife back."

Prez considers, then declares, "Wraith, you stay here. I can't see any fuckin' point in you going back to where she was. Archangel isn't going to drop her back home, however much we wish he would. You can best help her from here. Eli, you go get this thing started. We'll keep digging this end."

"Yeah. Run out of here with your tail between your legs. *Again.*" My eyes go sharply to Marvel's, but he's cracking up as if he made a good joke.

In truth, it cuts too close to the bone, but I go along with it. "As long as you're not going to give me a beatdown this time." I shut my mouth fast when it looks like he's giving consideration to it.

Prez looks around. "We *are* going to get her back, and in one piece." He raises his chin. "Mouse, give Eli a burner phone and walk him through checking for bugs in his house. Somehow Archangel knew just what your movements were. I want to be certain it's only Olivia's phone that was tracked.

Oh, and Eli? We might not be visible, but never doubt for one second you've got all your brothers behind you."

It's crazy, I think to myself, as I sit beside the prospect giving me a lift back to my house. I'm actually feeling more like my old self than I have for months. But that goes with guilt that I'm feeling stronger, while my wife's been kidnapped and is currently suffering fuck knows what.

She's got to be alright. Both her and the baby. I wouldn't be able to live with myself if she's not.

Butcher doesn't know what to say to me, so we're quiet on the drive. I don't start a conversation. Anyone who's not a trusted member will have to believe the club has refused to help me find Olivia if we've got a chance of Archangel being fooled.

He stops the truck when we arrive at the coffee shop, and I get out without ceremony, then walk over to Liv's car. Luckily I have a spare key on my keyring. Apart from my bike, it's the only vehicle we own so I drive it whenever I have need of a cage.

I then take the short journey home and enter the house that's so quiet and lonely without Liv here waiting for me.

I follow Mouse's instructions, satisfying myself I'm fairly confident there are no bugs in the house and so Archangel's information is limited. At last, I take Liv's phone out of my pocket. Drawing in a deep breath, I call the number of the person who'd texted her.

I hear the phone answered, then, silence.

"Er, is this Gabe?"

"Sure," the voice replies cockily.

"Gabe, I wonder if you could help? My wife, Olivia, has disappeared. I've just found her phone. It appears she was going to meet you for coffee. The waitress told me she was unwell when she left. Did you give her a lift somewhere? Anything you can tell me would help. I'm worried something's happened to her."

"Sounds like you're as fucking stupid as your wife is." His snort reaches me down the line. "Gabriel should have given it away immediately."

"I don't understand what you mean?" I let my voice rise, trying to put on the tone of a distraught man who can't think straight, and a worried husband. "Er…"

"Gabriel? Think about it for a moment. I've got time." But after a just a few seconds, like a person who wants everyone to acknowledge how clever they are, he impatiently expands, "Think about angels."

I let my pause stretch out, then act as if the penny has only just dropped. "*Archangel*?" I query, with more than a hint of disbelief in my voice. At his grunt of delight as though I'm a child solving a puzzle, I continue, strengthening my voice. "What the fuck do you want with my wife?"

His voice now carries ire. "I want revenge on your club. It was because of you I got locked up and now have a fucking price on my head. I want every single one of you to suffer."

"So why take my wife if you've got a beef with the Devils? It's with them, not us. She's not part of the club. Neither am I," I rasp out. "I left. I wanted nothing to do with them, and they none with us. Today, for fuck's sake," I let genuine distress enter my voice, "today I found out we mean nothing to them. When I couldn't find her, I went to them for help. They sent me away. They sent me a-fuckin'-way," I repeat for emphasis. "They don't give a damn about me or her. They've washed their hands of both of us."

"Don't give me that," he scoffs. "Your father's in the club, hers too. You were both born and bred there. You think I'll believe for a moment they won't be going crazy trying to find her?"

"Think what you damn well like. If you want revenge on the club, taking her will break me, but what am I now? A normal citizen. It won't do anything to them. We don't exist to them anymore. We took our chances when we left. You're right, we've both got fathers there, but even they've turned their back on us and no one else cares. You want revenge on Wizard and his brothers, well this is not the way to get that." I let desperation seep into my tone, while I'm rapidly thinking. "They destroyed you, Archangel. But they've destroyed me too. Give me back my wife, and I'll help you hit them where it really hurts."

Another silence, then, "What are you suggesting?" he asks, cautiously.

"I've got no reason to love the club. Look what they did to me?" I don't know what Liv's been discussing with him, so I decide to stick close to the truth. "I've had a fuckin' mental breakdown, and what did they do? They chucked me out instead of getting me the help that I needed." I'm crossing my fingers that Liv won't have said anything to contradict my version of events. "We're expecting our first child, but that made no difference to them. They gave me a beatdown that was so vicious, I couldn't even get a job to support my wife and child. After all I've done for them, they turned their backs on me and Liv. We lost our house, livelihood, *everything*." I squeeze my fingers tighter, hoping he hasn't tracked the ownership of this house back to them.

"Your proposition? I assume you have one?" His voice sounds bored.

"We fuckin' destroy them. I know everything, I was the fuckin' VP. I know where their armoury is and exactly what's in it. I know where the bodies are buried. I know everything about their strengths, weaknesses and how to get to them."

"Sounds like they made a fucking mistake letting you walk away. I'd have killed you instead of allowing you to leave."

"It came close, they did nearly kill me. But as you said, I'm family. Their old ladies wouldn't let them."

"Fucking bitches. If the Devils have handed their asses to their women, sounds like they'll be easy to take." Women mean nothing to Archangel. We know that only too well. That he can't understand the lengths real men will go to for their old ladies only strengthens my position at this point.

"Give me back my wife, and I'll help you."

"I'll think about it. Oh, Olivia and I have been getting on famously. I'm not tired of her company yet. I'll just hang onto her for a little while longer—"

"You hurt one hair on her head," I threaten, my voice deadly cold, "and all bets are off, Archangel."

"Hmm. Sounds like you're as pussy whipped as all the others."

"Hah," I bark. "She's my property. Mine, you hear me? I want her and my baby back unharmed." Property and owner-ship. Words a man like Archangel will understand.

"I don't believe you're in a position to threaten me, Hawk. But I'll think on your suggestion. Keep this phone on you. I'll use this number if I call."

"Call me Eli," I correct him. "I don't go by Hawk anymore."

He chuckles into the phone. "And you can call me your darkest enemy."

The line goes dead.

CHAPTER TWENTY-TWO

*O*livia...

I awaken confused and disorientated while slowly how I got wherever I am starts coming back to me. *Gabe.* He gave me something. It must have been in my drink or in that cake. I hold my breath and my hands go to lie on my stomach, terrified as I can feel no movement there. Suddenly, when a hard kick reassures me, I almost cry out in relief, but still I'm afraid. I've been so goddamn careful throughout this pregnancy, terrified to even have one cup of real coffee, doing everything that the doctor told me. Now, despite my greatest care, I've been subjected to some kind of chemical.

"Ah, you're awake."

I don't waste time on pleasantries, not that I'd have any to share. I hate this man who's taken me. "What did you give me?"

"Rohypnol," he replies, casually, not even pretending to misunderstand.

"What if it affects my baby?"

"You sound like you think you're talking to someone who cares." He shrugs off my question and sits on a chair. "Seems we have a few things to get straight between us. Firstly, I never was your friend, you were just too stupid to see that. Secondly, you can't appeal to my conscience, I haven't got one. You're not going anywhere. You can't escape, so don't try to."

"Who are you, and why have you taken me?" I try to keep the panic out of my voice and refrain from asking what he wants with me. I have an idea I don't want to know.

"You really don't have a clue who I am?" His eyes widen slightly.

"No. but I suspect you're not called Gabe."

His shoulders rise then fall. "Gabriel isn't my given name, but it's useful to go by at times. I'm mainly called something else though. Surely you've heard of Archangel?"

I dig deep into my memory, but shake my head. "No, I can't say I have."

He smirks. "So the Devils really do keep their women out of club business."

I've grown up in the club, heard those words more times than I can remember. I know the club thinks the reasoning behind keeping us in the dark is sound. Though I'm scared, I feel a burst of anger. Had I been warned a man called Archangel was after the club, had I been given any description of who to watch out for, I'd have run a mile the first time I'd seen Gabe. I should have realised the same man popping up time after time was more than coincidence. I'm a fool, but then, I've always had people watching out for me. I never looked out for myself.

As I look at the face I had thought endearing at one time, I now realise his natural expression is hard. *He must have been acting. Every time we met.* Now he's removed his mask, this is the real man sitting in front of me.

My baby kicks again, as if reminding me to be strong. I'm a Satan's Devils' woman, I should act like one. Keeping a picture in my head of Drummer's old lady, I channel my inner Sam. I won't give this man the satisfaction of seeing me fall to pieces. "You still haven't said why you've taken me. Eli and I don't have money. He won't be able to pay to get me back."

Archangel throws back his head and starts laughing. "I want nothing from your *husband*. Instead, I want my revenge on your club."

The club. At the speed of light my brain starts working. "Revenge? Revenge for what? Anyway, it's not my club anymore," I spit at him. "Eli and I are living citizen lives. We're nothing to them now." Mentally I cross my fingers. Dad will be frantically doing what he can to find me, but Archangel might be better off not knowing that. I doubt he'll be worried about having the wrath of the Devil's heaped down upon him. He's far too arrogant for that.

Something tells me downplaying my importance to the club will serve me best. If it's revenge he wants, I'll have to convince him that won't work.

He chuckles. "I think you're wrong. You are theirs. And to answer your question as to the reason?" Once again, his face hardens. "Thanks to them, I was sentenced to life without parole."

"But you're here." I don't understand. Had he been waiting to start his sentence?

"I served five fucking years." His face darkens with rage, then, the mask falls again. "I escaped," he explains nonchalantly, adding with more than a touch of scorn tinged with pride, "No prison can hold me."

Which means he must be a wanted man, but that doesn't mean the knowledge will save me. Not unless the police discover where he is and come knocking on the door. I suspect that's very unlikely. "The Devils won't give you anything to get me back." I say the words which I hope are wrong. *Will Wizard do whatever this man asks? Am I still important to them?* I am to my mom and my dad, but the

Satan's Devils in general? There's a question mark about that.

"Who says I want anything from them?" He pauses, waiting for me to ask what he's doing this for. When I don't oblige, he continues, his voice deepening, and his eyes flare. "I want them to hurt. Just as they hurt me. By taking you, by taking the one of their next generation, I will break them apart."

If I wasn't already scared, I'd be terrified now. He's suggesting I won't be returning home, and Eli will never meet his baby. My brain can't compute what he means to do with me. I'm a wife, a soon-to-be mother. How can all of that come crashing down?

When he sees I'm not going to ask the question I'm not prepared to hear the answer to, his tone changes once again. "I told you about my wife and her unborn baby," he remarks conversationally, as though we were back in that coffee shop again. "Of course, she wasn't quite as far along as you."

I'm wondering where he's going with this. There's only one reason I can think of. "Satan's Devils didn't have anything to do with your wife's accident." While not knowing the facts, that's something I feel deep inside. Devils go after the men causing a problem, they wouldn't target a woman or child. Unless there had been a mistake, and they'd thought it had been Archangel driving.

But instead of telling me he wants revenge, again, he laughs. "I know they didn't cause the accident. *I* know, because I paid the man who did."

For a moment I forget to breathe. My eyes open wide as they fix on him.

"Yes." He dips his head down then raises it. "I arranged for my wife and that brat of hers to die."

It's at that point the thought solidifies that there'll be no appealing to this man's better nature. He clearly doesn't have one. But still, I ask, "Why? Wasn't the child yours?"

"Sure." His unaffected response made in such an off-hand manner demolishes any remaining hope my child and I will get out unscathed. "My wife had grown annoying. I decided I didn't want to be saddled with a woman I no longer wanted, and a kid I never did." His eyes blaze with fury. "I'm a fucking careful man, Olivia. I make sure to cover my tracks. I knew the feds thought they were closing in, but they weren't. I was too fucking clever, always a step or two in front of them."

"But they caught you in the end." I can't stop myself saying, "To be sent down, you must have fucked up."

Twin patches of red appear on his cheeks. "They couldn't prove shit on the organised crime, violence, drugs, the money laundering, or the slave trafficking. Do you fucking know, Olivia, what brought me down?"

Of course I don't. I refrain from making an unnecessary comment.

"I'd covered all my tracks except in one area." His eyes glaze and seem to focus on something past me. "I ran a lucrative trade, only used trusted men. Men who remained loyal when I was inside, and men who've stepped up now I'm back out. Real Americans." He pauses as though it should mean something to me. It doesn't, except... *Have I heard about them on the news?* Maybe, but citizen stuff never really concerned me when I was living on the compound.

When he sees his comment hasn't meant anything, he continues, "Mutual benefit, of course. I can bring the money in, and, I know where their bodies are buried. It was an inconvenience to them when I was sent down, so they helped me escape. I'm resuming my business, of course, but it's hard picking up strings which someone else has retied. There are always people who step in when a market isn't being fulfilled."

"I don't understand what you're talking about. Or why you feel the Satan's Devils were involved. They wouldn't have picked up your business. They don't deal in drugs, or anything else you've mentioned."

"Feds are stupid. It's easy to give them misinformation, keep them chasing their tails. It was a fucking game I enjoyed playing. I was running rings around them, and others, the Wretched Soulz for example. Stupid fuckers thought I was going into business with them, instead, I stole theirs. Your fucking club didn't like the fact I was taking women off the streets in Tucson—which included one of their strippers one night."

I gasp. I remembering hearing about a girl who had gone missing from Satan's Angels, the strip club the Devils run. She never turned up. I didn't think anyone knew what had actually happened to her. But if my dad and Drummer had, they'd have done their best to find her. I could easily see how that may have led to them crossing swords with Archangel.

"When I got out, I wanted to know how I fucked up. Learn from your mistakes, isn't that what they say? I wasn't sent down for running drugs or dealing in women. You know what got me in the end, Olivia?" He stands and marches across to me, grasping my chin painfully and making me look into his face. "I was sent down for murder in the first degree. For plotting and arranging the death of my wife."

He lets me go so violently I fall to the side, then right myself, my arms protectively surrounding my stomach.

He's pacing the room. "Such a simple thing. Pay a man, set her up. But it wasn't how I normally did business. There was CCTV, licence plate number recognition. The man I hired was tracked down… Somehow all the information was found and was presented to the FBI tied up with a fucking ribbon." He takes a deep shuddering breath. "My business dealings weren't even spoken of in court. All they wanted was for me to be put away for whatever reason would suit their purpose and life for premedicated murder certainly achieved that. I was fucking set up, and your MC was at the root of it."

I could see how Mouse and Wizard could have dug that information up. Seems Archangel, usually cold and determined, failed to apply his normal careful modus operandi to the killing of his wife and child. Passion, maybe? Had she overstepped and he'd arranged it too hastily? But yes, the club has the expertise to follow leads up. I don't doubt him for a moment. Set up? He's already admitted he'd done the crime. He just didn't want to do the time.

"I know nothing about any of this."

"You don't need to," he says, coldly. "Poor innocent kept-in-the-dark, Olivia. Doesn't mean fuck if you know or not."

His phone rings. A sadistic smile crosses his face as he walks to the door. I hear him say, "Sure." Then he listens as his hand turns the doorknob. Just before he pulls the door shut with him on the other side, I hear him say, "You're just as fucking stupid as your wife is." Then I don't hear anything else.

Eli. It sounds like he's talking to Eli unless he's stolen another wife away. How did Eli know who to ring? Or has he got Archangel's number programmed into his phone? But no, he couldn't. He had to get a new one when he left the club.

Phone. My phone. Where is it? Did I leave it in the café? Has Archangel got it? I can't see my purse and can't remember if I had it with me as he helped me out of the shop. That and being pushed into his car is the last thing I remember.

If Eli has my phone, maybe he'll see I've been texting to and meeting with Gabe. My face blushes red, until I remember, I changed my passcode for that exact reason. Though it was totally innocent, I'd felt guilty.

Mouse. Or Wizard. A passcode wouldn't stop them. Perhaps Eli's gone to the Devils for help, or my dad anyway. Dad. He'll be out of his mind with worry. Why, oh why was I so stupid to go out alone?

Because he hadn't quantified the danger I'd be in.

Damn Dad and his club business. I'm involved through no fault of my own except for ignorance.

Baby, please stop moving so much. He or she is jumping around on my bladder. A need I'd successfully ignored while Archangel was distracting me is returning with vengeance now.

I look around. The room I've been left in is some kind of living room, it's got just the one door. I hadn't heard a key turning. *Perhaps it's unlocked?*

I don't want to anger the man who killed his wife and unborn baby, but if he's left the door open, maybe there is a way for me to escape? Or, at least, find a bathroom which, at the moment, is at the top of my priorities.

I stand and walk across the room. Gingerly I reach out and turn the doorknob. It moves easily, but the door doesn't budge. It's locked. As I expected.

It would serve him right if I wet myself right on his sofa. Doesn't he know pregnant women have needs?

"Hey." I bang on the door and cry out, "Hey. I need a bathroom."

Perhaps he doesn't care, if he's going to kill me, anyway?

"Help!" I shout louder, not expecting my cries to be heard, let alone answered.

But the door opens as if the person behind had been waiting outside. He's a man with military bearing hair shorn short, shoulders pulled back and, what gives it away, is the rifle slung over his shoulder. *Is that a swastika on his front pocket?* I cringe, expecting no mercy from him.

"What do you want?" he asks, leering at my body as though he's got a thing for pregnant women.

I shift uncomfortably, from the way he's examining me, and from my body's needs. "I need a bathroom."

He sighs, then jerks his head with an expression of distaste. "This way."

I'm conscious of his armed presence behind me as he

points out where I should be heading. *Would he shoot me if I ran?* Well, I'm not going to put that to the test. Or, at least, not until I've used the facilities.

He opens the door, then with another movement of his head, indicates that I should go inside. I do. As I throw the bolt, I realise the lock is one of the kind you can open from the outside in case a child shuts themselves in.

Wasting no time, I relieve myself and take the time to look around me. There is a window with frosted glass, but even if it opened, it's not big enough for a woman with a belly the size of mine to squeeze out of.

I've no other option but to wash my hands, then open the door. The guard is standing outside in a sentry pose.

I decide it's worth a try. Putting my hands on my stomach to emphasise my condition, I ask, pleadingly, "Will you help me find a way out? I'm pregnant."

"I can see that." He leers again. "A nice big target to aim for if you try to run."

Meekly, with no other option, I let myself be escorted back to the room I'd recently left.

Alone, with no pressing bodily function to focus on, I admit the dire situation that I'm in. The thought I might never see my baby born or my husband or family again, over-whelms me.

The need to cry engulfs me, but I won't give in. Crying would mean letting my guard down, weeping would mean giving up.

It might be hard for me to escape, overpowering my guard or Archangel an impossibility. But I won't give up. The only weapon at hand is in my head. The only way out is to keep my wits about me. I'll just have to think how best I can use it.

It's hard, but I know once the tears start, I won't be able to stop.

CHAPTER TWENTY-THREE

*E*li...

Immediately after I speak to Archangel, I take out the burner phone Mouse had given to me and place a call to Wizard. I can't call him Prez, he's not that anymore. But for now it's enough that he's a friend.

"It's Eli," I tell him, knowing he won't recognise the number. "I've spoken to the motherfucker."

"And?"

"He's taken Liv for revenge as we'd expected. I had to think fast, Wizard. I've come up with something. I don't know if it will work..."

"Eli, I know you've been doubting yourself for some fuckin' time, but you're the one on the ground. You've spoken to the motherfucker. Give me your thoughts."

Yes. I'm the one with the direct contact. I want, need, my wife back. And, it appears, I'm her best hope of that. *If* Archangel buys what I'm selling.

"I've told him the club beat me up and threw me out. That all ties have been cut. I've explained Liv and I are on our own, and..."

As my voice trails off, he prompts, "And?"

"And you won't give a damn whatever happens to Liv."

"What else, Eli?" he growls, sounding like he dislikes hearing me say it even if it is what was agreed.

I take a deep breath. "I've told him I know everything about the club, that I know where to hit you to make it hurt. That I'll help him destroy the Satan's Devils."

He's quiet. The silence stretches out. *Have I gone too far?*

Suddenly he gives a short laugh. "Fuck, Eli. This is why I wanted you at my side. Because you think outside the fuckin' box. It's fuckin' brilliant. If Archangel buys into your bullshit, we can set him up. Lead him into a fuckin' trap. Love it, Brother."

"If Archangel falls for it," I warn.

"Yeah." Again, he goes quiet. "Assuming he does, what are you thinking, Brother?"

"How do you want to play this, Pr… Wizard? I mean, do we deliver him to the feds so they can put him back inside?"

"We end his miserable life," he snarls. "If they couldn't hold onto him once, he could get free again. I want this ended once and for all."

"I'm so fuckin' happy you said that." Despite the constant fear for my wife and baby churning in my gut, I grin. I want Archangel six feet under where he can never be a threat to me and mine ever again. "So here's what I'm thinking." I'd come up with the plan fast, with no idea whether Wizard will think it's feasible. "I encourage him to launch an attack on the compound." I tap the fingers of my hand not holding the phone on the tabletop while I pull some more threads of my thoughts together. "He thinks we're soft about the women, and we all know he's not averse to hurting females. I can let him know our, *your* security is focused on the gate and main entrance, and that the entry via the forest is unguarded. I lead him in that way with the carrot he can hit you where it hurts, by harming the people you hold precious. But instead of unguarded old ladies, he'll find brothers waiting instead."

Wizard takes a moment, then speaks, "I like that idea. Like it very much. It's hard to get to and you can let him think we're overconfident, or blind to that as an entry point. I'll get Mouse to take the CCTV cameras down and the alarm on the gate so there will be nothing visible to warn him. Archangel will think it's totally unguarded."

"You think this will work?" Suddenly I doubt myself. I'd have preferred Wizard to have shot me down and come up with another idea himself.

"I haven't thought of anything better. Know this, Eli, I'd offer myself in exchange for Olivia if I thought that would help."

"He wants revenge. He took the bait when I offered to help him destroy the club. Wizard…"

"What is it?"

"Do you trust me?" I say the words fast. "You don't think I…"

"Really want revenge for yourself? Fuck it, Eli. I know you better than that. You're still the man who prospected and earned our trust. It wasn't you, our brother, that left, it was the man with a fuckin' disease in his head."

"Which I'm still battling," I admit.

"Which you're now fighting and getting the help that you need."

My palm hits the table. "What if I freeze, Wizard? What if I can't do this? What if I give something away? What if I fuck up and Liv… and Liv…"

"Nothing's going to happen to Olivia. Brother, you speaking to me like you did just now? You planning, thinking things through? That's the old you, the real you that's been hidden inside."

He's right that I'm fighting, struggling to keep back the demons that tell me I'll fail this time right when Liv and my unborn child need me.

"You can do this," Wizard says firmly into my ear. "If

there was some way I could step up and do it for you, I would. Not because I have any doubts in you, but I know your illness makes you doubt yourself."

"I'll be alright," I reply, knowing I've no other option. Not if I'm going to see Liv, and then our child when it's time for him to come into the world. "If he's hurt her…"

Wizard growls. "He's not going to get that chance. We're relying on you, Brother. Try and get him to buy into your plan. Tell him you'll only help if you get proof of life."

I almost drop the phone at the suggestion my wife might already be dead.

"Eli," Wiz snaps as though he can see me. "Don't slip back now. Olivia needs you. We fuckin' need you. Now listen up. Are you hearing me, Eli?"

I grunt to show, yes, I'm listening. I'd wavered, had a wobble, but now I'm back.

"If I were him, Eli, I'd take your phone and keep you secured so I couldn't warn anyone of a place or time. He won't trust you. I doubt he'll give you a chance to contact me again."

"You're right."

"We've got this, Eli. We'll be prepared. I'll move all the old ladies, the families and Tommy down to the clubhouse. They'll have to stay there until we hear further from you. Come at us anytime, we'll be ready."

I hear the sound of a vehicle stopping outside. "Gotta go. Got company."

There are no goodbyes exchanged as I waste no time ending the call and slipping the burner phone down the side of the couch. Amateur place to hide it, but hopefully no one will look. I'm only just in time as straightening, hidden by the side of the window, I see Archangel step out of a truck, accompanied by four of his goons.

Just the sight of them gives me chills.

Clubs like the Satan's Devils attract men who've served in

the armed forces, a substitute for the camaraderie and also the regime during the time they were deployed. Other organisations attract the same sort of men, men who like discipline and a routine, but who have a disdain for citizen rules. A line of command which turns a blind eye to the worst excesses of men which wouldn't go down well in society at all. The four who accompany Archangel aren't deadbeats looking for cheap thrills, these men are white supremacists who've probably also served. It's clear to see by the way they immediately surround him, their eyes scanning for danger in every direction.

If this is a sample of the army Archangel commands, taking him down won't be easy.

But the Devils will be protecting their home. Nothing is more worth fighting for. And, it's my hope, Archangel won't command such loyalty in his men as that they'll stay and fight for him. Once he goes down, they won't sacrifice themselves for a corpse. It's the cause they're fighting for, not the man, too self-seeking to give their lives for each other.

Or, so I hope. *I could be wrong.*

My fists tighten at my sides. *I've got to believe I'm right.* The course of action I'll be proposing to Archangel not only means Liv's in danger, but our families and the members of the club who I still think of as brothers.

I go to open the door before Archangel knocks on it.

Two of his men barge their way in. When it appears they're going to search me, I stand with my arms held out straight, thanking fuck I wasn't still carrying the burner phone. They take my knife, my gun, Liv's phone and finally my wallet.

"Careful," I growl as a straying hand gets too close to my junk.

Ignoring me, they thoroughly investigate every place I could be carrying, then lift my t-shirt presumably to make sure I'm not wearing a wire. I'm asked to kick off my boots so they can check for tracers.

Finally, when they're satisfied I've nothing left on me that could possibly be a threat, Archangel jerks his head and they place all my possessions down on the table. Clearly they're not taking the risk of me having anything with me that could enable me to be tracked. Archangel clearly doesn't trust me. Well, that goes both ways.

"Come with us," he instructs.

"Is Olivia okay?" I question, not prepared to go anywhere unless I'm assured my wife is unharmed.

"For now," he replies, ominously. "Whether she stays that way is up to you, and whether you've been telling the truth."

A second's hesitation in case I'm laying it on too thick, then I decide to go for it. "I've no reason to love the Satan's Devils. They threw me out of the club. Took me six fuckin' weeks to recover and my bones to heal." I pause for effect. "Sure, my dad's in the club, that's the only reason they didn't kill me." For the past couple of months, I've so often wished that they had. Now I'm glad they didn't. I'm here and have a chance to save Liv. "But that was the extent of his fatherly concern." I shrug. "Only reason I haven't done anything myself is that I'm one man on his own. I'll happily help you to hit them where it hurts. But if anything has happened to Olivia, I'm not giving you shit."

Archangel seems to issue a lot of non-verbal instructions. Before I have the chance to interpret the slight gesture of his hand, a fist belonging to one of his thugs hits so hard in my stomach, I double up, gasping for breath. My eyes water as I'd had no chance to prepare for the unexpected blow.

"That's the least you'll get if I find out you're lying to me." Archangel grabs a handful of my hair, forcing my head up to face him. "You'll get a beatdown that will make your last seem like a picnic. I'll keep you alive for days, and you'll beg me for death. Especially when I rip that baby out of your wife's belly while she's still breathing. Hopefully it will be viable, as I can always find a buyer for a kid. Your wife will bleed out with the knowledge of what I did."

I don't doubt that Archangel would make good on his threat. For a moment, fear floods through me, but I've started this. I can't fail, there's too much at stake. I don't care what he does to me, but I can't allow him to hurt Liv, or our unborn baby.

I force myself to breathe as normally as a man who's taken a hard blow to the stomach can and stare at him steadily. "My desire for revenge is equal to yours. They took your life and fucked up mine."

He walks behind me and lifts my t-shirt a second time. "You've still got their mark on your back."

I huff. "For six weeks I was laid up. I just haven't had a chance to get it done."

As he comes back around in front of me, I notice he looks undecided.

"What have you got if you don't work with me?" I dangle more carrots in front of him. "You don't know how to access the compound, or have detailed information about the club. You can kill me, and Olivia, but Wizard won't give a damn." I inject a bite of anger into my voice. "They set you up, Archangel. They don't care about anyone except their precious club."

"You were VP. You played a part in me going down."

I shake my head and scoff. "Five years ago I'd not long patched in. I was nothing but a lowly member. Drummer was prez, Wraith was VP. I only got the VP spot as Drummer begged Wizard to give it to me. He fuckin' set me up when I couldn't handle what went down." I let a sneaky expression cover my face. "But as VP, I do know *everything*."

"I know who's to blame," he insists, dismissing my embellishment. "Your father and Olivia's. Hence why I should just take you out. Whatever you say, it will hurt your families if no one else."

"You're wrong," I tell him, mentally apologising to the prez of the club. "They just acted on the information Wizard found. If Wizard hadn't been the driving force who kept digging, they'd never have found out about your wife. It's Wizard who's to blame. It's he who decided I didn't have what it took to ride at his side. Wizard's the man we both should take down."

"And now Wizard's the prez." He seems to think my answer is plausible. His face darkens, then he slaps me hard on the back. "Seems we've both got reasons to take everything he values away."

I give a half-grin, half-sneer. "I've got a good plan for that."

CHAPTER TWENTY-FOUR

Eli...

I ride in the back of the truck, sandwiched between his men. Men who are stoic and not open to conversation. Not that I bother to start one, but just notice they don't talk amongst themselves.

The demon who seems to be constantly on my shoulder, whispering my inadequacies into my ear, tells me I'm out of my depth. That Liv's depending on me to save her, but my plan won't work. All I'll succeed in doing is dying alongside her. Well, so be it. If I can't save her, I neither want nor deserve to live.

My palms feel sweaty, and my heart starts to race. I focus on controlling my breathing, swearing at the demon to get lost. Telling myself I can, and will, do this. That there's too much else at stake. Trying to draw on my memory that while I have no faith in myself, despite what I'd told Archangel, my brothers saw something in me that made them vote me in as vice prez.

I didn't get that spot out of any nepotism. As a prospect I was tested more than the rest. I earned a reputation for thinking before leaping, directing the club to do what was best. *Have I ever failed at anything?*

I try to think back. The only wrong decision I made was to walk away from the club and not to share what was going on in my head. But I was someone who men looked up to, how could I admit to feeling lost? How could I tell them the effort it took every fuckin' day just to raise my head off the pillow, let alone get out of bed? How could I speak to them when I hadn't the words to describe my own thoughts?

Wizard referred to what I'm going through as an illness, a disease. The therapist told me there were ways I could regain my life and live normally again. Hound and Throttle accepted how I'd broken down in the street. Hell, they seemed relieved there was an explanation for behaviour they couldn't otherwise explain.

I might not have the flu or a cold I can easily shake, but I am sick, even though that's just bad connections in my head. My synapses aren't firing in unison, the neuro-transmitters failing to do their work. I've just got to fight this as I would a viral infection.

I can do this. If I fail, I lose my wife. Not to another man, but worse, she'll be dead. And my son? Well, I'd never have a chance to meet him.

Slowly my palms dry. My heart starts to beat strongly, but evenly in my chest. My slow breathing becomes natural and not forced as I prepare for the battle of my life. I clear my head of all and every insecurity as my determination grows. With the help of the Devils I will save Liv. I'll play my part to lead Archangel into a trap.

The truck makes a sharp turn and starts bumping down a track. We arrive at a fairly nondescript mid-sized house set back from the main road. It's not ostentatious, but then, Archangel wouldn't want to draw attention to himself. There are also no close neighbours.

When we come to a halt, the men surrounding me get out, and I follow the first two, knowing the others are behind me.

My eyes rapidly look around, cataloguing the environment. I notice an ancient saguaro riddled with bullet holes. The sight pains me, realising they must use it for target practice. Born and bred in Arizona, it's a slight to my culture. The cacti are protected by law, even dead ones have to be left where they fall. The disrespect shown is just another black mark on Archangel's stained soul. Soon, I comfort myself, he'll be another fallen angel, explaining himself to Satan instead.

As I follow Archangel into the house, I see a guard standing outside a locked door. My heart beats faster, but with anticipation, not fear.

"I want to see my wife," I demand.

Archangel halts his forward momentum and turns to face me, one eyebrow raised.

"I want to see for myself she's unharmed. I'm not saying one word until I speak to her."

He considers for a moment. I jut out my lower jaw and purse my lips.

Blowing out a breath, he turns to the guard and raises his chin. Another non-verbal communication which has me wondering whether I'll need to learn sign language if I'm going to work with him.

A bolt is thrown, the door opened, then shut and locked again after I step in.

Liv stands disbelieving as she tries to process the apparition that's appeared. Then she's moving, flying at me as fast as a waddling heavily pregnant woman can, almost unbalancing me as she throws herself into my arms.

I hold her, breathing in that perfume which is so familiar, feeling that long silky hair brushing against my hands. I love this woman with everything that I am and always have. *How could I ever have thought I could survive without her?* I've been a fool. She's as necessary to my life as oxygen.

Gently I push her away, just an inch so I can look down into her face, examining her features, looking for bruising or any sign she's been hurt. Luckily I find no evidence else I'd not be able to keep my temper in check.

Liv and I grew up together. I can read every expression on her face. I know and understand every gesture. We communicated long before we learned to use words.

"I love you," I say out loud, then give a little shake of my head, a raise of my eyebrow to get her attention on my face, then I flick my eyes toward the door, while lifting a hand to my ear.

She looks confused for a moment, then nods her head. "Eli, what's going on? Has he caught you too? I've been so scared." Her face grows genuinely worried. "What's going to happen to us?"

"I'm going to get you out of here, soon," I promise, then give a shake of my head and close my eyes briefly before opening them again. This time she gets the full force of the steely stare I inherited from my father. "First, I've got to help Archangel take out the Satan's Devils. Seems we both want the same thing. Revenge on the club who've wronged us both."

I can see her brain working, computing my actions and words.

"How Eli? How will you get revenge?"

"Fuck knows I know everything there is to know about the compound, Liv. We were both there. No one knows better than me all the paths in which outsiders don't have a clue are there. Or where the security is and isn't."

"Are you sure, Eli? Sure you're doing the right thing?"

"Not one man, not one woman raised a fuckin' finger to help me, Liv. I fucked up, and instead of helping to find out what was going on, they made it all ten times worse. You know how badly it's affected me. I can't live with all this anger burning inside. And you've borne the brunt, haven't you?" I smooth my hand over her hair, acting like I'm trying to persuade her. "They kicked us both out, didn't they?

Though I begged them to let you stay until the baby was born."

That's complete fiction as we both know, but hopefully persuasive for any ears listening.

"My mom, my dad?" Her voice shakes showing she's genuinely scared for them, but I'm so fucking proud of my wife when she looks me straight in the face.

"They hurt us, Liv. Stood by and did nothing."

"I don't care about anyone else," she lies, calmly. "Not after what they did. But if you can, will you spare our family? I hoped they'd come around after the baby is born."

I hope my expression conveys I'll save everyone on that compound, but something else comes out of my mouth. "I know you did, Liv. But as I've said before, we've got all the family we need right here. You, me and our baby. We don't need anyone else."

When she sobs, she's not acting. I pull away her hand that's gone to cover her mouth and instead place my lips on hers briefly. "This is our chance to start a new life, baby. Put the past right behind."

"You're really going to betray them? I'm not sure…"

Her expression lets me know she understands the game I'm playing. "Sweetheart, whether you like the idea or not is not the point. I'm your fuckin' husband and it's your job to do what I say and stand by me."

The door opens. A slow clapping sounds. "Fuck, I wondered how long it would take for you to find your balls," Archangel's amused voice butts in. "Sorry to call a halt to this family reunion," he begins in a tone conveying he's anything but. "It's time to start talking, Eli. Leave the little woman behind."

I stare down at Liv again, memorising every feature of her face, then, rest my hands on where my baby lies inside her. "I'll be back," I promise. This time when I speak, total honesty shines out of my eyes.

She grips hold of the material of my t-shirt. "Eli..."

"Stay here." Stupid remark, she's got no choice.

Behind, Archangel snorts loudly. Then as I hear the stomping of feet, I pull away from her, preferring to walk out of the room voluntarily rather than unceremoniously being wrenched away by his men.

I stand with my hand to my forehead as the man guarding Liv locks the door to her prison again. She may be in fairly comfortable surroundings, but she's still jailed within four walls. I hate that I'm leaving her here. I know what I promised that I'd be back and take her home soon, but I wouldn't trust Archangel as far as I could throw him. He'd get the information out of my head then kill her and me as well without so much as breaking a sweat. I can't forget how he callously arranged the murder of his own wife and child. No one means anything to this man if he thinks it might get in his way.

I've got to be clever.

I love you, I tell her again in my mind, hoping somehow my thoughts will pervade through the wall separating us as I'm led away.

"This way," Archangel instructs sharply. "In here."

I'm pushed into an office and directed to a seat in front of the desk. I'm unarmed, but that doesn't stop a guard taking a sentry post in front of the doorway.

"Talk," the man instructs, wasting no time as he seats himself behind the desk.

I point to a notepad. Realising my intention, he tears off a sheet of paper and passes it across with a pen. Placing it in front of me, I start to sketch.

"This is the gate to the compound. The auto-shop is just inside. The clubhouse is further up the track."

I glance up to find Archangel paying close attention. His eyes reach mine. "You're not telling me anything that can't be seen on Google Earth."

I roll my eyes signalling *give me a fucking chance*. "Google won't show you the security, I can." I do so, laying it on thick, talking about non-existent compression points, trip wires, armed guards and of course, cameras with sensitive microphones to pick up sound, finishing up with, "You won't get in easily via the front gate, if you can make it in at all. Security is airtight, and so are the fences around the compound."

"Dogs?"

I shake my head.

"That's something. So, we come heavily armed. Explosives, percussion grenades."

I widen my eyes and shake my head. "Are you even listening to me? You don't have a fuckin' chance via the front gate. But," I hold up my hand and give a smug grin, "I can get you inside without them having a clue you're there." I have to stress they need me with them, else I'll be dead once they've milked the information from my head. And worse, so will Liv.

He's looking at me carefully. "You've just told me it's impossible. What do you propose? We drop in by fucking parachute?"

I snort as I'm supposed to. "Don't forget I know this place like the back of my hand. Look," I draw something else. "Up here, at the back of the compound is another entrance."

"One equally well guarded I suppose."

My grin widens. "Not at all."

"No? Well, what's up there?" His eyes sharpen.

"Houses." I look up to see if I can reel him in. "Where the members with old ladies live."

"Drummer and Wraith?"

I nod, trying to push down the feeling I want to vomit, wondering if I can pull off convincing Archangel I'd happily see my father dead. "Theirs were the first houses built. Others now live alongside them, Wizard, Heart, Rock, Joker and Lady—"

"I get the picture," he interrupts. "But surely security is tighter than a virgin ass?"

"Nothing much more than a trip wire alarm, and that's more than likely switched off."

His eyes widen.

"Oh, we tried all sorts of early warning systems, even a laser beam, but the wildlife kept setting it off, deer, foxes, even the odd javelina. We've never had an attack via the rear of the compound because there's no road to the forest, so you need off-roaders for a start, and even then you can't get particularly close. It's a long hike up from the road, so they've gotten lax. Most times the gate itself is unlocked and they rely on their reputation to keep people away from the compound."

"Vehicular access?"

"Nah, on foot only, as I just said. Is that a problem?"

"Maybe have to leave the tanks and heavier grenade launchers behind." Problem is, I don't think he's joking. "So you're suggesting we can get in that way. I presume it's best to use the cover of darkness. That area lit?"

After I shake my head showing no, it's not, Archangel drums his fingers against the desk. He fires off some more questions, and I answer them all, hopefully to his satisfaction, praying he'll take the bait and walk into the trap Wizard will have prepared.

"I like this idea," he tells me at last. "We get the lead members, maybe end up with some product to sell if we can take the women unharmed. Your woman alone has got three sisters." He gives me a look. "Can you control her if she kicks up a fuss?"

For the second time I swallow down bile. Liv would go crazy if Archangel got close to her sisters. She'd never forgive me. Fuck, I wouldn't forgive myself. If that happens, I won't be here to tell the story, I'll have died before I let anything happen to them, or to Isabel, Maya, Amy, Lisa, Rose, Hope,

Alexis, Sabrina, Maria, Tanya or Yiska. As I run through all the women and girls, I hope Wizard has got them locked down securely. Even Mouse's kids who normally live at his stables, and others who live off compound will have been brought in on lockdown.

This has to work.

He looks up at the man standing behind me. "Get everyone ready. We'll go in tonight."

Tonight? So soon. *Too soon?*

No. Wizard will have sprung into action after my warning.

I could have fucked up. He might be waiting to call church tomorrow.

Whoa. I again tell the demon on my shoulder to shut up, forcing myself to think of the man I supported as my prez, calming my heart rate down so I can relax. To Archangel showing how unfazed I am by clasping my hands behind my head. *Wizard won't have wasted one second. Even now everyone will be safe in the clubhouse, women moaning about the lack of space and teenagers seeing it all as a game. My brothers will already be on standby, some guarding their families, the rest at the top of the compound preparing the trap, ready for whatever is likely to approach. The main gate unguarded, of course.*

Archangel is watching me. If he misinterprets my pose as pleasurable contemplation of the forthcoming take down of my supposed enemy, that's on him.

"How many men have you got?" I ask him.

He studies me for a moment. "Enough." He taps the drawing. "I'll send in one team to cause a commotion at the main entrance. That way they'll be looking in the wrong direction. They'll all head down to the gate and be taken by surprise when we hit them where you suggest."

I force my features to remain composed as they are, again calming myself with the thought Wizard would do exactly what I would. *Mouse will be watching the monitors carefully and be on the lookout for a fake attack. Fuck knows, when there's danger about, that man never sleeps.*

"More security that end of the compound," I warn him.

"So they'll see us coming," Archangel smirks, "and all come running, leaving their families unprotected. Don't forget, they don't even know to expect me."

Oh, but they do. I stare across the desk at the man who tonight will take his last breath. The thought is a cheering one and makes me smile. "They don't know what's coming at all," I agree.

CHAPTER TWENTY-FIVE

*E*li…

We're back in the truck I arrived in, but now there are others following behind.

Archangel had picked my brains for how best to approach the compound. I took some joy in knowing we were in for a bumpy ride, taking the trucks as far into the forest as possible, then proceeding on foot. The men bitched about carrying loaded packs. In the end, Archangel relented and left some of the heavier artillery behind once he saw the terrain and understood just how far men would have to carry it. I revise my opinion about whether these men had ever served. Wannabe soldier boys just playing games, no way would they pass their fitness training as anything more than rifles, hand-guns and ammunition appear too heavy for them.

The discipline, I notice, also only extends to standing to attention and looking the part. Archangel took longer than I'd have expected getting them to move in something resembling formation. Once we got moving, several fell behind, and we were further delayed waiting for them to catch up.

As a kid I played in amongst these trees, as a teen I hunted for deer. I know the forest intimately. I could have been evil and taken them on a long, circular route but I'd tossed up tiring them out against getting this over and done with. Of course, the darkness also helps both sides. When dawn breaks, Archangel will see the trap he's heading into. The sooner we get there, the quicker we can get this finished, and Archangel will cease taking in air. Liv will be free and we can go home.

This time, I make a silent promise to her, *I won't clock out.* I'll be right there beside her. Belatedly setting up the nursery, making sure everything's ready for when the baby arrives. I'll get a job and we'll make a fresh start in Tucson. A sense of loss floods through me. I know they'll let Liv and I stay while I get my head straight and we welcome the baby, but at some point we'll have to strike out on our own. *My fault. I fucked up. Club life is behind me.* But we'll make do with our small family, which might even grow in time, and I reckon we won't be ostracised as previously, and maybe some of the brothers will stay friends.

There's a thrashing behind me as yet again someone stumbles over a downed tree I automatically stepped over. *My bad, I hadn't warned anybody.* Archangel had managed to find a small stock of night goggles from somewhere. I hadn't wanted to ask him what for. But insufficient to equip all his men. Unlike the Devils who'd have helped each other, his men didn't buddy up with the ones unlucky enough only to be guided by the light of the moon. I'm hoping on at least a twisted ankle or two to slow them down.

We reach the off-road racing track under which uncountable numbers of bodies are rotting. Road, an F.O.G. who transferred out years' back, was a trial bike rider, and used this track to practice on. It will probably need to be extended yet again after tonight, or hopefully. I wonder how many will die tonight, or whether Archangel's men will run when they realise their attack comes as no surprise. I wonder what welcome party Wizard has laid on, and trust it all goes to plan.

Shooting out my hand, I bring everyone to a halt.

"We're at the fire break," I tell them, speaking softly once they huddle around. "It's a hundred feet of cleared ground. Need to go quietly and carefully from now on."

"No cameras?" Archangel's scanning around.

"No. As you saw, it's not easy to get here this way."

"Trip wires?"

"There. About ten feet in from the forest, and another ten feet before the fence. But as I said, they don't work."

"Watch out for the trip wires," Archangel instructs anyway. "Quiet from now until we get to the fence."

Archangel's men are all dressed in black. I'm wearing blue denim jeans and a navy t-shirt. We'll be difficult to see emerging out of the darkness. I make a mental note that we, they, should have more security out here. But I hadn't lied and why we don't is quite clear. Even motion sensor lights are likely to disturb people's sleep when set off by a deer. We do normally have cameras though, and true to his word, Wizard has removed them.

Slowly we make our way across the hundred-foot-wide strip of cleared ground.

We're on our way, Wizard. Can you see? Can you hear?

A shout, a call would get me dead, and worse, warn Archangel away. I remain restricted to shooting off the telepathic warning in my head.

What if I'm wrong? What if Wizard's not as prepared as I expect him to be?

I'm a guide only. I've no weapon as Archangel doesn't fully trust me.

I do hear a collective sigh of relief when we reach the six-foot fence. Archangel peers through the slats.

"How many houses?"

I haven't really stopped to count. "Eleven, twelve?"

"We split up," he decides. "Eli, you're with me. Heath too. We'll take Wizard's."

To pre-empt his question, I point it out. I notice all lights are off, the illusion being everyone is in bed asleep. As they would be at three a.m.

"Open it." He nods at the lock.

I left the compound with my bunch of keys, which includes one to the back gate which is lucky as it's locked. Wizard must have realised it shouldn't have looked easy. Fuck knows why the key wasn't taken off me, but Archangel's pleased when I explain that our entrance will be easy. As far as I can tell, he's not suspicious. The apparent lack of security seems to have given him a sense of superiority. Men as lax as these will be easy to take.

Once inside, Archangel doesn't waste time, giving the signal for everyone to split up and move, his non-verbal signals giving instruction as to which group goes where.

This far up the compound, far away from the well-guarded gate and Mouse's security system, no one bothers to lock their front doors. Except, I'd expected and hoped for the extra precaution tonight—a lock shot off, a door kicked in which would alert everyone something was up. But Wizard's front door opens easily, and Archangel pushes me inside, with his gun to the small of my back. Another sign he still doesn't quite trust me.

I can't do much else but obey the finger to his lips signal and keep quiet as we move through the house. I'm tense, expecting Wizard to jump out at any moment, and hoping he recognises me before he shoots.

But nothing moves.

"Master bed?" Archangel whispers directly into my ear.

After I point it out, a prod with the gun gets me moving that way.

Yeah, sure. This is a good idea. Walking unannounced into the bedroom of a prez of an outlaw MC in the dead of night.

What's his first reaction going to be? Yeah, right. Shoot the intruder first then ask questions later. Archangel isn't stupid, he's using me as a human shield.

Archangel moves to one side, then flips on the light. Wizard sits up fast, his hand reaching for his gun.

"I wouldn't," Archangel says, showing his got a line straight to Wizard's head.

I inch back. I know this place as well as my own. All of us keep spare weapons ready and handy, and I happen to know Wiz has a spare gun taped behind his door. He'll probably have to rearrange shit when his kid's born, but for now... I reach behind me breathing a silent sigh of relief as I find it exactly where I expect to.

The quiet thump of a man dropping to the floor behind me isn't unanticipated. It coincides with Wizard barking out, "What the fuck are you doing in my house?"

Archangel didn't hear he's a man down, instead he sneers at Wizard, "Where's your pretty wife?"

"On night shift at the hospital."

I feel easier now I have a gun in my hand. I don't like anyone pointing a gun at my pr... Wizard for too long. Fingers can get twitchy on triggers. My eyes find Wizard's and I blink twice.

"What the fuck you doing here, Eli?" Wizard gives himself an excuse to stare at me. "You turned traitor now?"

"Something like that," I respond, giving myself the excuse to come alongside Archangel.

Then, fast as a flash, I whip my hand around his wrist, twisting and turning so his gun drops out of his hand.

"Nice work," Marvel says admiringly from behind me.

Wizard stands, already dressed in the jeans and boots he'd been wearing under the covers. "Tie him up," he instructs as he pulls on a t-shirt and his cut. He pauses and cocks his head at the sound of distant gunfire. That will be Archangel's distraction at the gate.

"That's my men," Archangel says, now from a prone position on the floor. It's hard to stand up when you're hog-tied. "You're surrounded."

Wizard shakes his head. "I think you'll find it's us who've got the upper hand." He tilts his head to one side. "Good job, Marv," he says. "And while I admire your handiwork with knots, I'd kinda like him to be able to walk."

With an exaggerated sigh, Marvel reties the knots and pulls the man now with just his hands bound behind him to his feet.

"One wrong move, shoot him," Wizard states, then steps over the man still lying across the threshold of the room. He shakes his head as he sees all the blood from the cutthroat soaking into the wooden floor. "Amy's going to have my fuckin' nuts," he complains.

"You're dead," Archangel tells me, his tone cold. "And so is your wife."

Wizard hears and throws me his keys. "Take my bike. It's outside."

"I can—"

"Go get your wife."

The concern in his eyes mirrors mine. It's possible Archangel left orders in the case that he didn't return. Orders that would ensure his depravity continued after his death.

I follow the others outside. From the rest of the houses, the brothers are all in various stages of bringing injured and captive men out. Glancing around, I see all of Archangel's men were taken by surprise, and all captured without one gunshot.

Even the shooting by the gate has ceased now.

"Olivia okay?" Wraith asks fast.

"When I left her," I tell him. "Unharmed, but scared."

"Go get her." Drummer catches my eye as he pushes his captive so hard he crashes to his knees on the ground.

Wraith's eyes narrow. "What are you fuckin' doing?" he

asks as I go to Wizard's bike. "She's fuckin' pregnant, you moron. Take Sophie's car."

I raise my chin at him, acknowledging his point. I exchange the keys, then slide into the driver's seat, having to push it back as far as it will go. The passenger door opens, then one at the back. I glance to the side, then behind me. Drummer and Wraith. I'm not in the least surprised.

The scene is bloody down by the gate, but none of it ours, *theirs*. Fuck, I don't know what to call the Devils anymore. Fighting alongside them tonight, leading Archangel into the trap, well, it was like slipping on some old familiar boots. A role that was comfortable, soothing, even.

It might not be my life anymore, but everything inside me makes it wish it were. I left under false pretences, things I was pretending to myself. Now I wish I could turn back time and cry out for help rather than bottling everything up.

"You did well, Eli. Your plan worked like fuckin' clockwork," Wraith tells me.

"Anyone hurt?" Drummer asks.

"Lady got a scratch, but it's only superficial," Wraith responds. "I don't think anyone else was injured."

"We had the element of surprise," I remind them.

"Thanks to you, Eli." That comes from Wraith. "You thought fast."

"Luckily," I tell them. "Archangel came for me as soon as I ended the call."

"Luck didn't have anything to do with it," Dad states firmly. "You had a plan. Like you always do."

I sigh. "That's pressure, Dad. The expectation that I'll always know what to do."

I can sense Wraith's head shaking. "Sometimes you won't. That's why the club isn't about one man. That's why we vote. Wizard brought your proposal back to the table and we all said yes. Could have said no, Brother. Could have come up with something else. You know that's the way we roll."

He's right. I know that. It's just got all back to front in my head. The weight on my shoulders hadn't been just mine, it belonged to the whole club. He doesn't know it, but he's given me something else to think about.

Thank fuck Archangel hadn't blindfolded me when he'd taken me from my house. I suspect if things had gone his way, neither I nor Liv would still be alive. It makes me worry whether Archangel had pre-empted things. I'm banking on him keeping her safe in case he had a use for either of us later.

I make my way directly to where she's being held captive, trying to push down the fear inside of me. I slip back into biker mode as I start to brake. "House is up that driveway. We'll walk from here. There'll be at least one guard on her. Maybe more."

"Where's she held?"

I notice neither man objects to me issuing instructions. "First door on the right. I didn't see much more than Archangel's office and where Liv is being held. I did notice a kitchen and a back door."

"You take the back seeing as you know the lay of the land better, we'll go in the front and take out the guard," Drummer suggests.

I'd rather it was me being the first to get to Liv, but I can feel my way around the house better, having taken at least some of the layout in when I'd scanned where I'd been brought. I'm mentally picturing rooms to check in case there are more guards lurking.

Once again my adrenaline rises as we approach the house. Light is streaming out of the windows, including the room where I know Liv is being held. My heart is in my mouth as I creep up close, staying in the darkness, then let my breath out as I see her restlessly sleeping, curled up on the couch. As I watch she jerks awake, as if she can sense I'm there. She looks exhausted as her eyes close again.

I give a thumbs-up to Wraith, and make a circle with my

finger and thumb, then I crouch down. Moving below window level, I make my way around the back of the house.

I'm counting down in my head. When I get to zero, I kick the back door in, simultaneously hearing a shot from the front of the house.

Drummer's voice sounds, "Clear."

I kick another door open. "Clear."

Four bedrooms all empty. Two baths, one empty and one… well, to say I caught a man with his pants down would be exactly right. A laugh is startled out of me when I see his face. He's half hovering over the toilet. Seems like I haven't quite scared the crap out of him.

Drummer appears. "Just the one… Oh."

A loud farting sound, the man's face reddens, he groans then there's a plop.

"Please, man."

"Do we let him finish, or kill him now?"

"Please," the man begs again. "Not like this."

"Dead's dead," says my dad, raising his gun, and shooting him in the head. "What?" He turns at my snort. "I did him a favour. He was clearly constipated. Now that's one less worry he has."

"No," I reply drily. "I think you cured that."

It seems death has loosened his bowels, and it's past time for me to leave. The stench is overpowering.

CHAPTER TWENTY-SIX

*O*livia…
I know Eli won't betray the club whatever they did. It's our family, by blood and friendship. The answer is he must have a plan. I have to hang on to that.

I'm going to get you out of here, soon.

But that's just my hope. However much I try to keep calm and soothe the baby growing inside me, I'm scared, terrified that however Eli thinks this is going to play out, there's a chance it could go wrong and not the way he expects.

Eli wasn't made VP because of his relationship to Drummer, he got it on his own merits. Old ladies aren't involved in club business, but we've got ears and eyes. So many times I've seen Eli being slapped on the back and congratulated as the club had gotten out of a fix, or made money, due to him being on the ball and coming up with ideas.

But will his lack of confidence in himself lately, the reason behind him leaving the club, make him overcautious? Will he pull back when he should move on? Will he second-guess himself?

Have faith in your man.

I would have. If he were the Eli I've known all my life, not the one I've lived with these past months.

The house is silent except for the slight whirr of the air conditioning, and creaks as the wood expands or contracts. *Has everyone gone?* Could I escape on my own?

I could try.

Going to the door, I rattle the knob. It's locked, of course. I'd hoped my guard would have left with Archangel and Eli, but no such luck. The door opens.

"What do you want?"

"Bathroom," I tell him.

"Again?"

I glare at him. "You try having a baby use your bladder as a trampoline. Yes, I do need the bathroom, *again*."

He shakes his head, but steps back and gestures in the direction I now know. "Don't try anything," he warns.

My eyes catch sight of a second man. I suppose it does take two to stop a waddling heavily pregnant lady escaping. But I do what isn't absolutely necessary, flush and clean up, then allow myself to be escorted back to my room.

No escape. All I can do is sit and wait. I think about Eli. When I'd seen him earlier, there had been flashes of the man he'd been before we were married. Was it possible that the shock of Archangel taking me forced him back to himself? Or, at least, started the recovery process? I realise I hadn't seen him since his hospital visit and wonder how that went. Had seeing a therapist helped?

Whatever plan he's working on now *has* to work. Not just because of me and our baby, but it has to succeed for Eli to start to trust himself again.

There's no bed, just a couch. I lie on my side and make myself as comfortable as I can. I'm tired, as I always seem to be nowadays. My head though, it won't switch off. But while I think sleep will evade me, my mind at last shuts down, taking advantage of that for now, my baby, too, is sleeping.

I wake with a start to what sounds like doors being kicked in and gunshots. I roll and awkwardly get to my feet and do an ungraceful dive behind the sofa. What protection it will afford me, I have no idea, but hopefully it will at least impede the progress of a stray bullet heading my way.

Now it's the door to the room that I'm in that's being broken down. *Friend? Or foe?*

Hating myself, I whimper slightly. *I just want to be safe and go home.*

"Olivia?" a familiar voice shouts, his voice panicked.

"Dad?" In disbelief, I pull myself to my feet, using the couch for leverage. "Dad?" I ask again, half thinking I'm still asleep and I've conjured up an apparition.

But when he crosses the room in two long strides and his arms come around me so tightly it's almost painful, I know I'm awake.

"You're safe, baby. Safe. I've got you. You're safe."

I haven't cried once since Archangel took me, but now the tears flow and don't stop. It's Dad, he's here.

"Eli?" I sob.

"With Drummer, taking out the trash." He jerks his head over his shoulder.

"He's here?"

Another gunshot sounds. Dad puts me behind him, but then the empty doorway is filled with the sight of the man I most want to see. I twist around my father and run to him.

"Eli!"

"Shush," he murmurs against my hair as I breathe him in, his arms surrounding me and our baby. "It's over, darlin'. Archangel won't be bothering anyone again."

"He's dead?" I ask, hopefully. A man as evil as him shouldn't be breathing the same air as me.

Drummer chuckles behind Eli. "As good as."

I'm a Satan's Devil's daughter. I don't ask for clarification.

Something tells me Archangel won't be let off lightly or be able to escape.

"Come on, darlin'. Let's go home."

"The compound," Dad clarifies. "Need you close to me."

"Need them both close," Drummer agrees.

"Er," I pull at Eli's arm when he turns and starts to head toward the front door. "I need to pee."

"Wait until you get back to the compound," Drummer says mysteriously, and Eli snorts.

"The bathroom's in use," he tells me at my questioning look.

"Yup," Drummer agrees. "Wouldn't advise going in there."

I start shifting from foot to foot. "Can we get a move on then?"

It's very early in the morning so luckily there's not much traffic about. I cuddle up to Eli in the back of the car, snuggled against his chest. One arm grips me tightly, the other gently rests on my swollen belly.

"Never, ever, losing you again, Liv. I couldn't live without you."

"Or I you, Eli."

"Are you okay? Is the baby good? Did he touch you, hurt you? Christ, I should have asked before."

"I'm fine, Eli." Well if the baby would stop jumping on my bladder I am. "Eli, I'm sorry. I should have told you about the man I met." Apart from surviving, this is what I've been worrying about. "Gabe, Archangel, whatever he calls himself, well, we kept bumping into each other, and I thought it was coincidence. There was nothing in it."

"He set you up, Liv." Eli sounds understanding, not angry. "I suspect he went on a charm offensive."

"He did," I agree. "He was easy to talk to, and…"

"And I wasn't listening to you." Eli's arms tighten slightly. "Liv, I'm going to be a better man for you." I hear his breath catch. "Christ, Liv. Being so up my ass meant I nearly lost you."

"Think we've all been up our asses," Drummer's voice comes from the driving seat. "Eli and Liv should never have left the compound. Fuck knows that Archangel was right, taking Liv, even taking Eli alone would have destroyed the club."

"Too fuckin' right," Dad agrees.

"What about Zane?" I ask. "He's off compound more than he's on. And what about my sisters? What if they marry civilian men? If we want to live outside the club, we should be able to."

Dad sighs deeply. "It's a difficult question to answer. I don't want to let any of my girls go. But Eli's come up with a plan for that now. If we know someone might be heading our way, we'll tell all the women who to watch out for."

Eli suggested that? It sounds like common sense. If I'd have known who Gabe really was right from the start, I'd have told Eli and never met him again. I'd have changed my shopping habits and stayed away, but their secretive club business had kept that from me. Hopefully it won't again. I snuggle against my man, trusting him now, only wishing he'd come up with that bright idea earlier.

"Now Archangel's gone," Eli says, his tone reassuring, "there's no one else with a current grudge against the club. Should that change in the future, then we widen protection for anyone connected with the club. Bring them in for safety, if necessary, or protect them where they are."

"Spreads us thin." Drummer voices an objection.

"We put together a workable plan. Keep it in our back pocket just in case. Have it as a church agenda item and revisit every few months to keep it current."

"That, right there," Dad says, tilting his head toward Drummer, "is why Eli became the VP."

Eli tenses beside me. "I used the wrong pronoun, sorry. I should have said you, not we."

There's silence from the front seats, and I don't know what's being left unsaid.

We pull up at the gates of the compound and wait a few seconds for them to open, then, Drummer's driving through, bypassing the clubhouse and continuing up the track to the homes where everyone lives. Well, everyone but us now.

As soon as the car stops, I throw open the door and start sliding out. Eli runs around to help me.

At the sound of our arrival, people start coming out. I notice they're all dressed, and no one seems to have been asleep. Mom runs toward me.

"Later!" I call out desperately. "I gotta pee."

After four pregnancies herself, Mom understands the urgency, and she clears a path through everyone waiting to greet me, shouting in typical Mom fashion, "Preggers lady needs the loo."

When I come out of the bathroom, she's waiting for me. Her eyes now examining me head to toe. "Are you alright, Olivia?"

"I'm fine, Mom."

"Baby moving okay? No pains?"

"Yes and no." I smile at her. "I was scared, but I'm okay. Though, he gave me Rohypnol…"

"We'll get you checked out." Eli and Dad have come in.

"Look, I'm good. I'm sure it won't have done any harm. Junior here is kicking just like normal." I really don't want to go off compound again. I want to relax, sleep and lie next to Eli.

"Livvy!" Hilda appears, quickly followed by Zoey and Eliza, my other sisters. "You alright?"

"Hey." Eli steps in front of me. "Liv's tired, she's been through an ordeal. She needs to unwind and get some rest. Can you hold your horses until the morning?"

"We only just found out she disappeared." Zoey stomps her foot, just like she used to when she was a child.

"And now she's back," Sophie says calmly. "Eli's right. You can catch up with her tomorrow."

"We've been planning your baby shower," Hilda says, her eyes gleaming. Then she turns her teenage eyes on Mom accusingly. "Of course we didn't know you were missing at the time."

Mom shrugs and looks at me. "Had to keep them amused somehow. And that was supposed to be a secret." She mock slaps Hilda on the ass.

Dad and Mom's house is getting crowded as two more people push in.

"You okay?" I'm asked again, this time by Amy.

Again I explain I am, but am worried about the effects of the drug Archangel gave me.

Amy purses her lips. "If the baby's moving and nothing seems abnormal, it shouldn't be a problem. This late in your pregnancy the baby's well protected. But I'd go to the hospital tomorrow just to make certain."

Eli's tensing beside me. "Can you all just give Liv some space? What she needs most is some rest."

At last they realise what's best for me. "Well, we'll say goodnight." Which is a misnomer as it's already daylight outside. I turn to walk out of the house to go home.

"Er, Liv." Eli stops me. "Our house…"

Shit. I'd completely forgotten.

"Has a bed." Wizard comes up alongside us. "Sent the prospects down into Tucson. They've already brought it back and got it set up." He passes Eli some keys. I recognise the ring that they're on. They're the keys to our house.

I feel tears at the back of my eyes, as emotion floods through me. I'll stay by my man's side through anything and go anywhere life takes us, but here is where I really want to be.

Wizard bends his head and speaks into Eli's ear. Eli nods and grins evilly. Then, at last, he puts his arm around me.

Leaving my mom and dad's house, we walk past the next two, then up to our own front door. Eli bounces the keys in his hands for a moment.

His reluctance to open the door worries me. "Do you think this is a backward step?" The significance of Wizard handing them to him hadn't been lost on me. It's not just the house to stay in tonight, I suspect he's given us the chance to move back to the compound.

Now just staring at the keys he's holding, Eli starts to speak, "I fucked up, Liv. I dragged you down with me when I reached the lows of my life. If I hadn't had run from my problems, Archangel would never have gotten near you—"

"He might," I snap, interrupting him. "I'm not chained to the compound, Eli. I go out. Amy works at the hospital, other girls have jobs. He could have taken anyone, but he took me, your wife. And if anyone was going to turn the tables on him, that was going to be you."

"But it was *you* who was taken, and I made it easy for him."

"You won. That's the main thing. Archangel's not a problem anymore." I turn him around so he has to look at me. "Did you lose any men?"

He shrugs. "No."

"So, whatever you did, worked. I'm safe, the baby's safe, and we can come back here, if that's what you want."

Now his hands clasp my arms. "There's nothing I want more, Liv, but there's a lot to sort out. The club won't want me back. I can't just pick up where I left off. I'll still need a job."

"All that will sort itself out in good time. But we've got our family back, and you're with me. And soon," I grin, "our daughter will make three."

He shakes his head and raises an eyebrow. "Not having a girl, Liv. You know this."

When I start to chuckle, knowing his feelings only too well, I stop when he again says my name.

"Liv." The seriousness of his tone worries me.

"What?" I reply, uneasily.

"I want you." Then he turns away, brushing back his long hair with one hand. "Christ, I'm a selfish asshole. You've been drugged, kidnapped, scared. You're—"

Three little words I've longed to hear over the past few months. It's been so long since I had my husband inside me. Nothing sounds better to me.

I'm smiling again as I look up and interrupt, "Pregnant women have needs, Eli. Especially those who haven't had their husband in so long. And especially those who've been kidnapped and want their man."

"I'm so fuckin' sorry."

"You will be, if you don't open that door and take me to bed."

With a hand that's not one hundred percent steady, Eli at last fits the key to the familiar lock and turns it.

CHAPTER TWENTY-SEVEN

 *li...*

Home.

I paused on the threshold assailed by emotion, mainly about the rightness of this, about to step inside the house that I had designed with my wife. If I read Wizard right, the handing over of the keys together with the words he'd said were symbolic. I might not know what the rest of my life will look like, but at least I know it will be centred here, in the home where I, and my family, can once again live.

Being back like this, as the last vestiges of adrenaline fade, I wonder why the fuck I ever left. Why didn't I cry out for help? Why was my answer to everything doing it all by myself? So many people would have been there to pick me up when I fell, yet low as I'd become, I never once expected them to hold out a hand. So disgusted with myself, I expected to see that also reflected on all the faces around me.

Instead, as I now know, I wouldn't have seen expressions of ridicule and disappointment, I'd have gotten understanding instead. If I had reached out, my brothers would have helped take the load off until I was ready to pick it up again.

Whatever she says, the woman I'm ushering in through the door has suffered due to my selfish actions and nearly paid the ultimate price. It's that knowledge that has me leading her straight upstairs to the bedroom, wanting to be as near to her as I physically can, or as close as her advanced state of pregnancy allows. My body wants her, but it will be enough just to hold her if that's all she wants.

Apart from the promised bed, the house is empty and our footsteps echo as we climb the stairs. But tonight, a bed is my only requirement, it's more than enough. Tomorrow we'll start the process of bringing the rest of our furniture back. I can't wait to see everything returned to its normal place, here in the home we both love.

Liv is clearly as eager as I as she starts to undress immediately as we reach our bedroom. I stand, transfixed, watching her disrobe, her belly looking so large and impossibly hard, as though she's about to burst. *That's my baby. Almost fully grown.* For the first time I realise I'm ready, impatient, to meet him at last.

Then I worry. I place my hand on her arm when she's down to just bra and panties. "Should we?" I wave at her stomach, suddenly guilty. "Liv, I don't want to hurt the baby. Perhaps we should wait until after you get checked out."

"I feel fine," she reassures me, confidently. "You heard what Amy said. Getting checked is just a precaution. As for harming the baby, you won't. Though we'll need to get inventive." Her eyes narrow, but her mouth curves as she adds, "No backing out on me now. I've been waiting months for this. Months to have you hold me like a woman again."

"I'm so fuckin' sorry." Apologising is all I seem to be doing tonight.

"You couldn't help it, Eli. You've been, are, still ill." She moves closer, or as close as she can, and her hand finds my cock still restrained by my jeans. "Sure I worried you'd lost interest in me, but now," she glances up with an impudent wink, "seems I've no concerns in that direction, or not tonight."

I cover her hand with mine, not to remove it, but as I roll back my head, I know it's to cherish the feeling of the only woman I ever wanted feeling up my rock-hard cock. "I didn't mean it," I tell her quickly. "There's never been, and never will be, anyone else. It was me, not you, the entire time, babe. I couldn't control the thoughts running through my head."

"I didn't either, Eli." She squeezes her fingers, applying just the right pressure, not too firm which would make me go off, but just enough to make me breathe in sharply, my breath whistling through my teeth. "Perhaps it was good that we had a chance to evaluate our feelings, now we've both circled back around and know it's only each other we want. But hell, I've missed you, missed this."

"Fuck, Liv," I manage to get out, her touch now starting to send me wild. "I couldn't, then. But now?" Now I can't remember why her touch, fuck, just her being in my range of sight hadn't turned me on. The shit going on in my head could have caused me to lose her. It had almost sent her into another man's arms. It hadn't been lost on me while it had been Archangel working to his plan, Liv's Gabe could actually have been someone who'd found my wife attractive in her own right and worn her down, eventually stealing her away. "You're mine," I remind her, my tone leaving no room for argument. "Mine," I repeat in a growl.

"And you're *mine*," she insists, as her fingers squeeze my cock. "All mine."

I gasp again, and this time do pull her hand away. "Liv, you're going to have to stop." I have to move her before I come like an overeager teenager. I'd had enough experience of that when we'd been little more than kids, experimenting in places her father wouldn't catch us.

"You're overdressed," she replies, her eyes glowing expectantly.

As she takes a step backward, I rectify that omission fast. I can feel her eyes watching so intently it's almost like a brand burning into my flesh. Her possessive eyes showing me, like she'd said, I'm all hers.

Naked, my cock juts out proudly, the veins red and pronounced, the head purplish as it strains to contain all the blood that's rushed down into it. I'm surprised I don't feel dizzy or weak. In fact, I feel on top of the world, the best I have for months. I know my problems aren't all behind me, but tonight is showing at least one is.

"Get on the bed," I instruct, my voice uneven as I suddenly choke up. Only hours ago I'd had to contend with the thought I'd lost her forever. Now I need to be as close to her as it's possible for a man to be with a woman.

I want to touch her, taste her, breathe her in. I want to gaze on those parts no one other than me and her doctors have ever seen. I might never have seen or touched another pussy, except for glimpses of those of the sweet butts in the clubhouse, but I really have no need. Perhaps if my father had met Sam when he was in his teens, he'd have settled down earlier. Instead of envying, or thinking I should emulate him, now I feel sorry for him instead. He'd had to wait until half his life had passed before finding the woman of his dreams, while mine had always been there for me.

She lies, first on her back, then quickly grimaces and turns on her side. I reach for her bra and unsnap it, then remove it, revealing breasts which are plump, full and ripe. For a second I just stare in reverence, they're so much bigger than when I'd last seen.

"They might leak," she warns me.

To which I just grin. *Another taste for me to savour.*

She raises her hips so I can take off her panties. It's a bit clumsy given the position she's in, but I make it work. I feel an ass that I've checked out during most of this pregnancy. Instead of relishing seeing her body grow as it nurtures my son, for a reason I can't now understand, I'd wanted to keep my head in the sand and pretend I wasn't going to be responsible for another human.

"I can just hold you, Liv," I tell her as I get onto the bed, sliding behind her and pulling her against me. I'm still concerned about the baby, about harming him, and mindful of the ordeal she's just been through.

"Are you kidding?" she asks, her hand reaching around to rest against my skin, as though reassuring herself I'm really with her. "I've waited so long to feel you inside me again."

Another reminder of what an asshole I've been. "I'm—"

"Don't you dare apologise, Eli. What if I'd been ill? What if I'd had a difficult pregnancy like Allie had back in the day? Would you have blamed me for not feeling horny?"

I place a kiss to that sensitive spot just under her ear. "It's hard to get my mind around how my brain betrayed me," I tell her, softly. "I promise you, Liv. I'll willingly take all the help that I need to get my head back on straight. I promise I'll—"

"Please, Eli. Please, just fuck me."

Chuckling softly, I pull up to rest on my elbow, leaning over her. She turns her head so she's in just the right position for my mouth to touch her lips. She opens for me, our tongues joining and caressing and it feels like I've come home.

Every intimate touch, every kiss, has always belonged to her. From awkward teenagers taking the first step toward becoming lovers, to each action we've fumbled our way through and learned until it's an action so familiar, she knows my every response as well as I do hers.

How could I have ever thought I was missing out not experimenting with other women? I don't want anyone else. I don't want to learn someone else's reactions. I don't want to experiment with a casual hook-up.

There's a wealth of emotion just behind the innocent

meeting of our mouths and tongues, as well as the physical expression of our love for each other. Tonight, there's an added element, an acknowledgement of what we could have so easily lost.

Eventually I raise my head and look down into her eyes, noticing how her pupils have dilated. "Thank you," I tell her, meaning it from the depths of my heart, "for not giving up on me."

"Never," she breathes. "I need you to complete me."

My eyes close briefly as I acknowledge that I also need her. I can't imagine a life without her in it. There were times when I thought she'd be better off without me, but truthfully, I'd never survive without her.

Suddenly I realise it's been far too long since I've tasted her. I pull up my body so I'm hovering over her, then manoeuvre downwards.

She starts to giggle as she realises my intention. "Not sure how we're going to make this work."

I growl softly, my voice vibrating against her skin causes her body to jerk. "I like a challenge, I've got this."

I pause my journey to lavish attention on her tits. They are indeed leaking, but I don't give a damn. Just another flavour to be savoured, and it's a reminder that soon my son will be suckling there.

"I'm too sensitive," she cries out, to stop me. Her wriggling shows not only discomfort, but what effect my administrations are having on her hypersensitive nipples.

Showing mercy, I continue to my destination, finding she's more swollen than I remember, not just with arousal, I remind myself, but her body's getting ready to bring my son into this world. A child born of me and her. Fuck, was there ever a man so lucky?

I hook one of her legs over my shoulders, and manage to get situated so I can indeed, as I promised, make this work.

"You okay?" I check in.

"I've missed you, Eli. I'm so ready."

She's wet and ready for me. When my tongue meets her clit, she gasps. "Eli!"

She feels different as I ease a finger inside her, curling around to find her G-spot. My twin assault soon has her tensing.

Is this okay? I lift my mouth. "Fuck, Liv. Are you sure this is going to be alright for the baby?"

"Eli, you asshole. Don't you dare stop!"

Who am I to deny a lady? Once again I lower my face and give her all I've got, my movements honed over the years knowing exactly what she likes best. Her hips tighten around my head almost painfully, but I don't complain. Her muscles contract and it doesn't take long before she's screaming out my name. My heart clenches as I realise there was a time I'd thought I'd never hear that sound from her lips again. My woman coming is the best music my ears ever want to hear.

I bring her down gently, then ease away, slipping my body beside her, her back to my front. Again I position her leg. With one arm over her belly, I start to enter her from behind.

"Tell me if this is too much," I beg her, scared that despite what she's said, fucking a woman eight months pregnant might not be a good idea.

"I will," she promises, gasping. "I want all of you inside me, Eli. I want you so fucking much."

That's exactly where I want to be. It's not just to get relief for my aching cock, it's the ultimate connection between us. With us it's always been much more than just sex.

From the first time when we had to work out what to do we seemed to just fit. Of course, we knew what went where, you don't grow up as we had to not have seen that in action, but it had been different putting knowledge into practice. I'd not wanted to hurt her, never had. Right now it feels like that first time all over again, me pressing in gently, giving her time to stretch and accommodate my length.

Strangely, I feel more linked to my baby than I ever have been. To my son which, despite her protestations to the contrary, I'm certain she's going to have.

"Eli, move, please."

"I don't want to hurt you."

"I'll fucking hurt you if you don't."

Her growled threat makes me chuckle, and then I oblige. Little pumps to start with, but when she simply pushes back with her hips, I pick up the pace, thrusting harder.

"Fuck, Liv. Babe, I'm not going to last." It's been too long and I'm on too light a trigger. I reach around to play with her still sensitive clit.

"Eli…"

"Babe," I rasp out.

"Oh God, Eli."

The moment she starts tensing around my cock, I lose it. I hammer in, then hold it as I feel cum spurt out of my dick.

"Christ, Liv. It just gets better."

"Hmm mmm," comes her satisfied agreement.

I rest my head against her shoulder, nuzzling a kiss to the sensitive spot below her ear. I'm reluctant to lose the connection, so let my cock soften inside her, ignoring that we'll be making the bed wet.

I've missed this so fucking much, even when I hadn't realised that I did. The months that had gone by without being inside her seem ridiculous to me now. Despite her understanding, I have to apologise again.

"Liv, I'm so fuckin' sorry. I was out of my head. I didn't mean to hurt you, but I know that I did. Whatever you want, babe, I'll give it to you. Whatever you need, I'll provide. I'll get help, make sure I don't slip back. Not going to check out again, babe. I love you too fuckin' much."

A gentle soft snore is my only answer, making me smile against her skin.

Relaxed and at peace for the first time in months, I follow her into sleep.

It only feels like a few minutes later when there's a knock at my bedroom door.

"You decent in there?" Liv's mother shouts.

Making a quick assessment, it's clear that we're not. I'd fallen asleep with my cock inside my wife, and sometime during the night it's slipped out. The mess on us, and the bed, is drying and sticky. Liv's lying just as she fell asleep.

"Er, no," I respond honestly, trying not to laugh.

"Well, you need to get up."

"What is it?" a sleep-heavy voice queries.

I kiss Liv on the shoulder. "Your mom. I'll go find out what she wants."

I stand, and grimacing, pull on my jeans, tucking my much-in-need-of-a-shower cock behind the zip. Leaving Liv resting, I go to the door and slip out.

"What is it, Sophie?" I enquire of the woman who's making herself at home, brewing coffee with the equipment I last saw in Heart's old house. It looks like the prospects have been busy while we've been asleep.

And still are, it would seem. As I stand there, our sofa appears, carried in by Butcher and Nathan.

"Olivia's got an appointment with the doctor at three." Sophie offers the reason why she disturbed our sleep.

"What's the time now?"

"One-thirty. We let you sleep in as long as we could, but she needs to get herself and the baby checked out, Eli."

I know that she does. "Okay, I'll go wake her. Is that for me?" I point to the cup on the counter.

"Her," Sophie corrects with a grin. "It's decaf." She laughs at the expression of disgust on my face. "I'll have some of the real stuff ready for you when you're dressed. Unless you'd prefer tea?"

My look of horror probably indicates I'd prefer Liv's decaffeinated coffee to that.

Liv's not at all happy at being disturbed and made to get out of bed, but deep down I think she needs the reassurance that the baby's alright, as after a few initial grumbles, she makes no more fuss. She gets showered and dressed while I change the bedclothes, finding clean ones in the boxes the prospects had packed and brought back from the Tucson house.

There is part of me which feels a failure returning home with my tail between my legs, having accomplished nothing while I'd been away from the compound. But I just have to suck up any feelings of inadequacy. Here is where Liv needs to be. Here with her family and a place where we can safely raise our kids. While it hadn't just been down to me, no one had really appreciated, you could take Satan's Devils off the compound and dress them as civilians, but the past couldn't so easily be escaped. While I don't know what the future holds, I'm never going to be putting Liv at risk again.

We go to the hospital and get our minds put at ease. Everything looks fine with the baby, and the drug Archangel gave her shouldn't have caused any harm at this stage. I take the opportunity to ask the doctor whether sex is okay, realising it's a bit late if the answer is no. But his response was to be guided by Liv. It won't hurt the baby. If she wants to be fucked, I'm okay to fuck her. Well, he might not have worded it in precisely those terms, but that had been my translation.

When we get back to the compound, Wizard is waiting for me.

Liv's too intent on updating her mom and mine on what the doctor had to say, that she barely notices me leaving.

CHAPTER TWENTY-EIGHT

*E*li...

It's on no one but me that I'm not a member of the club anymore. Do I regret it? No, I do not. I was right to walk away when I knew I couldn't contribute as I should anymore. Do I wish things had turned out differently? Fuck yes, and never more so than when I walk into the storage room and see Archangel close to taking his last breath.

It should have been me who'd been questioning him, making him hurt, but by not being a member, my chance had been taken away.

Archangel had taken my woman and potentially caused harm to her and my child. If I hadn't stopped him, he might even have killed her. But any secrets he'd given up rather than take to the grave had been for Satan's Devils' ears and not for those of a civilian like me.

Wizard has brought me here as they've offered me a concession, that I be the one to fire the bullet which would dispatch him to meet Satan.

Throttle's done his work well, too well it would seem. I have to look twice to be certain Archangel's still breathing. Whatever I could do couldn't make the man hurt anymore.

It's symbolic, me killing him, I don't even think he's aware who's taken the shot.

It's done. It's over. The Satan's Devils have one less enemy.

There's no cheering, no celebration. A few sighs of relief, and the sound of hands meeting leather as backs get slapped.

Wizard cups his hands around his mouth and whistles loudly. "Time for church," he calls out when he's got everyone's attention.

I feel a pang of there being a hole deep inside of me that will forever be empty as I see the members walking out. Shoving my hands in my pockets, I step out the door and turn in the direction of my house.

Suddenly I'm being dragged back by my collar.

"What the—?"

"You're coming too. We got things to discuss," Wizard growls into my ear.

For a second I'm bewildered, then I realise maybe they want to lay down some ground rules.

It's fairly obvious they don't object to Liv and I coming back to live on the compound, else they wouldn't have moved our furniture back in. But maybe it's only going to be temporary, time to sort ourselves out, for me to find a job and for Liv to give birth. Fear churns inside as I'm only too well aware of the dangers that lurk when ex-Devils try to live in the citizen world.

Or maybe they'll want to explain the boundaries they'll be setting about us living here, and what I can and can't do with the club. It is hard not to act just as I used to. I was a Devil for seven years, six as a patched member. Perhaps they want to remind me I won't have prospects at my beck and call anymore.

Just like the last time I was here, I'm directed to the seat Drummer's vacated at the opposite end of the table to prez. I wait for everyone to settle, feeling awkward and out of place, my shoulders feeling light as I envy everyone else wearing their leather. When Prez bangs the gavels, and starts to say my name, I'm not surprised. They'll get what they want to say to me said, then ask me to leave.

Wizard sits back in his chair resting the sole of his foot against the table, hands interlocked behind his head. "You did good, Eli," he tells me. "Since last night we haven't had a chance to catch our breath, and I haven't had a chance to tell you that yet."

"Yeah," Joker butts in. "Some of us were working and burying bodies while you were balls deep in your wife."

"Like I was saying," Prez subjects him to a glare, "we haven't yet met to discuss what went down. Just wanted to kick off with giving respect to you, Eli. Fuckin' good thinking on the fly coming up with that plan. Archangel had no idea we'd be waiting."

I shrug, brushing away any compliments, but I do explain my hastily thought rationale that had let to me suggesting the approach which had luckily worked. "Archangel thought he'd taken me unawares and had no idea I'd already spoken with you. He was so fuckin' self-centred he totally bought that I hated everyone here. Swallowed it hook, line and sinker."

"He called you a few choice names," Drummer puts in from the VP seat, a smirk on his face. "Some were quite inventive."

"While he was still capable of speaking that is." Throttle grins, looking decidedly pleased with himself.

Wizard just rests his eyes first on his VP, then the enforcer. That's all it takes. When he can be sure of speaking without further interruption, he addresses himself again to me. "When push came to shove, you did what you had to, Eli. There isn't a man here who didn't think you had their backs last night. Not one person voiced a doubt you'd play your part anything but admirably."

As everyone's looking at me, I raise my chin one way, then to the other. I get a few sharp nods in return.

Wizard looks to his right and makes a gesture toward Hound, who gets to his feet and comes down to the end of the table. It's only when he approaches, I see him carrying something. When it's placed on the table in front of me, my eyes open wide. It's my cut, with most of the patches in place. The only one missing is the one that read VP.

I start to reach out, but Wizard snarls. "Few conditions before you put that on. You better hear what they are."

I drag my eyes away from the leather I never thought I'd have the chance to ever wear again, emotions swirling through me. Hope, for the first time in months, and love for these men around me and their heart-warming ability to forgive.

"Anything," I tell him, suddenly knowing I'd give my right hand to be back with my brothers around me. I left due to my fear of letting them down, not for any other reason. I've missed them, *needed* them. I never expected I'd get another chance.

"That's a big fuckin' pledge there, Eli," Peg chuckles from my side.

Blade reaches over and fist bumps him. "We may need some time to come up with our demands in that case."

Rock snorts. "Still think he should start from the bottom and prospect again. Get him back for all the times as VP he was riding my ass."

Mouse looks at me and winks. "Nah, what about as a hangaround?"

I roll my eyes as I realise they're joking.

"Fuckin' F.O.Gs," Hound says.

Wizard clears his throat loudly, and his hardened gaze shuts the conversations down. "First, to take your place around this table, you come back as a member and not an officer."

I nod my head vigorously. I don't want the responsibility of being VP, and no man around this table would want me to be.

"Second, you go to therapy and do whatever the fuck you're told to. No ifs, no buts and no excuses."

My head continues its up and down movements, no hardship there. I've already made that promise to Liv.

"Third, Drummer has agreed to sit to my left for the duration, but he's not going to be in that chair forever. Once you've recovered, you come back as VP."

Now I change my action, and my head moves side to side. "No—"

"Don't contradict me. We've voted on it. There's no one else here who is better suited to the position. Yesterday you made the right call, Brother. If it hadn't been for your quick thinking, and how you made it work, blood could have been spilt on our side—"

"It fuckin' was," Lady interrupts, holding up his arm which is lightly bandaged. "I got stuck like a pig."

"Screamed like one more like," Marvel observes. "All over a little scratch."

"I had stitches," Lady insists.

"Will you shut up and let me finish?" Wizard roars. I press my lips together to stop myself grinning. *I've missed this.* "If it hadn't been for you, Eli, then there might be gaps around this table today, or women missing. The problem is, you don't trust yourself right now, but we, on the other hand, trust you."

If I felt emotional minutes earlier, I'm doubly so now. I glance up to see all eyes are now on me. There's one thing puzzling me. "When did you all agree to this?"

Peg snorts. "While we were questioning Archangel. Seemed as good a time as any to have an impromptu church."

"Particularly as he ranted and raved every time your

name was mentioned. Mental torture at its best." Blade smirks.

"Thought he was going to go into convulsions at one point." Joker chuckles.

"Course I had to cut his tongue out after a while," Throttle says, cleaning his nails with a knife. "He kept shouting us down."

"You going to put that on or not?" Wizard, no, *Prez*, bellows.

My greedy eyes land on my cut. My hands inch toward it. I notice I'm shaking as I pick it up, and when I slide my arms through the holes, breathing in the distinctive smell of oil and leather I make a vow and voice it out loud. "I won't let you down."

"Of course you fuckin' won't, *Hawk*." Prez lets his stare land on me, then looks around. "Moving on. We can cross off Archangel from our list now."

"His associates going to cause us a problem?" Hound asks, his brow furrowing.

"Nah." Mouse glances at prez and continues at his chin rise, "Archangel was too busy dodging the feds to be able to set up any type of organisation that's likely to carry on without him at the helm. I'll keep listening to the chatter, but it's gone silent on that front now. I'm not even sure he got any of the true Real Americans to stand by his side. Sounds like just a local group of wannabe supremacists supported him last night."

"And that Tucson cell is dead and gone," Throttle notes. "Anyone who comes for our families will not get a second chance, which they found out last night."

I nod, completely on board. There are clearly no survivors left from last night. Something I'll lose no sleep over, though it seems I'd missed some of the fun.

"It's been a long day." Wizard brushes his hand over his face, as though to emphasise his words. "If no one's got anything urgent, I say we go get a drink and celebrate Hawk's return."

"Seconded!" Rock yells loudly.

Joker fist bumps Lady, and others show they're in full agreement with that.

It's later, when I've just gone to the bar to get my second beer, Dad comes up. He rests his hand gently on my shoulder.

"You doing okay?"

I know to be honest now. "Better," I tell him. "Still got fears swirling around in my head." I shudder. "What if I'd been so up my ass, I hadn't called Archangel, or if I hadn't been able to act convincingly? What if I hadn't come up with a plan and told Wizard?"

Drummer tightens his grip. "Don't you think we all feel that shit? Years back, when your mom disappeared, I went through hell *after* I'd gotten her back. It's natural to go through the what-ifs and have nightmares when everything goes to shit."

"How did you cope?"

"By holding her tight and thanking fuck she came back where she belongs. By swearing nothing bad would ever happen to her again. And you know what, Son?" I raise my eyebrow. "Shit never did. Oh, the compound's been threatened like last night, and there was the time I sent her away, when Ella and Slick got married." His eyes glaze slightly as he remembers. "Fuck, I haven't thought about that in years."

"Thought about what?" Heart's come up alongside, motioning to Butcher for a beer.

Drummer snorts. "When you were out of your head and Sam and I were looking after Amy. Keeping her out of the hands of her doped-up grandmother."

Heart gazes at me for a moment, then takes the bottle the prospect has just handed him, and raises it toward me. "Guess I do understand, Brother. I couldn't see a way back through my grief, but I made it."

"Before I was born, Brother." I wink.

Heart shakes his head. "I'd rather you didn't remind me." He raises his chin to us, then walks off.

"Got a couple of things to say to ya, Hawk." Dad waits until I meet his eyes. "One, I'm not going to get comfortable seated where I am around the table, but counter wise, I'm in no hurry to step down. You take as much time as you need, Son. Just let me know when you want to take up the mantle again."

"What if I'm never ready?"

Drummer purses his lips. "Just take it a day at a time, Hawk. One day at a fuckin' time.

"Hey, Eli."

I spin around, my arm already open in invitation. "How you doing, babe?"

Her eyes sharpen. "You're wearing your cut! Oh my God, Eli! You're back in the club?" Liv's hand covers her mouth as though she can't believe what she's seeing.

"He certainly is," Wraith's voice barks from behind me.

"Are you happy?" I ask, suddenly anxious, worried in case she thinks it might set me back again.

"Happy?" Her eyes go wide. "I'm fucking ecstatic. Us, back where we belong. You back with the club? Life couldn't be better. Mom, Sam… Did you know?" She turns to the two women who've walked in behind her.

Sophie does an exaggerated eye roll. "Of course we didn't. It's bloody club business."

Liv copies her mother's gesture, but the shine in her eyes shows me exactly how pleased she is with my acceptance back into the life where we both belong.

"The baby's okay?" Wizard asks, stepping up and motioning Butcher to pass him a bottle. "What did the doctor say?"

"He's fine," I tell them, hugging my wife to me. "The doctor's happy with how he's coming along." He'd patiently answered all my questions, ones I would probably have known all the answers to had I previously bothered to attend the appointments with Liv.

"She's doing great," Liv says at the same time.

"Babe," I tell her, staring down and smirking. "That was a dick we saw on the scan." I'd been in awe watching that screen, and felt like such an asshole that I hadn't taken an interest before.

"That was the cord," she replies. "No dick in sight."

Drummer chuckles. "Think you've just got to accept it Liv, history is going to repeat itself. My boy will be having a son."

Wraith looks up to the ceiling then back down. "You're never going to let that drop, are you, Drum?"

I snigger. The story goes that Dad had boys, but Wraith never got his son. I believe Sophie put her foot down after Hilda, their fourth daughter was born, and Wraith had the snip and lost his chance. The rumour is Dad only had Zane and me as he didn't want to take the risk of having a daughter and giving Wraith the opportunity to throw shit back at him that he'd been quite happy to dole out.

"What can I say?" Drummer tells him. "The Felis swimmers produce males."

"What's so wrong about daughters?" Liv asks.

Wraith opens his mouth, then shuts it again, while Drummer guffaws loudly.

Sam puts her arm around her daughter-in-law. "Absolutely nothing at all," she tells her, with a stern look toward mine and Liv's dad.

CHAPTER TWENTY-NINE

Eli...

I've got a daughter.

Fucking hell. What on earth am I supposed to do now? I stare at my exhausted wife, and the scrunched up bundle she's holding in her arms.

The last twenty-four hours have been a mixture of terror and exhilaration. Liv had woken me in the middle of the night having contractions. I, in turn, had woken Amy, who'd come right away, and suggested I get her to the hospital immediately.

Seeing Liv suffer as she laboured to bring my son into the world had torn me apart. I was part full of admiration for the way she was coping, and part afraid that her body couldn't cope. As the hours had passed, I'd been more and more convinced it had to be a son she was having, an obstinate child who wanted to delay his entry into the world.

I'd been holding her hand when at last his head appeared, then his body. Then came the words, *Congratulations, Eli and Olivia. You have a daughter.*

A big girl too, she weighed in at eight and a half pounds.

I'd told the doctor he was mistaken, he had assured me, he was not.

"You look like someone's slapped you around the face." Liv chuckles softly.

I rake both hands through my hair. "I feel like it. A *daughter*? Hell, Liv."

She's openly laughing now. "Don't worry. It will be awhile before you need to think about borrowing Dad's shotgun."

I cross over to them. She taps the bed and I slide on, putting my arms around them both. "Wraith tried to keep you and I apart. It didn't work. Fuck, Liv. I feel sorry for him now. I fuckin' know how horny teenage boys behave. What if Wizard and Amy have a boy?"

"Oh, God. Eli. Don't make me laugh so hard, I'm sore. But that would be fate, wouldn't it? History repeating itself. The prez's son hooking up with the VP's daughter."

"I'm not the VP now," I remind her, unable to take my eyes off the baby who's my *daughter*, who I already love with every fibre of my being.

"You will be," she says firmly.

She could be right. Over the past month I've rediscovered my place in the club and have made progress in strides with the support of my brothers around me. I've seen the therapist a number of times. Now I'm a father. *A father.* I've no choice but to step up, if only to make sure no boy ever goes near her.

Gingerly I reach over and pull down the blanket to look at the face that already looks perfect to me. "She's beautiful."

"Layla," Liv says, decisively.

"Not Sage?" I knew that's what she'd suggested, when I'd been ignoring everything. Over the past few weeks we'd had discussions, but of course, my suggestions had all been boys' names. Layla's come out of the blue, but as I try it out, I'm happy with her suggestion. "She looks like a Layla to me," I agree.

"Have you got over the shock now?" She grins at me. "Because I think it's time we let everyone know."

"Do we have to?" I ask, knowing what I'll be in for as soon as I open the door.

"We can't hide in here forever."

No, we can't. I kiss Liv, then Layla. Then…

"Oh fuck, this is ace." Wraith's clutching his stomach. "This is what you get for defiling my little girl." He can hardly speak for laughing.

"She's beautiful." Sophie rocks her granddaughter in her arms having gone straight for the baby the moment I'd let them in.

"My turn," Sam demands.

"I'm not fuckin' old enough to be a grandad," my dad complains.

"Where's our niece?" Zoey, Hilda and Eliza demand as they rush in through the door together.

"Hey, girls. Give your sister some space." Sophie tries to corral her daughters up, but unsuccessfully.

It's utter confusion for the next hour as brothers, old ladies, and all the club's grown and teenage children come in to meet our new addition. When Wizard and Amy appear, I snarl at them.

"You're keeping any son of yours a-fuckin'-way," I tell them, loudly. My words only serve to make Wraith crack up again.

Then his face falls as he realises Layla's his granddaughter. "Better bide by what he says," he growls in warning.

Wizard's eyes are dancing when he holds up his hands. "We don't even fuckin' know what we're having yet," he complains.

"As long as it isn't a boy, we'll be fine," I warn him. "And if it is, we're keeping them apart from the fuckin' start."

"I've got a shotgun," Wraith stage-whispers beside me.

Amy rolls her eyes, pushes past and goes to Liv. "Men."

"Men," my wife agrees, grinning widely.

When finally the nurse comes in and clears the room, I'm left with Liv and our daughter. As my wife drifts off to sleep, I gaze down at the bundle making gentle snuffling noises in the crib.

Over-brimming with emotion, I gently touch her cheek. "You, little madam, are going to be the death of me. I know that already." I could deal with a son, be strict, impose rules and set limits. This baby girl already has me wrapped around her little finger, and I know I'll never be able to deny her anything.

Except a boyfriend. She'll live as a spinster, I've decided that. If Wizard and Amy have a son, they won't have a chance to grow up together like Liv and I did.

Who am I kidding?

My wife is perfect for me. Without her, I'd have fallen apart completely. With her by my side, well, I can accomplish anything—even coming back from my darkest hour. If Layla turns out to be like my wife, she'll make some man, or woman, or whoever she wants to spend her life with, very happy.

"Layla." It's a coincidence for certain, but her brilliant blue eyes open and stare straight at me. I crouch down by the crib. "You and your mother, you're the reason for me to live."

"I love you, Eli."

I stand, closing the gap between us. "I thought you were asleep."

"Bring her to me."

Carefully I pick up Layla and pass her to her mom. Then I lay down beside them, wrapping them both in my arms, watching in awe as the baby with innate ability tries to latch on and feed.

I'm not kidding myself or anyone that all my dark thoughts have gone, but slowly I'm learning to cope with them, to deal, rather than always feel I have to run. Now I've got two reasons to keep them at bay.

"Not going to fail you, Liv." I swear my vow softly.

"You never did," she tells me. "You're vulnerable, Eli. Just like any man. And just like anyone, you're going to fuck up. It's part of life, hon. If we fall down, we'll just get back up. We're going to make mistakes, all parents, all spouses do. But that's not being a failure, it's being human."

I'm a work in progress, I know that. But it's what my therapy is doing, making me re-examine how I look at things, changing my reactions from being inappropriate to those healthier instead.

I'll get there. My reasons for doing so are right here next to me in this hospital bed.

BEING LOST

Lost

All my life, it seems, I've made mistakes. Once, I lost everything. Failure seems to follow me around.

I didn't spot what a snake Snake was—he planned a mutiny right under my nose. Yeah, he did well when he appointed me as his VP, I followed him blindly, never suspecting anything.

Now Snake is dead and I'm the prez. I still spend my days doubting myself, but I've got the whole MC depending on me and I can't let them down. If I get it wrong, it won't just be me who goes down.

Then I meet her, a woman who needs me to keep her safe. I should warn her to stay far away, tell her I'm not a man she should lean on. I'm not a person to trust when I don't have faith in myself.

Patsy

Choices, always choices. I thought I did right when I left everything behind to make a new life, choosing which of my two adult children needed me the most now.

We should have been safe in our new life—nobody knew who we were.

But we've been found.

Luckily, before danger strikes, the Satan's Devils ride up to our door.

I'm no spring chicken. I'm not looking for a man in my life. But I need protection, I need help. It's time to make a stand and not run anymore.

There's only one man I can depend on to keep us safe. The trouble is, he's Lost.

Amy's Santa (Next Generation #1)
Ink's Devil (Colorado Chapter #5)
Devil's Spawn (Colorado Chapter #6)
Coming Soon
Being Lost (San Diego Chapter #1)

Note 1:

Each book can be read as a standalone, but to get the best reading experience for the Satan's Devils, read the books in the order above.

Note 2:
While the Blood Brothers series is completely separate to the Satan's Devils series, there is some crossover. Turning Wheels continues the story of a minor character who appears in Second Changes, and some characters appear in both series.

OTHER WORKS BY MANDA MELLETT

<u>*Blood Brothers – A series about sexy dominant sheikhs and their bodyguards*</u>

Stolen Lives (#1) Nijad and Cara

Close Protection (#2) Jon and Mia

Second Chances (#3) Kadar and Zoe

Identity Crisis (#4) Sean and Vanessa

Dark Horses (#5) Jasim and Janna

Hard Choices (#6) Aiza

Satan's Devils MC - Arizona Chapter

Turning Wheels (Blood Brothers #3.5, Satan's Devils #1) Wraith and Sophie

Drummer's Beat (#2) Drummer and Sam

Slick Running (#3) Slick and Ella

Targeting Dart (#4) Dart and Alex

Heart Broken (#5) Heart and Marc

Peg's Stand (#6) Peg and Darcy

Rock Bottom (#7) Rock and Becca

Joker's Fool (#8) Joker and Lady

Mouse Trapped (#9) Mouse and Mariana

Blade's Edge (#10) Blade and Tash

Heart Mended: A Satan's Devils MC Novella

Truck Stopped (#11) Truck & Allie

Satan's Devils MC Boxset 1 Books 1-5

Satan's Devils MC Boxset 2 Books 6-8

Satan's Devils MC Boxset 3 Books 9-11

Satan's Devils MC - Colorado Chapter

Paladin's Hell (#1) Paladin and Jayden

Demon's Angel (#2) Demon and Violet

Devil's Due (#3) Beef and Steph

Devil's Dilemma (#4) Pyro and Mel

Ink's Devil (#5) Ink and Beth

Devil's Spawn (#6)

Satan's Devils MC - Next Generation

Amy's Santa (#1) Wizard and Amy

STAY IN TOUCH

Email: manda@mandamellet.com

Website: www.mandamellet.com

Sign up for my newsletter to hear about new releases in the Satan's Devils and Blood Brothers series.

Facebook reader group: https://www.facebook.com/groups/mandasbadboys/

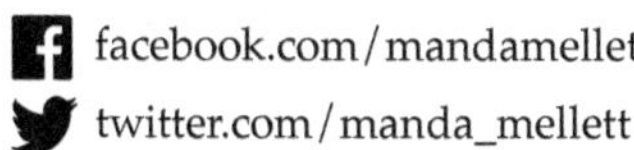

facebook.com/mandamellet

twitter.com/manda_mellett

ABOUT THE AUTHOR

Manda's life's always seemed a bit weird, starting with a childhood that even today she's still trying to make sense of, then losing her parents in the late teens. Going from the tragic to the bizarre, who else could be unlucky enough to have had two car accidents, neither her fault, one involving a nun, and another involving a police woman?

There isn't enough space to list everything that's happened to Manda, or what she's learned from it. But by using the rich fabric of her personal life, psychology degree, varied work experiences, and amazing characters she's met, Manda is able to populate her books with believable in-depth characters and enjoys pitting them against situations which challenge them. Her books are full of suspense, twists and turns and the unexpected.

Manda lives in the beautiful countryside of Essex in the UK, the area's claim to fame being the Wilkin's Jam Factory at nearby Tiptree. She can usually find jars of jam which remind her of home wherever she goes. As well as writing books and reading, Manda loves walking her dogs and keeping fit. She lives with her husband of over 30 years, who, along with her son, is her greatest fan and supporter.

Manda is thankful that one of the more unusual, and at the time unpleasant, turns her life took, now enables her to spend her time writing. Confirming, in her view, every cloud has a silver lining.

Photo by Carmel Jane Photography